Between Friends

D0673549

Between Friends

D.L. Sparks

www.urbanbooks.net

Urban Books, LLC
97 N18th Street
Wyandanch, NY 11798

ISBN 13: 978-1-60162-407-9
ISBN 10: 1-60162-407-7

First Mass Market Printing April 2014
First Trade Paperback Printing January 2012
Printed in the United States of America

10 9 8 7 6 5 4 3 2 1

Distributed by Kensington Publishing Corp.
Submit Wholesale Orders to:
Kensington Publishing Corp.
C/O Penguin Group (USA) Inc.
Attention: Order Processing
405 Murray Hill Parkway
East Rutherford, NJ 07073-2316
Phone: 1-800-526-0275
Fax: 1-800-227-9604

For Monica Renee Bowie
You are loved and truly missed.
Missing since July 5, 2007

This book, along with all my others, is dedicated to missing women everywhere. The ones who don't have the powerful voice of mainstream media, or the far reach of the movie camera. To you and your families I say: Don't give up hope because I haven't and know that you are not alone and I am praying with you for you loved ones safe return.

Unique Harris–Washington, DC
Missing Since 10/09/10

Evelyn Shelton-Spartanburg, SC
Missing Since 5/20/11

Chioma Gray-Ventura, CA
Missing Since 12/13/07

Sonsaray Warford-Richmond, KY
Missing Since 6/28/10

Dorian Suarez–Lavergne, TN
Missing Since 1/21/09

Shaquita Yolanda Bell-Alexandria, VA
Missing Since 6/27/96

For more information on these women and the scores of others please visit:

Black and Missing Foundation, Inc.

www.bamfi.org Facebook Twitter Youtube

Hunting is not a sport. In a sport, both sides should know they're in the game.

—Paul Rodriguez

Chapter One

Trip

"Come get you from where?"

"Atlantic Station, in front of Fox Sports Grill."

I sat up a little and craned my neck to look at the clock on the nightstand next to the bed.

It read: 12:50 a.m.

I put my head back down on the pillow and closed my eyes.

"How you end up there?" My voice was still heavy with the four hours of sleep I had managed to get before I got this call.

"Long story. Just come get me."

"A'ight, I'm on my way." I tossed my phone onto the bed next to me.

No sooner had I closed my eyes and convinced myself that I had just dreamt that whole conversation, the phone rang again.

I picked it up without opening my eyes. "Spencer."

"Man, get up and come *get* me!"

Thirty minutes later my partner, Philip "Big Phil" Porter, was climbing into the passenger seat of my truck. Standing upward of six feet two, and weighing no less than 200 pounds, Phil's large, muscular frame commanded respect. I wouldn't want anyone else kicking in doors with me during a bust.

"You wanna tell me what the hell is going on?" I yawned.

He hit the button and let the seat back. "Man, you know that chick I was with earlier?"

"Yeah, the one with the big ass."

He nodded. "Yeah. She was married!"

All I could do was laugh and shake my head. "How did you find out?"

"When her crazy-ass husband ran up on her car when we were leaving Copeland's."

"She wasn't wearing a ring?"

"No, she was wearing one."

I looked at him in disbelief. "And you still took her out?"

"She said she got it as a gift for herself."

"And your dumb ass believed her?" I laughed even harder.

"Come on man, you know women do shit like that all the time. They always on some old independent woman–type stuff."

"Yeah, it was a gift all right," I agreed. "A gift from her *husband* on her *wedding* day."

He cut his eyes at me. "Just shut up and take me back to the hotel."

I looked over at him. "Aw, and you got all dressed up for her and everything."

"Fuck you," he said, trying to sound hurt. "She could've been the one."

"Yeah, the one for this area code. I see you managed to get something to eat," I said, motioning to the white take-out bag on his lap.

He sat up like he'd forgotten he had it. "Oh yeah, I'm always gon' do that."

He opened the bag and started going through the Styrofoam container.

"Yo, hold up! Don't start pulling food out in my truck," I protested. "I still ain't got rid of that smell from the Chinese food you spilled the other night."

"Man, chill out," he said, shoving a handful of fries into his mouth.

My phone went off; a few seconds later his did the same. He pulled his from his hip and checked the display.

He wiped his hand on his pant leg. "Don't look like either one of us is getting any rest tonight, partner."

I checked the rearview, hit the sirens and made a U-turn in the middle of Northside Drive; and headed toward Lee Street, where the text came from.

I pulled the truck to a stop in front of the address we'd been given.

"You got any thing I can change into in the back?" Phil asked.

I nodded. "Yeah."

I hit the latch and we jumped out. A few moments later I heard him call out, "Yo, you got anything bigger than toddler size back here?"

"Hey, you can go up in here in your Smokey Robinson gear, for all I care."

"Fuck you."

He came alongside the truck and tossed me a vest. I watched as he squeezed into a Drug Enforcement Agency T-shirt, which was clearly too small for him. I looked at him and shook my head as he tried his best to make it work. I easily filled out an XL, so I knew Phil was definitely an XXL.

He looked up at me. "What?"

I chuckled. "Nothing." I turned and headed inside.

The stench inside the tiny house was overwhelming; I couldn't help but feel nauseated. The linen face mask, which the coroner had given me, was doing nothing to keep the smell of death from penetrating my nose. The front door was destroyed, completely off the hinges. Definitely, whoever had kicked it in had been on a mission.

I scanned the room and counted three bodies in various places, all black males. Two appeared to have been killed execution style; the third showed signs of having been beaten. He was beaten beyond recognition and lying in a puddle of his own blood.

I found the ME in the other room. "What we looking at?"

"The two by the door took a thirty-eight in the back of the head. The other one—blunt-force trauma."

"Any identification?"

"According to records, the corpse over there is Eddie Tucker."

"The kingpin?" I asked, surprised.

The Atlanta Police Department officer nodded. "Yeah, shocked us too."

When I saw all the drug paraphernalia, I damn sure wasn't expecting to find forwarding addresses or family portraits in the house, but I also wasn't expecting to find one of the most wanted kingpins in Atlanta and New Orleans either. We'd been tracking him back and forth across the state line for years and could never get a hook in him. Katrina had flushed out a lot of dealers and most were hopping back and forth over the state line into Georgia trying to avoid getting snatched up by us. Eddie was just one of many.

"What time frame are we looking at?"

"According to liver temps, one, maybe two yesterday morning. Got one more in the back bedroom."

"Who called it in?"

"Anonymous."

That didn't surprise me either. "Thanks."

I made my way past a cluster of detectives and APD officers and headed toward the back of the small apartment. As I entered the already crowded room, my eyes immediately went to the bloodied body on the bed. From what I could tell, it was female.

I clapped my hands together. "All right, guess this is my official welcome home so what else we got?"

The officer standing there started talking. "Twenty-something female, beaten and raped. GSW to the right temple."

I walked over to the bed and looked down at the girl. The twisted look on her face caused my heart to lurch. Her hair was plastered to the side of her head with dried blood from where the bullet had entered. Blood seeped from the gunshot wound to her ear and pooled on the bed next to her head. I couldn't help but think about my sister, Trinity. The girl had no business here and she definitely didn't deserve this.

"We think it's the same MO?" I asked, scribbling notes in my pad.

Phil nodded as he signed the ME's report. "It's definitely the same MO. Robbery, drug related."

"Damn, man. This is getting out of control."

"That Four Horsemen bust definitely messed up a lot of dealers' books. This could be coming from any number of people."

The millions in drugs and money recently seized during that bust sent the streets into a tailspin. From the small-time dealers to the cats hidden behind gates in their upscale communities, everyone had took a hit, and they were all pissed. Now they were scrambling, trying to regain a stronghold that the bust shook loose.

The increase in stupidity on the streets of Atlanta wasn't the only thing that earned us our first-class ticket back to my hometown; it was that and the fact that the bust was believed somehow to have ties to the Fulton County Jail.

I walked back out into the living room, which was now crawling with even more DEA agents and a few APD officers.

"Special Agent Orlando Spencer."

The voice coming from behind me was all too familiar. I smiled and turned around. "Hello Captain Lewis?"

My former Captain smiled. "I see they called in the Golden Boy, all the way from New Orleans."

I laughed. "Yeah, something like that."

We gave each other a courteous handshake.

"They need you in the back, Captain." An APD officer came up and interrupted our reunion.

He nodded in his direction. "I'll be right there." He turned his attention back to me. "Duty calls. It's good seeing you. Good to have you back in town."

"Good to be here Captain," I lied.

He gave me a head nod. "We'll have to have drinks and catch up, Trip."

I cracked a smile as he made his way to the back where his attention was needed.

I'd earned the nickname of "Trip," short for "triple," by being the third Orlando Spencer in the family. It was something my father started calling me when I was little, and it stuck. As a matter of fact, even in school, teachers rarely called me by my real name. I've always been known as Trip Spencer.

In the Tahoe, Phil was now eating the rest of whatever food he had rescued from his failed date. He smiled as I slid into the driver's seat.

"So that's your old captain." He wiped a fake tear from his cheek. "It's so good to see you two reunited."

I cranked up the truck. "Shut up and don't spill no shit on my floor."

He laughed. "Don't get mad at me. You the one everyone treating like the second-coming around this camp."

"Go 'head with that Phil," I laughed.

He bit into his sandwich. "I'm just sayin' can I get some love? I'm a special agent *too*," he said, pretending to whine.

I just shook my head and looked at him. "How can you eat that?"

He looked at me. "Don't start with that healthy diet, no-eating-after-midnight bullshit. My grandfather lived to be eighty-three years old and ate whatever he wanted." He stuffed the last of his sandwich into his mouth and popped the last of his fries in as well.

I shook my head. "Yeah, okay."

"Stop worrying about my food and let's go," he said. "I just got a text from my informant. We gotta be over off Bankhead in fifteen."

"Let's ride."

Being back in Atlanta opened up a lot of boxes in my mind full of memories that I had long ago packed away—some good, some not so good.

When I initially left this city behind and took the spot with the agency, over six years ago, I had no intention of returning. An opening in the New Orleans DEA office offered me the perfect escape from everything that I had grew to hate about Atlanta. So NOLA's unfortunate loss of an agent turned into an opportunity for me to leave behind a city full of baggage. But this case had brought me back, once again, and all I could do was hope the baggage in my closet would stop shifting long enough for me to get the job done and retreat back to New Orleans.

I listened as Phil tried to get his CI on the phone. He wanted to see if his confidential informant had any information about what happened tonight. The informant claimed not to know anything about the killings, but he did give us a heads-up on a potential bust. He was hooked up with the informant through an Atlanta undercover he knew who'd been working the case with us the past few months. The UC assured Phil the informant was reliable and set up communications as soon as we touched down. We all agreed that bust was too big, which meant there was entirely too much at stake for no one to be talking.

We pulled into the dark parking lot in front of the Family Dollar on Bankhead and cut the lights on the truck and waited. The dilapidated area in the heart of Atlanta spoke volumes about the state of mind of the people it held in its arms. There were no 401(k) plans or money market accounts for these people, only what the streets had to offer; and we were constantly trying to take that away from them.

After about five minutes I started to get agitated. I wasn't sure if I was on edge from knowing I was in the same city with Idalis again, or if it was just the intensity of what was going on. But whatever it was, I was ready to get it over with and head back down I-20. I looked at the clock on the dash; it was almost three, and I was officially running on fumes. Our day began almost two days ago and, thanks to napping in the truck when I could and eating drive-through meals, I was hurting for a good eight hours of sleep and a real meal. Not to mention, I still hadn't made it to see my mother and sister.

I reached up and rubbed the stress knot in my shoulder. "Man, where's this informant?"

"Calm down," Phil insisted. "He'll be here. Give him a minute."

I let out a sigh and started jabbing the scan button on the radio.

"Seriously, what's your problem?" my partner asked.

"This city is my damn problem."

Phil chuckled. "You been back in Atlanta airspace for forty-eight hours and you already tripping?"

"Man, shut up."

"Why don't you just go?"

I shook my head. "I don't know, man."

"I'm just sayin', I think you'd feel better."

"Shut up, Phil."

"Whatever." He pulled his phone out of his pocket. "You know what you need?"

I laughed. "No, but I got a feeling you're about to tell me."

"A woman. I'm about to find you one."

I hit the button on the side of the driver's seat and laid my seat back a little. "Just broke up with one, remember? Plus I don't need any ho you met on Twitter or desperate married chick that you got trolling around on your Facebook page."

He laughed. "Some of them women are off the chain on there. You should see some of the pictures that hit my phone, and most of the time without me even asking."

"I know *you*, so I believe you." I laughed.

He laughed too. "Whatever, man. Anyway, that's the third chick you broke up with in the last year. That's why you so damn cranky." He leaned back, causing the passenger seat to strain against his large frame. "That's exactly why a brother like me is single."

"No, a brother like you is single 'cause you got a fucked up attitude about women." I laughed.

"Oh, you got jokes? Man everybody can't be the ultimate male model like you," he laughed. "Locs freshly twisted, line-up every week, muscles all buff."

I busted out laughing. "Yo, partner, you trying to date me now too?"

"Fuck you man, I'm just sayin'," he said, cracking up.

I reached up and smoothed my goatee. "That disposable attitude you have toward women is gonna get old after a while. You need to ease up and maybe one will stay around long enough to remember how to get to your house."

"I like it that way." He grinned. "Don't have to worry about getting stalked."

"Yeah, okay."

"I must be doing something right, 'cause you all tense and my phone is blowing up."

I chuckled. "Come on, man, it's blowing up with desperate-ass married women with crazy husbands."

We both laughed.

I reached up and scratched my temple. "Say what you want. One day you gon' stumble across the right one and when you lose her"—I looked over at him and smiled—"and your dumb ass probably will lose her, then maybe you'll understand and we can continue this conversation."

Phil chuckled. "Please. That's why I don't catch feelings. 'Cause when you mess around and catch feelings, it ain't long before you sitting in an unmarked police truck crying to your partner."

We both couldn't help but laugh at that.

I looked up and saw a dude running toward the truck. "Is that your boy?"

"Yeah." Phil hit the button and the tinted window on the Tahoe hummed downward. "What's good Darius? What you got?"

"House right around the corner, 1275."

I asked, "You sure you can cop what we need?"

"Yeah, man," the informant answered, agitated. "Just be there in five minutes."

Phil rubbed his goatee. "I'ma call you in four. Answer your cell, slide it in your pocket and keep it on so we can hear everything." Big Phil slid him a stack of marked hundred-dollar bills. "Don't fuck this up. No less than six."

He nodded. "Just show up. I got you."

"When the bust goes down, we're gonna have to arrest you too, to make it look legit," I added.

Darius cut his eyes at me. "Yeah, I hear you."

This time I hit the button and rolled up the passenger-side window. I didn't care if he got mad or not. I didn't like him.

Phil laughed. "Why you gotta do him like that?"

"Something about him I don't like."

He shook his head and laughed. "You don't like nobody."

I got on the radio and gave the information to the backup that had been strategically placed around the neighborhood. All of them would be within a left or a right turn away when the bust went down.

Exactly four minutes later, Phil dialed the CI. He answered and Phil put his cell on speaker so we could listen to what was going on.

"What's up, man? What you got for me?" we heard him ask.

"I got six, like you wanted," the supplier said. "Right here. You got the money?"

"Right here."

"Cool. Cool," the supplier said.

There was a brief silence, followed by the sound of chairs being moved around, and then what sounded like a door opening and closing.

I heard Darius ask, "That all of it?"

"Yeah."

I jumped on the radio. "Units, move in! Units, move in!"

The Tahoe I was driving lurched forward when I hit the gas and bent the corner on two wheels. Phil jumped out, gun drawn running toward the house before I pulled to a complete stop. The other three units screeched to a halt in front of the house.

Murphy was up the front steps ready to blow the door. He yelled out their arrival before kicking in the door. "Search warrant! DEA."

I sprinted around back and saw two guys face-down on the ground with a knee in their backs being handcuffed.

"Get down! Get down! Let me see your hands," Phil yelled from inside the house.

It wasn't long before the informant and two other men were being led out of the house in handcuffs. I walked over to the supplier, grabbed his handcuffs and twisted his hands up behind his back.

"Ahh!" he screamed out.

"Man, shut up," I barked. "Look, I got a proposition for you."

"I don't want to hear shit you have to say," he spat back.

"Hey, it's up to you. You can either do a minimum twenty"—I bent down close to his ear—

"and that's federal time, playa, not that revolving door downtown on Rice Street, or you can help me out."

Phil walked over, smiling. "I suggest you do what my partner says. Somebody called and interrupted his beauty sleep and he's *pissed*!"

Phil chuckled at his own joke.

He twisted his body to see Phil more clearly. "Help you how?"

"You give us your supplier, and we never met," I said.

He turned and scowled at me. "Just like that. You gonna let a brotha go?"

I shrugged. "It's up to you. You can either help us out or get comfortable at Club Fed." I asked, "What's it gonna be?"

He dropped his head. "Look, I usually go through a runner and all I know about his connect is his street name. I ain't ever met the dude, but I know they call him Geech."

I smiled. "That'll work."

Chapter Two

Idalis

I'm in town baby girl.

That's all the text said, but I guess coming from him that was all it needed to say.

Trip and I were inseparable growing up. We had our own set of friends but we always managed to wind up together somehow. From the immature halls of elementary school to fun-fill halls of Booker T. Washington High all the way to the tense halls of Clark Atlanta University, we were two peas in a pod. We helped each other navigate our way through and made sure we made it to the next level together. It wasn't until that things started to change for us.

I tossed my keys onto the dining room table; they landed next to a stack of wedding magazines and a box of favors, which my sister had promised to help me put together. I picked up the stack of mail and flipped through the pile. It was mostly bills and junk, so I tossed it back onto the table and kicked my shoes off before grabbing a bottle of water from the refrigerator. It was so hot outside and I had been running in and out of stores all afternoon. I couldn't wait to peel off my clothes and shower away the layer of sweat that was covering my body.

Once had showered and was comfortable in shorts and a tee, I called my twin sister, India. She and I might have been twins, but that's definitely where the similarities ended. She didn't have any kids and I had a son, Cameron, and was about to get married in less than two months. Recently she had moved back in with my mother and was working on her master's in business.

The music she was blasting, Jill Scott's *Blessed*, came across the line before she did. "What's up, Twin?"

"Can you turn that down please?" I complained.

I heard her mumble something smart before the volume lowered. "You happy now?"

"Yes, thank you."

"What do you want, Idalis, other than to regulate how loud the music is in my car?" she asked.

"I got a text from Trip earlier, he's in town."

"You talked to him yet?"

"No, not yet. I might call him later."

"*Might*?" she questioned.

I sucked my teeth. "You heard me, might."

"Okay, whatever, we still meetin' tomorrow for lunch?"

"I'll let you know."

"What you mean?" she asked, attitude all in her voice.

"I'll have to see."

She sucked her teeth. "You mean you have to see if you're allowed out."

"Don't start with me," I said.

"You're a loser. Call and let me know. Bye."

"Bye." I hung up.

I stood up and made my way to the kitchen with my empty water bottle. It was still early and the house was quiet. Too damn quiet. Cameron was with my mother and I was lost. I was used to having hustle and bustle going on around me. I looked at the clock and realized that I still hadn't heard from my man all day. I'd sent him a few texts but he hadn't responded to any of them. I scrolled through my call history, found his name and hit send.

He answered, "Briscoe."

"Hey." I stood at the kitchen counter, picking at the edge of a dishcloth.

"Hey, mama, what's up?"

With the sound of his voice, my body warmed.
His throaty tones had always been so hypnotic
to me. I didn't know who sounded sexier sometimes, him or T.I.

"I've been texting you all day."

I heard paper rustling around. "Man I been
busy. Plus I thought you'd be somewhere catchin'
up with ya boy."

"Wow. Seriously, you're going there?"

"What?" he asked, laughing a little. "He your
best friend right?"

"Whatever." I tossed the dishcloth onto the
counter.

"Don't be like that, girl. What you doin'?"

"Getting ready to go get Cameron in a little
while."

"You at home?" he asked.

"Yeah."

"Thought you were going by the club."

"I did, but I had to run some errands for the
wedding and they took longer than I thought,"
I said.

He let out a sarcastic laugh. "Did your errands
include a trip downtown to Spring Street?"

"No they didn't, smart ass. I had this appointment booked at the reception hall weeks ago."

He didn't say anything. That was my opportunity to mention the text message, but I already

didn't like the direction of this conversation so I didn't.

"Hello?"

"I'm here," he said.

"I know you're not tripping," I said.

"Nah, I'm straight, but I need to go."

Reluctantly I asked, "What time are you coming home?"

"I don't know. But I'll call you when I'm on my way."

"All right."

"Yeah."

I sat there for a second after disconnecting his call tapping my phone on my leg. I suddenly found myself with too much free time on my hands and nothing to do.

Maybe I should have gone to the club, after all.

Nervous energy propelled me around the house. I made my way upstairs and tossed some dirty clothes into the hamper and folded some clean ones, but even that wasn't enough to stop my mind from wandering.

After a while I stretched out on the couch, hit the power button on the remote control and started flipped channels. For a while I sat there scanning stations, not really looking for anything or for that matter, watching anything. It didn't take long before that got old and I ended up moving from the living room to the kitchen then back again.

I was restless.

And I knew why.

"It's only five o'clock," I said to out loud to no one.

I headed upstairs to my room, swapped out my shorts for workout clothes, grabbed my bag and keys, and headed to Metro Fitness, off Metropolitan Parkway. At times it was technically a meat market but that's not why I went. I went to work out and let off some steam. India hated it; she said there was too much ass hanging out for her.

When I got there, I was actually surprised by how crowded it was for the middle of the week. I actually had to wait for a treadmill. When I finally got one, a short dark-skinned girl, with way too many muscles, told me that there was a thirty-minute time limit. I nodded before placing my cell on the display and began to try to outrun my stress.

Or maybe it was my past.

I huffed and puffed; and somewhere around mile five, the wind got knocked out of me when someone came up behind me and spoke.

"Excuse me, ma'am, are you gonna be long?" the voice asked.

I slowed my pace, but I didn't stop.

I smiled, speaking without turning around. "No, sir, I'm almost finished."

I took a deep breath; I could smell his cologne. He was officially in my space. I slowed down my pace until the machine shut itself off. I picked up my phone and blotted my face with my towel.

"What's up, stranger?" I said, turning around and looking up into my best friend's eyes.

He smiled a beautiful smile. He looked good—I couldn't deny him that. He scooped me up in his arms and wrapped me in a hug.

"What are you doing here, Trip?"

"My partner, Phil, dragged me out here."

I scanned the room. "Where is he?" I had never met his partner. At that moment I was reminded that there were so many parts of his life that I didn't know about. Considering how I used to be a huge part of his life—and now I was almost a stranger—the thought stung a little.

"In the weight room, supposed to be working out but trying to push up on some girl."

We smiled as a couple years' worth of tension weaved in and out of the space between us, filling in gaps of space that we couldn't seem to fill with words.

He stared at me for a second, then spoke. "You want some water?"

"Sure."

We walked to the juice bar. He bought two bottles of water and turned his attention back to me. "Look, I want to apologize about . . . " he started.

"No need."

"Yes, there is. That whole situation was just—"

I cut him off. "I understand. Your dad had just died; you had Camille back in New Orleans. Things were crazy. I'm just glad to see you."

We grabbed our water and walked toward the basketball courts and took a seat in the bleachers. There were a lot of brothers living out their NBA dreams at the gym. A few looked damn good; others looked a hot mess.

He took off his leather weight-lifting gloves and laid them on the bleacher next to him. I watched him as he opened his water and instinctively reached for mine so he could open it. I passed it to him, but not without our hands touching.

My mind was cloudy.

Thoughts bounced around like giant beach balls.

I looked up and a guy on the other side of the court caught my eye. He looked familiar, but I couldn't place his face. Just as fast as he had appeared in my line of sight, he disappeared.

Trip said something. I cleared my head and my throat, then took a sip of water. "I'm sorry, what?"

"You always come here to work out in the evening?"

"Not usually. My son's with my mom and I was home by myself," I said.

A smile spread across his face, which made my legs weak. "What? Your fiancé didn't want to stay home to keep you company?"

I let out a small laugh. "You got jokes."

He winked. "Nah, I'm just playing. When is the wedding?"

I looked down at my ring finger. It was empty. I had left the ring on my dresser. I didn't like wearing jewelry when I worked out. "August."

"Do I get an invitation?"

"Gotta have an address to send it to."

Again he flashed that smile.

"You look good, Idalis." His eyes scanned my body. "A little skinny for my taste, but you still look good."

I slapped his arm. "Shut up."

"Surprised his controlling ass still hasn't dragged you across the broom."

"Don't start," I said.

"What? Y'all been engaged for a minute."

I rolled my eyes. "You know what. I have been playing referee with y'all since college."

He gave the basketball court his attention. Made a few sounds like he enjoyed what he was seeing. I pulled the ponytail holder out of my hair, letting it fall down across my back and shoulders. I ran my fingers through it, never taking my eyes off Trip. I allowed myself to become reacquainted with his features: the creamy color of his fair skin, his striking hazel eyes, and the perfect lines that framed his full lips, which made up the mustache and beard that blended flawlessly into his goatee.

My eyes took in the way his long, thick, dark eyelashes framed his almond-shaped eyes. How his dreadlocks fell past his shoulders and rested on his back when pulled into a ponytail. I remembered when he started growing them in college; he was one of the few men who looked damn good with them. He kept them neat, got them re-twisted on a regular. He still looked the same to me; the only thing that had changed about him was the fact that his features were more mature.

He spoke without looking at me. "Why are you staring at me?"

I bit my bottom lip and laughed a little. "No reason."

Then he turned to look at me, reached up, and tucked my hair behind my ear. "Waffle House?"

"You still love that place," I said laughing.

"No doubt." He smiled.

"Guess I should be grateful you didn't suggest the Varsity."

A look came over his face like he was actually considering what I'd just said.

"Trip, no!"

He laughed. "Come on let's go."

I waited by the front door while he went to let his partner know he was leaving. We headed out, with me following behind his truck in my car. Once I was in the car, I called my mother to check on Cameron and she reassured me that he was fine.

My car trailed Trip's truck into the parking lot of a Waffle House, which wasn't too far from the gym. Once inside, he ordered steak and eggs; I ordered a waffle and a cup of coffee. For a moment we sat in silence, pretending we were interested in what the other patrons were doing. Finally he spoke, snapping me out of my trance.

"So what's up, baby girl? How you been?"

I looked up from my cup of coffee. "I'm good. How have you been?"

"I'm good. Been a minute since I been home."

"What? This is still home for you?" I joked. "You act like you can't come up I-20 anymore."

He chuckled. "You got jokes."

"I'm just sayin'." I took a sip of my lukewarm coffee.

"You still working at Four Seasons?"

I shook my head. "No I'm at 404."

"Oh, you working at that club over on the west side? What you managing?"

I took a sip of my coffee. "No, I own it."

He made a face like he was impressed. "Wow, so you big time now?"

"I guess you can say that."

"How you like that?"

I nodded. "It's different running a whole spot, but I like it."

"You must like it a lot, you driving that C-Class."

I laughed. "Why you sizing up my whip?"

"You ballin' and I'm driving a departmental issue truck."

"Whatever, that's by choice. Don't think I don't know about that BMW 550i you got parked in your driveway."

He looked at me and shook his head. "You still nosy as hell. What else is going on?"

I took a bite of my waffle. "Oh! Remember Dionne? She manages it for me."

His eyes got big. "For real? I haven't seen her since college. She still wild as hell?"

I nodded. "Yeah, she works the bar too, but I would be lost without her help."

"Remember that fight she got into at the soph-omore skate party at Cascade with Lisa Travers?"

I started cracking up. "Yes! Because I got caught in the middle of it and ended up with a bloody nose trying to pull her off that chick."

He doubled over laughing. "That shit was hi-larious."

"Yeah, and you just stood there watching."

"Are you crazy? Break up a girl fight,"—he shook his head—"not gonna happen."

I rolled my eyes. "You're stupid."

The waitress appeared at our table, getting both our attention.

Her brown skin had a refreshed glow about it, like she had gotten a good nap before her shift. Her micro braids were pulled back in a ponytail, and she had huge hoop earrings on, with a tattoo of something in cursive on the side of her neck. She smiled as she placed our plates in front of us.

"E'rythang look good?" she asked.

I looked from my plate to her big brown eyes. "Yes, it's fine. Thank you."

With a smile and a nod, she left, taking her southern hospitality to her next table.

I took a bite of my waffle and felt Trip's eyes on me. I glanced up and smiled.

"Are you gonna watch me eat?"

He laughed. "Yeah, I just wanted to make sure your skinny ass still ate food. All the weight you've lost, you never know."

"I got a wedding gown to fit into, I can't be all fat walking down the aisle."

We laughed a little, but just a little.

With the mention of my wedding the sparkle in his eyes flickered and went out, like someone blowing out a candle. I pretended not to see and he turned his head toward the window, probably hoping I didn't notice as well.

While we ate, we visited the past, talked about old friends and new ones. He told me about his recent promotions and how he'd made a comfortable life in New Orleans.

"Trinity is never moving out, you know that right?" I said, when he mentioned his sister.

He laughed in agreement. "Yeah, you're probably right. How's your sister?"

"India is still India and still playing by her own rules."

"She still in school?" he asked, shoving a piece of steak into his mouth.

"Of course she is. She wouldn't be India if she wasn't taking some class somewhere." I laughed.

I truly believed my sister was trying to make college her career. Other than occasional work-study programs, the money that our grandfather left us, and the fact that our father had enough foresight to be well insured before he died, she'd never held down a regular job.

I asked, "What's up with Camille, y'all ready to walk down the aisle?"

He chuckled. "Excuse me?"

I smiled. "You heard me. You and Camille? Married?"

"No wedding bells this way, we stopped seeing each other a little while ago."

I rolled my eyes. "What's up with that?"

He smiled and took a sip of his orange juice. "So," he started, "how's your little boy? What's his name again?"

"Oh so I guess we changing the subject?" I asked.

"You would be guessing right."

I took a sip of my coffee. "Cameron. His name is Cameron."

"Cameron, that's right," he repeated. "Hopefully, I get to see him before I leave. Last time I was home he was still a baby and I definitely wanna stop by and holler at your mom."

I nodded and smiled. "Definitely. Last time you came I didn't even get see you, I had to hear about it second-hand."

"I know that was my fault. I came in to handle some things for my mom and I dipped back out. How's your grandmother?" he asked.

"She's okay. Last winter she fell and broke her hip so Mama moved her in with her."

"Oh wow, I'm sorry to hear that."

"She was outside on the ground for almost an hour before someone realized she was there and came to help her."

He shook his head and took a drink of his orange juice. "Wow. Well it's a good thing she's with your mom now."

Sitting there with him I had so many things going through my mind—emotions that I didn't recognize and some I knew all to well. I knew how much I was risking, sitting here with him, but it felt good to be around him again. I missed my best friend; I missed talking with him like we used to do. Throughout college he was constantly a shoulder for me when it came to Lincoln. He was always good at picking me up and dusting me off, and assuring me that things would always work out—eventually.

My thoughts were interrupted by his voice.

"Well I'm really glad things are good with you."

I smiled up at him. "Yeah, things are pretty good. I can't really complain."

His face softened. "Then seriously, I really am happy for you."

"Don't get it twisted, we have our issues but what couple doesn't? His hours are crazy, but we make it work."

He took a bite of his steak. "I don't think I could handle being responsible for anyone else."

"So you don't think you'll move back at all?"

"I doubt it," he said between bites. "There's nothing here for me."

I sank back in my seat and looked at him. Different emotions took jabs at me with his statement, my mind was cloudy and I was crossing lines that had been drawn in the sand a long time ago.

He held his hands out for me to take, and I did. I looked up into his eyes and was surprised to find sympathy living in them. The warmth of his skin against mine caused my heart to pick up speed.

"Come on, you know what I mean."

I slid my hands free from his. "You're good."

"Just because I don't live here anymore doesn't mean I don't still care about you," he continued. "You know that right?"

"I know." I smiled. "I just miss my friend."

"I miss you too, but I can't come back here, Idalis."

"Why not?"

He winked. "Because Atlanta's not big enough for me and your man's egos."

I let out a small laugh. "You make me sick. But you do have a point. Let's go."

He paid the bill and walked me to my car. Both of us moved slowly as we made our way across the parking lot. For the first time I became aware of how humid the air was as it hung over us, weighing me down even more.

I asked, "Where are you going now?"

"Back to my hotel. You gonna be okay?"

He got close to me.

He looked in my eyes, as if trying to read my thoughts.

Being this close to him after all this time was surreal. Part of me wanted to reach out and touch him, to make sure he was really here. Another part of me wanted to turn and run and act like I'd never seen him.

I felt like the world was spinning and I was standing still. "Yea, I'll be fine."

I took a step back.

Put much needed space between us.

I pulled my keys out of my purse and hit the button on the remote. My car's lights flashed. "I gotta go, Trip."

He hugged me and I inhaled him deeply.

The hardness of his body, the firmness of his grip.

I wanted to take him all in.
Commit everything to memory.
It wasn't until I was tucked safely behind the dark tint of my windows that I finally exhaled.

Chapter Three

Trip

Tension had a grip on my neck which was making it hard to focus as my loud-talking SAC addressed the packed conference.

Lenny DeLuca was our special agent in charge. I watched Lenny's stocky frame as he paced the small floor in front of the conference room. His square jaw and dark Italian features were tucked beneath a black DEA cap.

At first glance you'd think he was in his mid-forties, even with the salt-and-pepper goatee that he sported. It was hard to believe he was over fifty.

He'd been DEA for over twenty years and had served a stretch in the U.S. Marines before that. We were told that his no-nonsense attitude was what had propelled him up the ranks. Everyone under his watch respected and trusted him with everything.

There were about ten agents, from both Atlanta and New Orleans, crammed into the conference room. We were all being briefed on the situation in Atlanta. Phil was next to me, and he was devouring a sandwich he'd gotten from Quiznos. He had the conference room lit up with the smell of steak and onions. I was ready to get out of the room and get some fresh air.

"Atlanta P.D. is ready to cooperate fully with this investigation. They weren't happy about us stomping around in their backyard, but I did a good enough job at helping them see the big picture," Lenny informed the group.

"Wow, Lenny, you took over their city like that?" a voice yelled out from the back of the room.

The agents from New Orleans couldn't help but laugh. Mainly because we knew that whatever Lenny wanted, Lenny got when it came to investigations. He was connected on levels that I had yet to discover. And when he decided that he wanted you to see things his way, that's exactly what you did.

He smiled. "Damn right. They wanted help, well they got it."

Laughter erupted in the tiny room, mostly from those of us who'd traveled up I-20 and invaded Atlanta's territory.

He held up his hand. "Okay, okay, ladies," Lenny joked. "That's enough. I think we all have the same goal here. We need to plug this hole that's funneling the contraband into the jail. Just last week an inmate shot another inmate with a gun that was smuggled inside.

"Somebody is picking off big-time drug dealers, one by one. We don't know if there is a new dealer in town or just someone trying to make a name for himself, but we need to find out, and we need to do it fast."

He picked up a folder and spread the contents on the table. The officers all took turns eyeing the paperwork inside. "Spencer, you and your team are over off Moreland." He dropped a folder on the table and pushed it so it slid toward me. I reached out and stopped it. "Atlanta informed me this morning that they have a couple UC's working on this as well. So keep that in mind when you're out there shaking trees."

An agent down front asked, "Are they gonna give us a heads-up?"

He shook his head. "As of right now, no. They know who they are, and will share reports with us tagged with the officer's ID number only. It's for the officer's protection, and to try to maintain some integrity in the investigation."

"Lemme get this right. They obviously got holes in their organization big enough to drive a car through, but they wanna keep secrets from us?" I asked.

Lenny ignored my blow at Atlanta's mediocre cop work. "Okay, you all are in this room because you're the best at what you do. Let's get this case wrapped up guys so I can go home. I don't like Atlanta. The traffic is horrible, and I can't get a decent jambalaya."

After the meeting I made my way to the kitchenette at the end of the hall for a cup of much-needed coffee. As I poured a cup of the steaming liquid, my partner walked in and laughed.

"Whoa, what's up? Your night must've turned out better than I thought. You never drink coffee."

"Man, shut up." I laughed, pulling out a chair and sitting down at one of the dingy white tables that the secretaries and desk workers used to eat lunch.

Phil pulled out the chair across from me and sat down. "So what's up? What happened last night? You and your girl hook up?" He opened a bag of chips.

"It's not like that. We just talked."

He looked confused. "That's it?"

"Yeah, we left the gym and went to Waffle House."

"Really?" Phil leaned back and gave me a sympathetic look. "I'm sorry to hear that."

"You stupid." I shook my head. "What did you think was gon' happen?"

"From what you told me about her, I figured you two would've ended up back at your hotel room, with you blowing her back out."

I busted out laughing. "Nah, we just cool. It's been that way ever since we were shorties."

"So you mean to tell me you never hit that?"

I shook my head. "It ain't like that. We're just friends."

"Man, if she as fine as you say she is, then I really *am* sorry to hear that," he laughed.

I got up and dumped the strong black coffee in the sink. "Man, let's go. We got surveillance to do."

"No, playa, you got it wrong. *You* got surveillance work to do. You driving and I'm taking a nap. I didn't get any sleep, but I got a good reason."

I stopped and looked at him. "And what's that?"

"Denise and Desiree."

"Twins?"

He just stood there, nodding and smiling.

I headed toward the door. "Let's go. You can tell me about it on the way."

Twenty minutes later we pulled the black un-marked Tahoe into a spot nestled about three houses away from the house that was under surveillance. As promised, my partner slid down in his seat and pulled his black DEA cap down over his eyes.

"Wake me up if you see anything interesting."

I couldn't help but chuckle. "Yeah, okay."

We both knew that surveillance work could take as little as a day or as long as a month. It was a matter of the luck of the draw. So for the next four hours, we took turns watching the dilapidated house on Hollywood Road. I did more watching than Phil, whose snoring was starting to get on my damn nerves.

Crackheads and dealers made their way in and out, oblivious to the fact that they were being watched.

"Get up, dude. Ain't that your CI?" I asked, nudging Phil with my elbow.

"Yeah, that's him. Hit the lights."

I flashed the headlights twice, and we watched as Darius checked his surroundings before he started a sluggish jog in our direction. He probably couldn't get up the speed to run because he was so big and sloppy, on top of the fact that his pants were down around his ass. When he approached the truck, I instinctively rested my hand on my gun.

Phil rolled down the window. "Yo, what you doing over here?"

He shook his head and looked up the street from where he'd just come. "Just chillin'. Ain't nothing goin' on over here. It's just the same crowd."

Darius kept eyeing me, and I did likewise. I didn't like dealing with a CI that I wasn't familiar with, but this dude and Phil had developed a good relationship. So if my partner trusted him, then I had to trust him as well.

"Damn," Phil said. "Can't you call someone? Let them know you're looking for weight."

Darius frowned at him. "What, you think we all hang out playing Xbox and texting each other and shit?"

I couldn't help but laugh at that.

Phil sank back in his seat. "Come on, Darius, I need something."

"Look, just gimme a couple days to try to come up with something. I might know somebody, a brotha named Twist. He always knows a little bit of something about everything. Let me see if I can catch up with him. Cool?"

"A'ight, call as soon as he get at you," Phil instructed.

"No doubt."

Phil rolled up the tinted window and looked over at me. "You ready to call it a night?"

"Whatever, you slept most of the time," I laughed.

"Told you I was tired."

After I dropped Phil off at his car, I checked the time. It was pushing up on eight, but I decided to stop past my mom's, anyway. I hadn't seen her or my sister since I'd been in town. Plus I was starving, and a drive-through just wasn't gonna cut it for me right now.

I pulled into the tiny driveway in front of the even smaller house situated over in southwest Atlanta. I swear, when I was growing up, this house and yard used to be huge. Now it seemed so small and inconsequential. Back then, however, I wasn't six foot two and 195 pounds.

The light in the living room was on, letting me know someone was up. I took a deep breath and killed the engine on the truck. Memories started flying at me like I was in a batting cage. Each one held its own dose of emotion. When I saw the curtains in the front window rustle, it was official.

I was home again.

I hopped out of the truck and made my way to the front door. Before I could rest my hand on the doorknob, my baby sister snatched the door open and wrapped her arms around my neck.

"Oh my God! Trip! When did you get here?" she shrieked.

"I got in town a few days ago," I said, walking into the house with Trinity still wrapped around my body.

She slid off me and placed her feet on the floor and her hands on her full-sized hips. "And you're just now coming by here? Mommy gon' be mad."

"I was doing some surveillance work, couldn't get away. This bust ruffled a lot of feathers."

She smiled big. "Well, now that my big brother is in town, it's all good!"

I cracked a smile. "Glad you have that much faith in me."

She looked around me, back at the front door. "Where's your fine-ass partner?"

"Shut up, Trinity and move." I brushed by her and made my way toward the kitchen.

My sister had grown from a scraggly, knobby-kneed teenager to a beautiful woman. She could rival the best of them in the looks and the body department. Her hazel eyes, which nestled beneath her long, thick eyelashes, and her high cheekbones combined to give her the kind of exotic look that most women were paying for at the cosmetic counter and plastic surgeon's. A few months ago she told me that she was starting to loc her hair, and it looked good.

"Where's Mom?" I asked.

"In bed, lying down. Her hip has been bothering her."

I changed my direction and headed toward the hallway that led to my mother's room. "Hook me up with a plate. I'm starving," I said to my sister. Then I tapped on the worn wooden door before slowly pushing it open. "Mama?"

Her small body changed positioned in the bed and she turned her focus from the television to me. "Orlando?"

"Yes, ma'am."

Her tiny hands covered her mouth. "Oh my Jesus! When did you get here? Come here and give me a hug!"

I made my way to the bed and wrapped my mother up in my arms. Myrtle Spencer was truly small. I was scared that if I squeezed her too hard, she'd snap in half. She smelled like Noxzema and cocoa butter lotion. The same scent she'd carried since I could remember. Trinity always tried to buy her new stuff, but she always went back to what she liked. I never told her, but I was always glad when she did. Those other smells were foreign to me; they didn't smell like home.

"I got here a few days ago. Been doing some work. Sorry it took me so long to come by."

She reached up and took my hat off my head. I laughed to myself. My mother had a strict rule: no hats on in the house. It was sign of disrespect as far as she was concerned. "Your hair is too long."

I smiled. Mama hated the locs when I started growing them back in college. But just as much as she hated them, she hated the braids I used to wear even more.

"Are you hungry?" she asked, starting to get up out of the bed.

"Mama, I'm okay. Trinity is fixing me something now. You stay in the bed. She told me your hip has been bothering you. Have you been to the doctor?"

She waved her hand in my direction. "Hogwash, they know about as much as I do. I just need to stay off it for a while. I'll be fine."

I laughed at her feisty attitude. I knew there was no way I was gonna convince her otherwise, but I was gonna make sure Trinity got her to the doctor by the end of the week.

"Where are you staying?" she asked.

I never stayed with my mom when I came to town. In my line of work, I didn't want to draw attention to my family if I could help it. All it took was one pissed-off drug dealer or runner and my world would be twisted up in an instant.

"I'm okay, Mama. Look, I'm not gonna stay long. I just wanted to stop by and grab something to eat. I'll make sure I call you tomorrow, okay?"

I bent down and kissed my mom's cheek. I loved my mother more than anything, but I didn't want to get sucked in and emotional. I couldn't afford to. Don't get me wrong. I loved what I did, but the price I had to pay at times made me wonder if it was all worth it.

I stood up and started across the tiny room to-ward the door when my mother's voice stopped me. "Trip, I know you're busy with your job. But your daddy's dead and buried now."

I stopped without turning around. "Yes, Mama, I know."

"It's time to let it go. Stop all this back and forth."

"I love you Mama, I'll call you to in the morn-ing."

I didn't respond to that, I just kept moving. Once in the kitchen, I sat down at the tiny table in front of the plate my sister had fixed for me: fried chicken, green beans, mashed potatoes, and corn bread. I assumed all leftovers from the dinner they'd had earlier.

"Thanks, Trin," I managed between bites.

She placed a glass of sweet tea in front of me before she sat down across from my chair. I looked up into her eyes and knew she was full of questions—and I wasn't in the mood to answer any of them.

"I can't believe you're actually here. Why didn't you call and tell me you were coming in?"

"Well, loan me twenty dollars so I can prove it and I barely had time to pack. I hope the shit I threw in my suitcase matches."

She laughed. "Whatever, big shot. You need to lend me some money. You the one who got the big promotion."

I looked up from my green beans. "You need a little something?"

She shook her head. "I'm good. I got the new check card for Mama's prescriptions and stuff."

Six years ago when I left for the DEA I started having money direct deposited every two weeks from my check into an account to cover my mother's expenses. I knew that her SSI and Medicare weren't nearly enough. When my ex-girl, Camille, and I split she started acting a little crazy and I had to change a lot of shit around.

I nodded. "Good."

"Camille still acting up?"

"Nah, she settled down, once I threatened to arrest her ass."

She laughed. "Was you really gon' arrest her?"

I glanced up at her like she was crazy. "Hell yeah! She keyed my damn car."

"That's not nice, Trip."

I smiled. "I wasn't gon' lock that chick up, calm down."

"Good."

She got quiet. Too quiet.

I took a bite of my corn bread. Without looking up I asked, "What do you want, Trinity?"

"A'ight look, don't get me wrong. I'm glad you're here, but how long are you gonna keep jumping back and forth across the state line, Trip?"

I took a drink of sweet tea. "I'm not."

"Yes you are."

"I'm not one of your social work cases, Trinity," I said, dropping my fork to my plate. "Stop trying to psychoanalyze me. I live in New Orleans."

Just then, my phone sang a jingle, cutting short what was destined to be an argument.

I checked the display and stood up. "I gotta go."

I placed my plate in the sink, kissed her on the cheek, and headed toward the front door.

"Yeah"—she called to my back—"you always do."

"The healthy man does not torture others. Generally it is the tortured who turn into torturers."

— *Carl Jung*

The nighttime skyline came into view as his truck cut down I-85 and exited the interstate and blended into the crowded downtown city streets. The city was alive with nightlife. On the outside, it was the equivalent of a beautiful woman, drawing you in with mind-blowing views of the beautiful Centennial Olympic and Piedmont parks.

Just like two supple breasts, Turner Field and The Georgia Dome captured a man's eye and pulled him closer. But just like that baddest bitch in the club, Atlanta had its secrets. And if you were to dig deeper, you'd find them. This beautiful city is just as grimy as the next gold digging bitch trying to make a come up.

He'd made this run a hundred times if he'd
done it once. He looked down at his dashboard.
He had just got a text and needed to head to the
other side of town so he needed to make this one
quick.

He caught a glimpse of himself in the rearview
mirror and didn't like what he saw in his eyes. It
was a look of a man who was slowly being backed
into a corner.

He knew the look all to well, because he'd put
the same look in the eyes of others men.

The screen in his dash began to glow along
with the phone in it's holder in the armrest. He
hit the button on his steering wheel.

"Yeah."

A sensual voice, with a Spanish accent oozed
from his speakers. "Hey *papì*, I thought you were
coming to see me. I miss you."

"I may not make it tonight."

"But—" she started.

"Listen here, don't start that shit. I got business to take care of, I'll get at you when I can."

He heard a soft sigh come from her end of the
phone. "Okay. Are you gonna call me later?"

"If I can."

He pulled up to his destination as he continued to listen to her attitude pour through his
speakers. He ran his hand across the top of his

head a couple times, tried to give her a second to get her shit right.

She didn't.

"Look, I ain't got time for this, I'm gone."

With a tap of the screen he disconnected the call, grabbed his cell and hopped out the truck. She knew better than to call back and try to argue so he didn't give it a second thought.

In front of the dingy townhouse situated off Center Hill Avenue he spotted two tall skinny dudes standing out front. One looked like he was texting and the other was on his phone. They both straightened up and gave him their full attention when they saw him approaching the steps.

The dark-skinned one spoke first, "Hey man, what's up?"

The other one nodded absent-mindedly like he wasn't sure what to say.

He nodded toward the house. "Twist in there?"

They both nodded.

He brushed past them and jogged up the steps and entered without knocking. The smell in the small house was enough to make him want to hurry up and get this over with. It smelled like someone burnt something and tried to cover it up with some nasty smelling air freshener that made it even worse.

He made his way to the back where he found
Twist and one of his boys playing Xbox. Twist
jumped up, surprised, when he saw him.

"Yo, I ain't hear you come in, what's up?"

"Maybe if you grow the fuck up and stop
playing video games you'd be more aware of
what's goin' on around you," he said, snatching
the game plugs out of the television. "Go get my
shit."

Twist made his way in the other room and the
dude Twist was playing the game with got up
and stood behind him, blocking the doorway.
He figured that was supposed to be a sign of
intimidation but he took it as disrespect.

Without hesitating, he turned around and
punched him in his throat causing him to double
over. While he was bent over trying to catch his
breath he hit him twice in his jaw.

"Yo! Is you crazy? Fuck away from me," he
growled, as dude scrambled into a nearby chair.

"Hey! Chill out Linc man, *damn!*" Twist said,
coming back in the room with a briefcase.

"Man shut up, that my shit?" he demanded,
turning his attention to him.

Twist flipped through the contents of a briefcase, which was now open on a table in front of
him. His ashy hands were trembling; he could
barely count the crisp new bills inside.

"One fifty large," he finally said.

"That's it?" Linc said. "Come on now. That figure you talkin' is gon' make some people unhappy, 'cause it just pissed me off."

"I—I can probably have the rest by next week," he stuttered. His eyes nervously glanced over at his boy, who was still trying to get himself together.

"Come on, man. You know how this works. Supply and demand," Linc said. "I supplied, and now I'm demandin' my damn money."

Linc paced the floor, while Twist stood fidgeting, not sure what was about to happen. The tension in the room made him feel somewhat godlike, and he got a high from it, which he loved.

The first time he'd shook down a dealer, over two years ago during a bust, it gave him a buzz—a feeling that not even the purest cocaine could replicate. When he realized just how stupid these dealers really were, that only fueled his appetite and from that point it was on and poppin'.

"The streets are cold. Everyone is underground."

Linc pulled his gun out of his waistband and tapped it on the edge of the table. "Well, get a shovel and start digging. You know I don't operate like this."

Twist nodded in agreement. "I know. I know. I just gotta make a couple calls, that's all. Just gimme some time."

"How much time?" Linc frowned at him. He really wanted to lay Twist's skinny ass out, but he needed him. Twist was good for running little bullshit errands, which Linc either didn't like doing or just couldn't do. And he was good for keeping him up on what was going on in other areas too. This fool had an ear and a hand in a little bit of everything.

Twist continued, "I don't know . . . a couple weeks. Right now, he's the only connect I know of that got pockets that deep."

Linc took a deep breath and processed his options. Things had been running pretty smooth up to this point, and he needed shit back the way it was quick. He walked over to the table and pulled a stack of money out of the case and then slid the case back in Twist's direction.

"Do it and you better not be fuckin' with me."

Twist nodded. "I can still deliver the rest of the merchandise to your boy from the jail tomorrow night."

"He's expectin' you over off Moreland with them cell phones."

Twist nervously shook his head. "I got'chu. I got'chu. I'll be there."

"You better be. Don't make me have my boys run up in here and bust you, Twist. You know I will."

For a split second, a very quick second, he actually felt bad for Twist. He knew he was just a low-life dealer trying to eat but the way he'd been fucking up lately was unacceptable. Linc had been rolling him for almost two years now and he'd been the most respectful and loyal out of all the dealers he'd fucked with. But right now he was fucking with his money and that was something Linc didn't take lightly. A few dealers had already been laid down because of that shit. Linc was careful that it wasn't by his hand or even by the hand next to his; but dudes knew his reach was far and wide and no one ever knew when he'd reach out and touch them.

"I know, I know. Just gimme some time to handle this other thing," Twist said.

The sound of Linc's gun being cocked echoed through the room, causing everyone to stop in their tracks. Linc pointed the gun at Twist's boy squeezing the trigger and putting a bullet into the wall next to his head.

He holstered his gun.

He pulled his phone off his hip and headed out the door.

"Make this right, homie, or next time I won't miss."

He was out the door before the piss made its way down Twist's leg and hit the floor.

Chapter Four

Idalis

I agreed to meet India at Applebee's before heading in to the club. I figured hanging out with her would chill me out and get me ready for the club tonight. She reached over and swiped a wing from my plate; I took a sip of her sweet tea.

"Are you going to be able to make the dress fitting next week?"

She nodded. "Yeah, but I ain't happy about it."

"Don't start, India. Dionne ain't complaining about her dress."

"That's because her dress doesn't make her look fat like mine does."

I rolled my eyes. "And your dress doesn't make you look fat either, shut up."

"I'm serious. Dionne looks like a damn model in hers. I think you did it on purpose."

"Give it up, India. You're wearing the dress."

Her cell rang, causing mine to chime right in. She gave me a frown, because she knew who it was.

Linc's name flashed across the screen on my phone, validating her dirty look.

When I came home last night after meeting Trip and picking up Cameron from my mom's, Lincoln wasn't home. And by the time he came in, I was already asleep.

I answered, "Hey, you."

"Hey, girl, where you at?"

"Applebee's, with India."

"You was sleep when I got home last night," he said.

"I know. You should've woke me up."

He let out a low laugh. "It was late. At some point we gon' have to meet in the middle."

"Yeah, we are," I agreed. "I miss you."

Our hit-or-miss routine had been going on for weeks now. If it wasn't for his dirty clothes and toothbrush, half the time I wouldn't know he lived there.

He kept talking. "You going by the club tonight?"

"Yea, I'm leaving here in a few."

"A'ight. I'll stop by there later."

"Okay, I'll see you later then."

I hung up and put my phone on the table. India was still into her conversation with whoever the flavor of the week was for her. I could tell from the giggles and the low tone of her voice that she was making plans, the kind of plans that I wished I had for tonight.

I waved down our waitress and ordered a piece of carrot cake and a cup of coffee. Hell, if I wasn't getting any, I might as well be fat.

India hung up. "Whoa, what are you doing?"

"I need something sweet."

"A'ight. You're gonna be the one looking fat in her dress if you keep it up."

"Whatever."

She shoved a few fries into her mouth. "Guess that was him?"

"Yes, it was."

She chuckled and drank her tea. "Y'all are funny."

"I am glad my relationship is amusing you."

"It's not," she said, taking another wing from my plate. "It's actually pretty sad."

"What do you mean by that?"

She raised an eyebrow. "Look at the way you let him control you. And don't even get me started on Trip, and I barely see you anymore—unless I look in the mirror."

I laughed at that last part. But I couldn't argue with her. "Just drop it, India. Who were you on the phone with?"

"Derek."

"I thought you were done with him."

"I was, but he has a hurricane tongue, and that's hard to let go."

I couldn't help but giggle. "You're a tramp."

"Don't try to change the subject. Why haven't you talked to Trip yet?"

I smiled. "Who said I haven't?"

She leaned back, surprised. "Ooh, girl! You holding out! When? What did he say?"

"We bumped into each other at the gym and went to Waffle House after. That's all. But I have to admit, it felt good to be around him again."

She took a drink of her tea. "I bet it did. Growing up, you two were joined at the hip."

It wasn't until Linc showed up during our sophomore year in college and enrolled at Morehouse that things started to change between Trip and I.

Linc grew up off Bankhead, a few neighborhoods over from us, and fought his way up from the streets by way of the football field at Douglass High.

His speed and strong throwing arm earned him a full-ride scholarship to the University of

Georgia, but when he found out he wasn't going to be starting he wasn't happy. So he whined and complained his way out of a scholarship into a bunch of student loan debt just to start on a mediocre football squad at Morehouse.

Little did I know that from that point on things would never be the same or that the hatred between Trip and Linc would quickly turned into more than just a rival between alma maters.

"He seems happy, though, and he looks good."

"I don't think Trip could look bad if he tried."

I laughed. "True. I didn't realize how much I missed him until I saw him."

"You think he misses it here?"

I shook my head. "No. He seems like he's content with where he is."

"Did you ask him?"

"Ask him what? If he wanted to move back?"

She scooped up a piece of my carrot cake. "Yeah."

"Why would I do that?"

"Because that's what you want. And the way he left was kind of messed up."

I shoved a forkful of cake into my mouth. "No, it's not. And you need to mind your business."

She gave me a look that let me know she didn't believe me. And I gave her a look that let her know I didn't care what she thought.

Her expression changed from playful to serious. "You know if—"

I cut her off. "I know, Twin, I know."

I drank some of my water and wiped my mouth. India started shredding her napkin and tossing it onto the table, a sign that something was on her mind.

Now it was my turn to grill her.

"What's up with you? Why are you making a mess?"

She leaned back in the booth. "I wanted to talk to you about something."

"What's up?"

Her chest rose and fell with a huge sigh. "Well, you know I'm supposed to graduate in the fall."

"Yeah."

"Well, I was thinking about—"

I cut her off. "I swear, India, if you mention another degree, I'm gonna fight you."

She balled up what was left of the napkin and threw it at me.

"No! *Damn*. Shut up and let me finish," she fussed. "There's a company that I've been talking to, and they might be interested in me."

"That's good!"

I jumped up, ran around the table, and climbed into the booth next to her. I hugged her, but she didn't seem as excited as I was.

I stopped my solo celebration and looked at her. "What? What's the problem?"

"The company is out in San Francisco."

I slid to the edge of the booth like she was contagious. "That *better* be the new nickname for downtown Atlanta."

She just sat there with this stupid look on her face, shaking her head.

"Oh *hell* no!" I got up and moved back to my side of the table and starting digging around in my purse.

"Where are you going?"

I pulled a twenty out of my purse and tossed it on the table. "I'm going to 404."

She looked up at me, almost pleading. "Come on, Idalis. Don't be like that."

"Love you. Bye, India. Text me when you get to my house and before you put Cameron to bed."

"Twin!" she called to me.

"I gotta go. I'll be home as soon as I get off."

I made my way toward the club without even turning on the radio. I let the window down a little and inhaled the fresh air. Again I found myself trying to clear my head.

California. *California?*

I couldn't believe that heifer was really trying to move 3,000 miles away. That was the last thing I wanted to hear.

Tension rode my back as I clutched my phone, scrolling through the contacts until I found the number I was looking for. The jury in my mind deliberated for a few moments before coming back with a verdict.

I hit send.

Chapter Five

Trip

My phone rang, but I silenced it without even looking at the display. We were standing in the middle of what could only be described as a massacre. The young lady's throat had been cut so deep that her head was almost severed.

I looked around the upscale home in Cobb County and couldn't help but shake my head. I wondered if these refined neighbors knew that they were living in the midst of a well-thought-out, well-orchestrated drug ring, right in their own backyards.

Just when I didn't think that things could get any worse, I noticed Lincoln Briscoe walking out of the kitchen. He was on his cell phone, which gave me a chance to go the other way.

I found Phil standing over the body, which was now covered with a white sheet. My partner was talking to one of the APD officers. There were a few agents there taking notes and gathering evidence.

"They found the knife. It's already been bagged," the officer said.

"Cool. She got a name?"

The officer answered, "Monique Lewis. Stabbed fifteen times, throat slashed. Apparently, she was running more than drugs out of this nice house."

Again I couldn't help but think about my sister.

Phil looked at me. "You a'ight?"

"Yeah, I'm good."

"Of course, he's good. You don't know? That's Supercop," Linc taunted. "Special Agent Orlando Spencer."

Phil looked over at him like he was crazy then looked back to me.

Linc walked up with a sly grin on his face that I wanted to slap off.

The sound of his voice made me wanna punch a hole in the wall. But instead, I turned around and growled, "Listen here, I'm an *agent,* not a cop. Matter of fact, why are you even here? Don't you have a speeding ticket quota to meet?"

"I see they called in the Top Cop, all the way from New Orleans."

I laughed. "As long as you notice."

It was no secret that Lincoln and I didn't get along, but we had managed to find a way to coexist back in college for Idalis' sake. We'd both known, since the day we met in Idalis's dorm room, we were oil and water. We didn't mix. And I was sure he hated me being back in Atlanta, almost as much as I hated being there. I knew me being DEA and digging up dirt in APD's backyard, his stomping ground, was pissing him off even more, but I didn't give a fuck.

"Well, I for one am glad to have you back in town," he said, sarcasm hanging on every word. "Does Idalis know you're here?"

With the mention of her name, my body got tense. "Why don't you ask her?" I shot back.

"I'll do that, Trip, when I get home. Right before bed."

Our eyes locked in a hate-filled stare until someone called him name getting his attention.

"They need you in the back, Lieutenant Briscoe." An APD officer came up and said.

"Duty calls. It was good seein' you," he taunted, as he walked away.

"Yeah, give Idalis my best when you see her," I said, cracking a smile. "If you can."

I was about to head for the door when I got a call from Clayton County.

"Spencer," I answered.

"Hey, this is Morgan. We're following a lead on the stabbing out here in College Park. Some girl named Santee Mitchell."

"A'ight, keep me posted."

I went and found Phil in the kitchen. "They got a lead. Some chick in College Park."

"Cool, they don't need us then. Let's be out then."

We were about to head out, when an officer came in and stopped us. "Hold up. We found a girl hiding in a closet downstairs."

We watched as a female officer led a thin, terrified girl into the crowded room. Her wide-eyed expression let me know that she'd seen way more than she ever wanted to see in her lifetime. Someone had covered her scantily clad body with an over-sized blanket. The room was silent as she sank down on the couch. I walked over to her and crouched down and got eye level with her.

"Hi, I'm Agent Spencer. I'm with the DEA. What's your name?"

She opened her mouth to speak but nothing came out at first. So she tried again. "Mya De-lowe."

I looked back at the officers in the room. "Did you see what happened here tonight?"

This time she didn't even try to speak she just nodded.

"We're gonna need you to give a statement, can you do that?"

Tears welled in her eyes as she nodded again.

I tapped her lightly on her leg and thanked her before standing up and making my way back to the door.

Just then Lincoln stepped in the room.

"There you go, *Lieutenant* Briscoe, handle that." I cracked a sinister smile.

Hatred flashed in his eyes, letting me know that if there hadn't been a house full of law enforcement, things would be going a lot differently now.

I gave him a wink before heading out the door behind Phil.

We got into the truck, and Phil pulled a Hostess cake out of nowhere and opened it up.

"Don't get crumbs everywhere," I said.

He held out the chocolate cake. "Want one?"

I just shook my head and cranked up the truck.

Once we were back downtown, we sat in the conference room and scoured stacks of paperwork for hours, trying to piece them together like a puzzle. Trying to find a pattern, a slipup, anything that would give us a clue on what the connection was between all of this and how it tied in with the jail.

"There's a lot of money and drugs being moved in and out of there for nobody not to know anything," Phil mumbled while studying files. "There has to be something we're missing."

"Not to mention this phantom dealer who's taking over territory under the radar. Atlanta got more problems than they realize."

"Shit, I know," Phil agreed.

I stood up and tried to walk off the tension in my back. I stretched a little and peered out the window. "We've been over this stuff a million times. Ever since the trail pointed in this direction, we've been on top of everything. We may never plug this hole."

"Maybe you not as good as they thought, pot'na."

I turned around and saw Lincoln walking in the room, followed by two city cops. A few seconds later, Lenny appeared in the door.

"What are you doing here?"

Lincoln sat down at the end of the table farthest from me. "Now, I know you didn't think we were gon' let you ride in town on your white horse without letting us play, did you?"

I looked at Lenny. "What is he doing here?"

"Lieutenant Briscoe is supervising the UC's over in Zone One and has a good bit of information on some dealers and their runners. It couldn't hurt to let him know what you've collected so far."

Phil stood up. "Why don't you have Lieutenant *Bankhead* here just give us his list of names and let us do what we came here to do?"

Linc mean-mugged Phil. Part of me wanted him to at least try to go after him to justify the ass kicking I've wanted to give him for years.

"Once this case crossed state lines, technically, it became our jurisdiction, Lenny," I countered. "We don't have to share lunch with this cop."

I heard Lincoln let out a disgusted sound. "Hey, we can do this the easy way or we can do this my way, don't matter to me, ya dig."

Lenny let out a sigh. "Look, don't turn this into a cockfight. This case is starting to take on a life of its own, and you two know it. So, Spencer and Porter knock off the Crockett-and-Tubbs act and close this case so I can get the hell out of Georgia."

With that, Lenny turned and walked out of the room.

"So, fellas, what you got so far?" Lincoln asked, leaning back in his chair.

"You can read, right, Briscoe?" I started.

Phil tossed the folder he was holding in his direction, causing the contents to fly out and scatter across the tabletop. The two city cops that were with Linc started picking up the scattered papers.

"Figure it out," Phil finished.

Phil walked out and I started to follow, when Lincoln stopped me.

He let out a slight laugh. "Yo, I ain't goin' nowhere, dog. You might as well get used to seein' me. Fed may trump city, but this is still my backyard, pot'na."

Fire rose in my chest and lapped around my neck and ears. I saw out of the corner of my eye that Phil had reappeared in the doorway to the conference room.

"Yo, Trip, he ain't worth it, man. Let's go."

I looked from Phil back to Lincoln. He had a smug look on his face that made it damn hard not to fire off a round in his chest. I turned and headed out the door and I heard him call out to me.

"I'm lookin' forward to workin' with you, Special Agent Spencer."

"Fuck you, Lieutenant Briscoe," I shot back.

Chapter Six

Idalis

Club 404 was packed to capacity. I knew we had to be violating some sort of fire code tonight. The DJ had the whole club jumping. His mix had everyone cramming onto what little bit of dance floor there was left. Customers were screaming their orders out to the waitresses over the loud music and bartenders were happily filling orders and collecting tips. After their confusing, shouting exchanges, the servers could barely maneuver through the crowds, back to the bar with their orders.

Before I had Cameron, I worked as a manager and an event planner for the Four Seasons, which kept me pretty busy. But once I got pregnant, Lincoln felt I shouldn't be working. He encouraged me to slow down—more like *insisted* on me slowing down. I didn't start working again until Cameron was almost two, when Linc surprised me by buying this spot. He was co-owner, but he always said that it was just on paper, that this was my project to do whatever I wanted to do with. And I had a lot of ideas for this spot. It took a little over a year but the word got out quick and Club 404 was on the map and I was making my own hours and home with my son whenever I wanted to be, making both Linc and me happy.

The black T-shirt and skinny jeans from *bebe* I had on were a good choice. I was comfortable but had dressed up my outfit with some accessories for the pictures that people always wanted to take with me since I was the owner.

My hair was pulled back in the front and hung straight down my back. I hated having hair in my face when I was sweaty and with all the running around I was doing tonight, I was definitely working up a sweat.

If I wasn't running around and pulling money from the bartenders' drawers, then taking it back to the office, I was taking pictures or networking with radio stations or local magazines trying to get ad space and more exposure. Tonight my good friend Si-Man Baby hosting on the mic and he was working the crowd. He came over and gave me a quick squeeze.

"You looking good in them jeans girl."

I smiled. "Thank you. I appreciate you coming out tonight."

"Anything for you, you know that."

A few patrons walked up, asked if they could snap a few pictures. Si-Man and I obliged and then he disappeared into the sea of people and started hyping the crowd.

"When I say Si-Man you say Baby!" he called in the mic, voice booming through the club. "Si-Man!"

"Baaaaaby!" the crowd responded.

I made my way to Dionne's station, and instinctively she placed a bottle of water in front of me. We'd been tag teaming at this for almost two years, it was like we read each others minds. I popped the top on the water and let its coolness hit the back of my throat and cool my insides.

I pulled my phone out of my back pocket and checked my messages. India texted me and let me know that she'd picked Cameron up from my mom's and was on her way to my house. She also let me know that she didn't appreciate me leaving her at Applebee's. I responded and thanked her for picking him up and told her I wasn't thinking about her or her trip to California.

Just when I was about to head to the back office, I felt an arm snake its way around my waist and a pair of lips brushed my neck.

I inhaled his scent and smiled. *God he smells good*, I thought.

"I wondered if you were coming," I said over the loud music.

Linc turned me around and I looked up into his brown eyes before planting a kiss on his lips.

"I told you I was, didn't I?"

"Yeah, but it was getting late. I didn't think you were gonna make it."

I cut my eyes for a second and I saw Dionne placing drinks on a tray in front of me. She hollered across the bar and asked me if I could run them to a table because apparently Marissa put the order in and had forgotten about them. I nodded before I turned my attention back to Lincoln.

He tilted his head and smiled. "So you got me punchin' a clock?"

I had wrapped my arms around his neck and squeezed. "I didn't mean it like that. How was your day?"

He leaned back onto one of the empty stools. "Man, it's been a crazy day. Did you hear about them findin' that chick with her throat cut?"

I picked up the tray off the counter. "Yeah, we were talking about it earlier. Does it have anything to do with your case?"

Before he could answer, his phone lit up on his hip. His hand instinctively went to grab it. He nodded toward the crowd. "Go 'head and handle yo' business. Let me get this. We'll talk when you get back."

I grabbed the tray off the counter and waded my way through the dense crowd of drunks and half-naked women gyrating to yet another song with a long list of promises of satisfaction in bed.

As I set the drinks in front of the customers, I looked up at the bar where Linc was standing covering one ear with his free hand and using the other to hold his phone. He was having what appeared to be an intense conversation. I watched his lips moving as he pressed his phone against his ear. His goatee was perfectly manicured against his chocolate skin. He had just got a fresh cut, his line-up was sharp, and he looked damn good. The lights from the bar bounced off his Breil Milano watch, drawing attention to the tattoo on his forearm. That watch was my Christmas gift to him last year.

A voice snapped me out of my peep session. I looked at the table of people, reacting as if they had just appeared out of nowhere.

"Huh? I'm sorry. What did you say?"

The female sitting directly across from me had attitude written all over her overdone face. Her fake lashes were so long and thick; honestly, I was surprised she could even see the drink to pick it up. She slid her martini glass back across the round table toward me.

"I *said,* I asked for a Cotton Candy martini. That's not what this is," she snapped.

I cocked my head and leaned in a little closer, because now *I* had an attitude. "Excuse me?"

"There ain't hardly any liquor in this. I ain't paying seven dollars for a glass of flavored water."

The guys she was with laughed, but the other lone female tried to get her to chill out. "It ain't that serious, Princess, dang. Why you always gotta try to get loud?"

Princess? Seriously? This weaved-up bitch's name was Princess. It took all I had in me to maintain my owner persona, because I really wanted to cuss her out and toss the drink I was holding in her face.

"You want something else?" I asked.

"No, I want the drink I asked for," she snapped, rolling her big fish eyes.

I stopped and glared at her for a second. "I'll send a waitress over with a new drink." I took the glass and headed back toward the bar.

I slammed the glass down on the counter. "Dionne, I need another Cotton Candy martini, heavy on the liquor, please, and this time make sure Marissa does her damn job and takes it over there."

Dionne took the glass and dumped its contents and started mixing another one. "What they say?" she asked.

I just shook my head. "Don't ask." I looked around. "Have you seen Lincoln? He was just standing here."

She nodded toward the back. "He headed back toward your office a few minutes ago."

Dionne's milk chocolate skin was glowing with perspiration under the lighting of the bar. Her short naturally curly haircut fit her face perfectly. He sweat caused some of the short wispy curls to hug her hairline. She was short and put together, but she wasn't one to be messed with either. I learned that from running around with her in college. We were always up in somebody's dorm, cussing out a chick for one reason or another. Usually, it was over a rumor that had made its way back to her. Dionne was into women, had been since high school, so it was never over a man; but the relationships she was in and out of with women seemed to cause just as many problems as a heterosexual relationship.

I turned to make my way to the back when I was stopped in my tracks by a slurred, gravelly voice.

"Hey, Miss Idalis! What I gotta do to get a dance?"

I smiled at Mr. Lewis as I walked by. I scanned his appearance. His salt-and-pepper hair, scruffy beard, and crooked smile were endearing. His wife passed, over a year ago, from cancer, I think, and that's when he started coming here. I think it was more for company than for anything else. He was a sweet man in his mid to late sixties, and he was always trying to convince me to dance with him.

I winked at him. "I told you, I can't dance with you until you're ready to marry me and take me away."

He smiled a big grin, revealing missing teeth. "Okay, now, I'll get the ring. You just better be ready."

"I promise I will be."

"Here you go." He handed me a twenty-dollar bill.

We'd had this ritual for months now. I had accepted the fact that my short, flirtatious conversation was the equivalent of a lap dance for him.

He didn't get a lot of attention from the waitresses, mainly because he was older and didn't have the best hygiene. The first few times I turned down his money, but then he confided that it offended him and that I should take it as a compliment—so began our weekly exchange.

"Thank you, Mr. Lewis," I said, shoving the bill in the back pocket of my jeans.

Our little conversation didn't stop my momentum. I wanted to know what had drawn and, more importantly, what was keeping Lincoln in the back for so long.

Before I pushed the door to my small office open, I stopped and tried to hear over the music what was being said. I couldn't make out much, but I heard Lincoln's voice and he was angry. I could only make out him asking if someone was "sure" about something.

When I finally pushed the door open, Lincoln was leaning against my messy desk in the middle of the room. There were papers all over my desk, because it was coming up on the end of the month, and it was almost time to balance the books. There were packages of supplies, which I hadn't opened yet, stacked up throughout the dusty office.

That's when it hit me.

Nate was the dude I'd seen at the gym.

Nate shot me a grin that made my skin crawl. "Hey, girl. What's up?"

"Hey, Nate," I answered back.

Linc looked up from his phone. He was agitated. "What you need, Idalis?"

"I was just wondering where you disappeared to—"

He cut me off. "I'll be out in a second."

I stood there for a moment, not sure of what was going on.

He looked up at me. "Idalis, gimme a few minutes to wrap this up."

I stared at him for a second, prepared to check his ass for snapping on me in my own office, and that's when I saw it.

Saw the anger swirling around in the same brown eyes that were so happy to see me just moments ago.

I turned around and headed back to the front of the club.

By the time I made it back to the bar, I didn't know what to think.

"You good?" Through my clouded thinking I heard Dionne speak. I looked at her. Tried to focus. I saw her lips moving, but I couldn't hear what was coming out.

I shook my head like I was trying to clear it. "What?" I asked.

"I asked if you were good?"

I looked down at my watch. It was almost one. I looked back toward where I'd just come from.

"Lincoln's in the back with Nate." I gave her a look that must've translated the confusion I was feeling. "I don't know what the hell his problem is."

She twisted her face. "What is he doing here? Ain't he supposed to be out chasing criminals or something?"

"He's been acting funny ever since Trip got back."

Her eyes got big. "Trip Spencer?" She leaned back and laughed. "I *know* he ain't happy about that shit."

I shook my head. "No, he's not."

I looked around and watched the pulse of the crowd, getting lost for a moment in everyone dancing and partying like they didn't have a care in the world.

"Well, don't let it get to you," she reassured me. "Once this is over, and Trip is gone, he'll be back to normal."

"Yeah, let's just hope that's soon."

Just then, I felt Linc come up behind me. He wrapped his arms around my waist, squeezed me close, and pressed his lips against my ear. The sense of relief, which started to wash over my body, was stifled when he whispered in my ear.

"You need to meet me back at the house, now."

My mouth fell open with disbelief. My stomach did a flip.

Before I could ask what was going on, he disappeared into the crowd. Dionne gave me a look filled with questions, which I had no answers for.

I had no idea what his problem was but Dionne agreed to do the last count down of the night and tip out the DJ for me so I could finish up in the office and head home. I slipped her the keys and headed out.

When I pulled into my driveway over an hour later, Linc's Yukon wasn't there. The fact that he wasn't home made my nerves worse. I woke India up so she could head home and I checked in on Cameron. He was sleeping peacefully, which calmed my nerves, but not much.

As I was making my way back downstairs, Linc was finally pulling into the driveway. I went in the living room and took a seat on the couch. I didn't know what the hell was wrong with him but he needed to get it out, whatever it was.

Once he came in the house, I sat motionless and listened as he shed his night, layer by layer. The sound of the Velcro yielding the release of his bulletproof vest echoed through the foyer. Next I heard the sound of his handcuffs clanging against the tile in the foyer. His footsteps moved into the distance as he moved to the den. The next sound was that of the strongbox, which housed his Glock, being unlocked and relocked. It was then placed back on the shelf, where he kept it, out of Cameron's sight and reach. He was barely three, but that didn't mean he wasn't a master explorer and we made damn sure that gun was nowhere in his path.

"Idalis!"

"I'm in the living room."

More footsteps.

This time headed in my direction.

I stood to my feet. My mind was running through every possibility of what his problem could be. His eyes were fixed on me, causing my face to flush hot. I took a deep breath and blew it out softly.

He didn't speak as he walked up to me.

Then again, he didn't have to say a word. The anger on his face said enough.

"Somethin' you wanna tell me?" he questioned.

Slowly I shook my head. "Look, I don't know what you're talking about. Or why you're tripping but—"

His hand shot up and clamped around my throat. He cocked his head to the side and spoke, "I asked you a question shawty."

I reached up and wrapped my hand around his wrist. Fear gripped my body and rattled my bones.

"I don't know—"

He tossed me to the couch and I bounced off the edge and hit the floor. "You don't know what?" he demanded. "I can't hear you Idalis."

My mind was in overdrive. I could feel my heart pounding in my ears. "What is *wrong* with you? What are you talking about?"

He lunged toward me and snatched me up from the floor by my hair. He put his face close to mine; I could see the tiny brown flecks in his eyes. His nostrils flared with rage.

"I'ma give you one more chance. Is there *anything* you wanna tell me, shawty?" he asked, through clenched teeth.

I was terrified. I wished I knew what he wanted me to say because at that point I would've said whatever he wanted me to say just to get him to stop.

"I swear, Linc, I don't know what you're talking about."

"Guess you ain't think I was gon' find out 'bout you meeting Trip at the gym?"

My chest grew tight and my eyes widened.

My mouth gaped opened, but the only thing that came out was a soft cry of pain from the grasp he had on my hair.

"Or about y'all hugged up at Waffle House."

That knocked the wind out of me. "Linc, it wasn't like that and you know it! We're just *friends* you know that!"

He tightened his grip on my hair. "Then what was it like, Idalis?" he growled. "I asked your ass on the phone if you'd talked to him and you told me no."

"I hadn't. I swear. He just happened to be there."

"Oh so now you think I'm stupid?"

Tears fell relentlessly from my eyes. "Linc, stop! Cameron is upstairs asleep."

He looked toward the hallway, then back to me. "Maybe I should go wake him up and school l'il man on how much of a liar his mother is."

"Linc, don't do that," I begged.

"You got me workin' fuckin' crime scenes with this dude knowin' he had already been hugged up with you and got him laughin' behind my back?" he yelled.

He released the grip he had on my hair. Before I could recover from the excruciating pain, his hand slammed across my right cheek, knocking me back to the floor.

Terrified, I scrambled to the couch and scooted into the corner.

He stood there for a moment glaring at me before he turned and walked away.

"You ever make me look stupid like that again, Idalis, I'll kill you," he said, as he headed down the hall.

A few moments later I heard his footsteps fade off in the distance as he made his way upstairs to the bedroom. Once I heard the bedroom door close, I got up off the couch and went into the bathroom in the hallway and checked my tear-streaked face. It was red, but nothing that I couldn't cover with makeup.

After all, I had become somewhat of a pro at covering up things.

Chapter Seven

Idalis

"Idalis, this is crazy! I can't believe he *hit* you."

The next evening I was sitting at my kitchen table as India handed me a washcloth with some ice cubes tucked inside. I placed it on my throbbing jaw. She came by after her evening class and brought us some takeout. I could barely get off the couch and had managed to keep Cameron happy with PB&Js and cheese crackers all afternoon.

"Keep your voice down. Cameron is in the other room."

"I know. And what if my nephew had woken up last night when he came up in here, acting like a dick?"

I put the ice pack on the table. "But he didn't. Can we just drop it?"

"That's it." She threw her hands up in the air. "I'm tellin' Mommy."

I stood up. "Don't do that, India. She already got too much to worry about with Grammie."

"Then I'm telling his captain! I'm telling someone. This is bullshit!" she yelled. Her voice was quavering, letting me know she was about to cry.

That was one thing about us that we both hated. It didn't take much for us to cry. Especially when we were mad.

My twin stared at me with tears in her eyes. She was a mirror image of me: right down to the back-length honey blond–highlighted hair and the tiny scar above our right brow.

My scar came when I was eight years old. I was running and playing out in front of our grandmother's house. Grammie's home had a brick wall, which framed the front yard, and I tripped and fell, hitting my head on the edge of one of the bricks. Twin insisted we didn't match anymore and we had to be the same, even down to scars. So she took Mama's house key and dug it into her head above her brow until she bled, leaving a scar to match mine. Of course, my mother wanted to strangle her, but I think it was then when she realized that the connection we made in the womb would never be broken.

I tried to make light of the situation. "So, can I slap you so we have matching bruises?"

She cut her eyes at me, letting me know she wasn't in the mood to laugh this off. I couldn't blame her for caring; after all, she was my sister. I wanted to say something to make her feel better, but I didn't have the answers myself. Linc had never done anything like this before. This was unchartered territory for everybody; I hated it just as much as she did.

"Idalis, you need to handle this. He's gone too far."

I stood up and made my way to the sink, dumping out the melting ice cubes. "I know, India. And I will," I assured her.

"I'm serious," she continued. "He needs to get his shit straight, or it's a wrap."

Her honesty, although appreciated, was starting to annoy me.

"Twin, I understand where you're coming from. I just need to sort this out with him, which I *will* do."

A few moments later we heard the soft chime of the alarm notifying us that the front door had been opened. My body tensed as India stood in the doorway of the kitchen.

I heard Linc's keys being placed on the table in the foyer and I stood to my feet as he made his way down the hall to the kitchen.

"What are you doing here?" India snapped, ready to fight.

"I live here," he countered. "Fuck *you* doin' here?"

I put my hand on her arm. "India, don't."

She looked at me, then back to him. "I'm going to check on my nephew."

We both stood motionless as she disappeared out of the kitchen. Once she was gone, he moved in my direction. I didn't know if I should run or grab a knife out of the butcher-block caddy.

"Idalis . . . I'm . . . I'm sorry."

I moved slowly and managed to put the island in the middle of the kitchen between us.

"What's going on with you, Linc?" I asked.

He reached up and rubbed the top of his head. "Man, this case just got me stressed. That's all."

"But you've had stressful cases before, and you never brought them home with you. Most of all, you've never put your hands on me."

He placed his palms on the counter. "I know. But this one's different."

"Why, because of him?"

I stood there, waiting for an explosion of some sort, but instead he kept his head down. He was hiding whatever truth his eyes might have been holding. I saw his chest expand and deflate as he filled his lungs with air and let it out.

Silence hung between us, longer than I wanted. I could hear Cameron laughing and what sounded like music coming from the television in the den.

"Do you wanna be with him?" he asked, when he finally spoke.

This time it was my turn to move toward him. I reached up and placed my hand on the back of his head. "Linc, I'm marrying you."

He turned his head and looked down at me. "That's not what I asked you."

"Trip is my best friend. We've been through a lot together. We have a lot of history. It's hard to label something like that."

He shook his head. "That don't mean nothing, shawty. Hell, we got history. You still ain't answered my question."

Just then, India and Cameron walked into the kitchen, taking our attention away from each other. She had car keys in her hands and Cameron's Optimus Prime overnight bag on her shoulder.

"What's going on?" I asked.

"Cam's coming to spend the night with Auntie India, right?"

My baby boy smiled big. "Can I, Mommy? Can I, Daddy?"

I knew what she was doing; and whether I agreed with her or not, I loved her for it.

Linc bent down and picked up Cameron. "You promise to be good for your grandma?"

"Yes, sir." He nodded, excited. "Mommy, can I go?"

I forced a smiled as I stared into my sister's sad eyes. "Yes, baby, you can go."

He raised his tiny fists over his head and started cheering. "Yay!"

I watched as Linc bent down and placed him back on the floor and he ran over to my sister. She scooped him up and looked from Linc back to me. "Call me if you need me."

"I will."

They headed down the hallway. I heard the front door open, then close. And just like that, I was alone with Linc.

I took a deep breath and rubbed the palms of my hands on the front of my jeans. I knew this night could end one of two ways: peaceful or chaotic. I personally was voting for peace.

He leaned back against the counter and crossed his arms against his chest.

"So you gon' answer me or what?"

I nodded as I moved slowly toward him.

I ran my hands up arms uncrossing them and resting my hands on his chest. I stood on my toes as I kissed his neck. His hand slid up my thigh and rested on the small of my back.

When I felt his body relax, I took his hand and led him upstairs to the bedroom.

Linc sat on the edge of the bed, watching, while I allowed my clothes to fall to the floor. The only time he took his eyes off my body was when he pulled his shirt over his head. I licked my lips and bit my bottom lip as I reached behind me and undid my bra, letting it fall to the floor. I moved forward into his embrace, skin against skin. He sucked one of my nipples into his mouth, moistening it before gently blowing on it, causing it to reach out to him. A moan rumbled in my throat as he called the other one to attention.

I looked down and watched him draw circles around my nipples with his tongue as I reached down and undid his pants. Once they were completely off, I laid him back on the bed. I held him in my hand and slowly began stroking him until I felt him begin to swell in my hand, and a groan escaped his lips.

"Put it in your mouth," he instructed.

"Yes, baby."

I did what he wanted and sucked him into my mouth.

"Like that, baby?"

"Yeah . . . just like that."

He moaned and I felt his hips move as I licked and sucked the head while I stroked him. His hands made their way to the back of my head as I sucked all of him into my mouth.

I moved slowly at first. Making sure I was able to take him all in without gagging. Then I let him work his hips and use my mouth for his pleasure.

I squeezed the base of his penis with my thumb and forefinger, making sure his pleasure lasted. I massaged the underside of the shaft of his penis, feeling the huge vein throb against my tongue.

"Mmm . . . you taste so good."

He reached for me. "Come here."

I crawled up his body until my center was directly over his. He sat up and sucked my nipples into his mouth as his hand moved between my legs. I felt his fingers enter me as I reached between us and began stroking him. As I straddled his thighs, I moved my hips against the rhythm of his fingers as we stroked each other.

It wasn't long before his hands were on my waist and he was lifting me up, guiding me down onto his waiting shaft. I couldn't stop the moan that rose and escaped from my throat as he opened me up.

He pulled me close and I wrapped my legs around him. He sucked on my neck as we rocked like that for a few minutes before he lay down and let me take over.

I worked my hips in small circles, watching him as he looked up at me, enjoying his show. He reached around and smacked my ass, and my rhythm picked up some speed.

"Yeah, girl, you know how I like it. Work that ass."

Sweat ran down my body onto his as he grabbed my waist and began thrusting his hips upward, causing me to cry out. I held on to the headboard and rode him faster.

"Uh! You . . . gon' . . . make . . . me . . . cum," he said, his breathing ragged.

Just then my eyes snapped open and I stared, emotionless, at the wall in front of me.

That's exactly what I'm trying to do, I thought.

I placed my hands on his chest and moved up and down on him. I was so wet; the sounds of my body filled the room.

I teased him—pulling him out, all the way to the tip, and then taking him all back in. I did that, over and over again, until I felt his hands grip my waist.

"Cum for me, baby," I whispered.

When I felt his body tense, I hopped off him, slid down his body, and took him in my hand. I worked him up and down. I licked and sucked his tip as he cried out. I felt him throbbing and twitching as he came; his warm seed spilled out onto my hand.

I got up and went into the bathroom for a towel to clean up. I turned the water on in the shower and let it run as I looked at the woman staring back at me in the mirror. Tried to justify the things she'd done in the name of love and family.

When I realized I couldn't, I climbed under the streaming water.

You do what you have to do, I thought.

I cleaned up and brushed my teeth. After brushing my hair back into a ponytail, I climbed into bed. Linc was already half asleep, but he pulled me close to him as soon as he felt my body next to his.

"You know I was thinking about something," I started.

He reached up and rubbed my hair. "What's that?"

"There's a lot going on and I can't focus right now, with Grammie being sick and you working on this case." I took a deep breath. "What if we pushed the date back for the wedding? Just for a little while."

He got quiet and I held my breath.

Held it so long that my lungs began to burn.

"Nah, date stays the same." He grabbed his phone and silenced the ringing, officially dismissing me.

"I mean, don't you think it would make sense—"

"Drop it. The date stays the same," he said, cutting me off. "Oh and Idalis."

"Yes."

"Don't get Trip fucked up."

My eyes went to the ceiling, and got lost in the fan's movement.

Became hypnotized by its smooth rotation.

I lay there, trying to find comfort in the midst of chaos.

Is that even possible? I asked myself.

I guess anything is possible, when you have control over nothing.

Chapter Eight

Trip

I slid the plastic key into the door to my rented home and took a deep breath. The suite at the W definitely wasn't my house back in New Orleans, but until this case was complete, it was home for now.

I tossed the files I had in my hand onto the glass coffee table before heading toward the bathroom. I was in desperate need of a hot shower. I opened the glass door and turned the knob. The marble-and-glass room quickly started to fill with steam as I pulled off my clothes. The Velcro from my vest cut into the silence of the room as I tossed it to the floor.

As much as I hated to admit it, my mind was on Idalis. We had history—a history that no one would understand but us. Hell, she was my first kiss. I smiled at the memory of us hiding under the back steps of her grandmother's house. We were only seven years old. I remember how she tried to act like she wasn't scared, but from the way she was shaking, I could tell she was just as nervous as I was. It was just a peck, but I remember walking away, feeling like I'd just become a man.

I also remembered how Idalis used to help me hide the bruises from the fights with my father with the makeup she would sneak from her mom's room.

"He gon' get his one day, Trip. You just watch," she would always say as she gently applied the tacky mixture to my bruised skin.

I turned the water on in the fancy sink, bent down, and splashed some water on my face before pulling my locs back in preparation for my shower. I looked up into the mirror. Stared at the man staring back at me. I tried to see past him—didn't want to see him—but I couldn't escape him.

It was my father.

I saw him in my hazel eyes, in the hardness of my jaw line. I'd even inherited his long eyelashes. It was his face. I was becoming him.

Everyone always told me that I looked just like him, and I fought hard to reject that my entire life. Always insisting that I looked like my mother. I didn't want to give that asshole credit for anything. He didn't deserve shit but the dirt resting on top of him.

I closed my eyes against the memory, but it hit me like a runaway train.

I was ten years old when I was awakened by my mother's scream. She was cowering in the corner of the bed that rested against the dark wall. My mom, my little sister, and I were all crammed into a twin-sized bed in a small bedroom on the second floor of my grandmother's house. My little sister was huddled with her in the corner. She was clinging to her nightgown, with eyes wide as saucers. I was at the foot of the bed.

I felt my mom's hand on my leg. "It's okay," she whispered.

All of a sudden my dad's voice came booming through the room. He was screaming at my mother, accusing her of sleeping around. I could tell he was drunk. He smelled of liquor and cigarette smoke. He was probably high off some weed or something, but I wouldn't have known the difference. The screams that escaped my mother's lips were due to the crutch that he was using to beat her.

"I swear to you, I didn't," she cried, barely above a whisper. She pressed her body closer to

the wall. Tried to sink into it. Holding my sister, trying to shield her. I stayed under the covers. Pulled them farther over my head. I didn't raise my head, only craned my neck enough to see my mother's face. The light from the hallway was falling across the bed; she had a look of terror in her eyes. It was a look I'd seen many times before.

He swung his weapon of choice again, this time catching her on her leg and clipping my foot. I scrambled to the head of the bed, ready to protect my mother with my tiny body. He looked at me and scowled, ready to challenge me as always, but the crutch broke from that last blow. I could hear the wood crack and the pieces hit the hardwood floor.

He threw what was left of the shattered wood to the floor. The crutch was my uncle's. He had had a motorcycle accident and had broken his leg a couple months before. The crutches were still around the house. He turned and walked out of the room. He was mumbling and calling my mother every name but what her mother had given her. I heard the change in his pocket jingling along with the keys in his hand as he stumbled out of the room and down the steps.

My mother looked tired, worn, and much older than her license said. The tears ran down *her face as she sobbed in the corner. After hearing the front door slam shut downstairs, my mother slid out of the bed, hobbled on her bruised legs, and padded to the bedroom door. She leaned against the door frame for a second; I guess she was making sure he was really gone.*

Her thin nightgown clung to her sweaty body. Her breathing was ragged and fast. She slipped out of the room into the hallway and then down the stairs. I heard the locks click and the chain rattle on the front door as she did everything she could to lock out her attacker. To lock out my father. My mother limped back in the room and crawled into bed. She grimaced out of pain and sucked in air. She stretched out next to my sister and me. And we all lay there until the sun rose pretending to be asleep, and praying he didn't return.

It's amazing how your mother's influence molds you. When you are in the womb, your mother's actions and movements influence your movements and sleep patterns. When you're born, you are trained that daytime is for waking and nighttime is for sleeping. That, too, is by your mother. As you grow, your parents teach you a lot about manners, rules, and how to act in public. But it's the unconscious things they teach you that seem to take hold of you like a pissed-off pit bull that refuses to let go.

I believe that you are taught to be the person you eventually grow up to be by watching your parents. Girls learn how to be a woman by watching their mothers; they also learn what to look for in a husband or a boyfriend by what they are exposed to by their father. Boys learn what to look for in a wife or a girlfriend from their mothers, but more importantly they learn from their fathers *how* to be a man and a father. So, inevitably, if something is wrong with the equation, then a person is involuntarily set up for a life that is way harder than it has to be.

My father taught me an important lesson.

Not just how to be a man, but how to be a better man than him.

The bruises. The black eyes. The trips to my aunt's that always lasted longer than they were supposed to. Everyone wanted to blame the drinking and the drugs, but I refused to give him a cop-out.

He made a choice, and it was the wrong one.

I made up in my mind I was never gonna treat a woman that way. The way I was prepared to protect my mother that night—as a man—I would always be prepared to protect. I guess that's what drove me to the force, and for whatever reason held me on the force.

I was compelled to protect those who couldn't protect themselves.

After my shower I dried off and stretched across the rented bed and tried to will myself to sleep, but my mind wouldn't stop. I checked the clock, and the restaurant downstairs, Savu, was already closed. I got up and got the files off the coffee table and sat down on the couch. I spread the evidence and files out in front of me like puzzle pieces.

I picked up the picture from the latest crime scene. The only thing more disturbing than the scenes themselves was how clean they were. No prints, no trace, nothing. The girl's twisted body lay peacefully. Outside of her throat being slashed, it appeared she was sleeping. I stared at her face, peaceful and beautiful. Guilt washed over me for a moment.

I couldn't protect her.

I placed the picture back inside the folder and dialed my sister.

I could tell I'd woken her up, but I didn't care. "Get up. I can't sleep."

She yawned. "Ooh! I hate you." I heard her moving around. "What's up with you?"

"Sitting here, going through these case files."

"Man, that shit'll give you nightmares," she said.

She had no idea how true that was. "So how's work?" I asked, trying to change the subject.

"It's work. Dealing with the public ain't easy."

I chuckled. "Who you telling?"

"We miss having you around. Especially Mama."

"I know, Trin. But I needed a change."

"So what made you come to that conclusion? You're all the way over there with no family, and you can't hold down a relationship longer than six months."

I kept telling myself that she meant well, which was the only thing that was saving her from getting cussed out.

"Just let it go, Trinity."

"I will, when you answer me this. Was it Pops or Idalis?"

Hearing both of those insinuations was a blow that I wasn't ready for. "It was time for me to move on. That's all."

"Come on, Trip, this is me. I was there, remember? And I know how you felt when Idalis got engaged too."

I reached up and pulled the tie out of my locs and leaned back on the couch. She was right. Through it all, Trinity had been there for me. She had been there through all the fights that I had with my dad—both the verbal and physical sparring, all in the name of protecting her and my mother.

Even when I went to college, and swore I'd never come back to that house as long as he was there, she made sure to come by the dorm and keep me updated on what was going on in the house. The older Dad got, the less violent he became physically, but that hadn't stopped the verbal abuse, which he still inflicted on them. The fact that my mother had refused to leave him left a bitter taste in my mouth, and it wasn't something that I could let go of, just like that.

"You know there was nothing you could've done, right? That's how their generation is Trip. They stand true to that 'death do us part'."

"I know."

"So why are you punishing yourself and for that matter everyone around you?"

I sighed. "I'm not, Trin. Damn, would you stop trying to fix me."

"Trip, Pops checked out of our lives long before he died, and you've been plugging that hole with the wrong things. You gotta let go of your anger. Because at the end of the day—in spite of him—we both made it. You made it. It's like you're still trying to prove something to him."

"No, I'm not."

"Then move back. Mama needs you. I miss you."

I rubbed my temple. "Can we talk about this after I close this case?"

She let out a hard sigh. "Whatever. Bye."

Just like that, she hung up on me.

I shook my head and thought about calling her back, then decided against it. My phone lit up again, and this time it was Phil.

"What's up?"

"They just sent some agents over to Perry Homes, off Odessa Street."

"Do we need to ride out?"

"No, Lenny called. He said they found two more dealers taken out, execution style."

I leaned back on the couch and stared at the ceiling. "Wow."

"Shit, I know. Said the place was tossed and their stash was taken."

I let out a sigh. "A'ight, I'm about to jump into the shower. I'll get at you in the morning."

I disconnected the call and tossed my phone onto the couch next to me.

We finally had the chance to catch up on some sleep.

But I had a feeling I wasn't going to get much of it tonight.

Chapter Nine

Idalis

Sunday afternoon I made my way to my mother's with Cameron. I was meeting India and Dionne at a bridal shop, off Howell Mill Road, for our fitting. My mother had agreed to watch him for me.

Once I made it to my mom's, I gave her a quick hug and kiss, then made my way upstairs to talk to Grammie. Mama told me she was doing much better and had even been getting out of bed and moving around. When I got to her room, she was sitting and knitting.

"Hey, Grammie."

"Hi, baby."

I hugged her. Part of me—the scared little girl—didn't want to let go. I wanted to crawl into her lap and let her convince me that everything would be okay. Instead, I just sank down onto her bed.

"Mama told me you were feeling much better," I said.

She smiled and nodded. "Yes, I am," she answered. "How about you?"

I took a deep breath. "I'm doing okay. Things are changing so fast. It's overwhelming; sometimes I don't think I can handle it."

"Yes, you can, baby."

I took in a deep breath and let it out. "Grammie I'm thinking about pushing back the wedding for a little while."

She asked, "Do you think that's best?"

All I could do was nod. I didn't dare tell her that Linc pretty much told me that date was staying the same no matter what I said.

I heard her lay her knitting down on the small table next to her chair; she motioned for me to come to her. Like a little child I slid to the floor and rested my head in her lap. She began stroking my hair, and tears escaped from my eyes. I quickly wiped them away in a weak attempt to hide them from her.

"You listen to me, baby. You owe it to that baby and yourself to make the best life possible for yourselves. He didn't ask to come here. Don't you think it's unfair to try to raise him in the midst of a bunch of foolishness?"

"Yes, ma'am."

My heart broke in two. Just the thought of her worrying about me and my problems killed me. I never wanted her to know about any of my issues; she didn't need the stress. She just needed to get better.

"Whatever is going on, take care of it, ya hear me?"

"Yes, ma'am."

"You have a lot going on, baby. Right now, you are holding the destiny of three lives in the balance. You need to draw on your God-given strength and make it right."

"I'm not strong like you."

She gently lifted my head and smiled down at me. "Baby, you are my granddaughter, and a child of God, you can do anything."

I couldn't help but smile at that. "Thanks, Grammie."

"You're welcome. Now go downstairs and get yourself a cup of tea."

"Yes, ma'am."

After one more hug I made my way to the kitchen. My mother was sitting at the table and sipping a cup of herbal tea. The strong fragrance of cinnamon and spice filled the small room.

"Mama, can I talk to you for a second?"

"Grab a cup and sit with me," she said, motioning toward the cabinet. At first I thought maybe India told her what happened between Linc and me, but I knew my twin wouldn't sell me out like that.

"What's going on?" she asked, taking a sip of her tea.

I heard the music signaling the start of *Sponge-Bob SquarePants* coming from the other room. Cameron would be glued to the television for at least another thirty minutes, and that song would be stuck in my head for at least a day.

I swirled the tea around in my cup with my spoon. "I'm thinking about pushing back my wedding date."

Her eyes went blank for a moment, like she was trying to choose her words wisely. I studied her. Looked for any sign that I need to get up and run for my life.

She set her cup down and spoke. "I try really hard to let you and your sister make your own choices, but Idalis I know something hasn't been right for a long time." She took a sip of her tea. "I was just wondering how long it was gonna be before you said something."

I sat back in my seat. "Mama, everything is okay, I just think we need a little more time that's all."

She shook her head. "No, baby. You haven't had that sparkle in your eyes for a long time."

I pushed my cup of tea away from me. The cinnamon-flavored concoction was no longer appealing. There wasn't an herbal remedy on the face of the earth that could make me feel better now.

I stood up and grabbed my purse. The best way to deal with my mother was in small, quick doses. I had made a mistake starting it, and now I needed to end this conversation quickly, like ripping off a Band-Aid.

She cleared her throat before speaking. "You're allowing Lincoln to control your life. You already let him come between a lifelong friendship with Trip," she said as she placed her own cup in the sink. "What's next? You won't be allowed to talk to me?"

I stopped and looked at her, surprised. "Mama, Trip is the one who moved, not me. Linc didn't make him take that job with the DEA."

She stopped and rested her hands on the stainless-steel bowl and let out a low sigh.

"What?" I asked.

She turned and looked at me. "I just want you to be happy."

I let out a hard sigh. "Mama, I know. Look, I gotta go. I need to meet India and Dionne at the dress shop in less than an hour."

"You can deny it all you want. But something is not right, Idalis, and I know it."

I hugged her. "Bye, Mama."

I promised her that I would call, kissed Cameron, and headed out the door toward Howell Mill Road. I found myself driving slowly, not in the rush that an excited bride should be in. I felt my phone vibrate and my heart fell into my stomach. I was relieved when I saw India's name flash across the screen.

"What's up, girl?"

I briefly filled her in on what happened at the house.

"Well, you can't be mad at her she's right," she said, matter-of-factly.

I let out a sigh. "Whatever, Miss California."

"Oh, so now it's on me?"

I switched lanes, and ignored her question. "Are you there yet?"

"Yeah, I just pulled into the parking lot with Dionne."

I exited Interstate 75 and caught the light just as I was about to make the right onto Howell Mill.

"I'll be there in a second. Just got off 75."

I disconnected the call and stared up at the light. The bright red light hypnotized me for a second. Transported me into a world of "what if" and "what could've been." It was only when the car behind me started blaring its horn that I snapped back to reality.

It was time to turn the corner.

In more ways than one.

Once I made it into the shop, India was already in one of the tiny dressing rooms, which lined the walls, trying on her dress. And Dionne was admiring her cute figure in the row of mirrors lining the room.

"Now, that looks cute on you," I said.

"Girl, everything looks cute on me," she said, smiling and twirling around.

I laughed as a short, thin white lady made her way toward me. She had a wide smile plastered on her face and her hand extended.

"You must be Idalis," she gushed. "Your twin sister is already trying on her dress, and I have yours waiting for you in that end dressing room."

She motioned toward a much bigger room at the end of the hall. All I could muster was a smile and a weak thank-you as I followed her. I tapped on the door that I knew India was behind.

"I'm here," I said.

She responded, "I'll be out in a second. And I do look fat in this dress."

"Don't start, India."

At the end of the room were two double doors. The hyper woman pushed them open, revealing a much bigger mirror-lined room with a stage framed by a three-step staircase.

Suddenly I felt like the walls were closing in on me and I couldn't breathe. I wanted to turn and run, but she was already ushering me toward a door that had my dress hanging on the outside.

"This is where you can change. And as soon as you're finished, you come on back out and let's take a look." She smiled even bigger, which I didn't think was possible. "But I already know you're gonna be beautiful!"

I pushed the door back and unhooked my dress. The changing room was huge. There was a pedestal in the middle of the room, and several cushioned chairs and benches lined the walls.

I plopped down on one of the benches, which I was sure had held much happier brides-to-be before me, and let out a sigh. My Coach bag slid off my shoulder and landed on the floor. I stared at myself in the mirror and hugged my plastic covered dress close to my body. I remembered the day I had picked this dress out. I had told India that it was perfect, that it was made just for me. Now I wasn't so sure. It felt more like a prison jumpsuit than the satin and crystal-encrusted happily-ever-after, which it represented.

I slipped out of my jeans and tee. I stood and looked at myself in the mirror. I'd dieted and sweated off nearly fifteen pounds in order for the dress to fit me the way I wanted it to. I smiled at the thought of running into Trip at the gym. Couldn't help but wonder what he was doing and if I was gonna see him again before he left.

"You need help zipping that up?"

I swung around. My sister and Dionne were standing in the doorway. They looked amazing in their short A-line strapless black dresses. The gathered ruffled skirt stopped just above their knees, showing off their legs perfectly. I was so happy they'd listened and brought the black shoes I'd bought them to try on with their bridesmaid dresses. The flash of red from the bottoms of the shoes was the perfect touch. The red accessories I'd picked out were gonna be perfect.

Seeing how beautiful they looked brought tears to my eyes.

I smiled. "Wow, India, you look amazing. You do *not* look fat. Dionne, that dress hits you just right."

My twin made her way to me and zipped me into my own gown. I stepped back and admired myself in the mirror.

The strapless Maggie Sottero gown's bodice was embroidered with Swarovski crystals, which winked in the room's track lighting. I forced a smile and began playfully putting my hair up, as if trying to decide to wear it up or down. I felt someone straightening out the bottom of my gown. My sister stood back and looked at me. This time it was her turn to have tears in her eyes.

"Oh my goodness Twin, I look beautiful," she laughed. "I'm just kidding. You look amazing."

"You do look beautiful, Idalis," Dionne added.

Their voices snapped me out of my self-induced fairy tale and our eyes met briefly. "Then why don't I feel beautiful?"

"I wish I knew, Twin. I wish I knew," India whispered. "I do know one thing, though." She wiped her tears.

I looked down at my dress, tousled the skirt on my gown, and smoothed it out. "What's that?"

She placed her hand under my chin and lifted my face to hers. Her hand went to my make-up-covered bruised cheek. Her fingers touched my face gently before she put her hand down.

"You're running out of time to fix this."

I turned away from her before the first wave of tears fell.

I admired my glowing silhouette in the mirror. Suddenly the dress I was wearing was so heavy—it might as well have been made of lead.

Chapter Ten

Idalis

I sat on the couch, tapping my phone on my leg.

Lincoln wasn't home, and truth be told, I was kind of glad.

After we left the dress shop, the three of us headed to Atlantic Station and during our late lunch they both managed to convince me to call Trip and talk to him about my situation. I fought hard against the idea, mainly because I didn't need the drama, and there was no telling how many different cans of worms I would be opening if I made that phone call. But one point that they did make was that Trip was the only person, other than India, who knew me better than I knew myself.

I remembered when we were in the fifth grade and this fat chick named Althea was bullying me. Trip pulled me to the side in the lunchroom and convinced me that I had the power to kick her ass and get her to leave me alone for good. Well, it didn't take long to find out, I didn't. India ended up having to jump in and save my behind; as a result we all got suspended for a week. But there was something about knowing that he believed in me that made that ass whooping worth it.

I tapped the screen on my phone and flipped through my contacts until I found his number.

I smiled when his voice came across the line. "Hey, you."

He laughed. "I was wondering when you were gonna call."

"Sorry, I been running around," I lied.

"I understand, I even went by the gym hoping to run into you again."

I let that comment hang out there, deciding not to touch it.

"So what's up?" he asked.

"You were on my mind, so I just wanted to call."

I heard him let out a slight laugh. "Is that right?"

I moved my phone to my other ear. "Yes. Is that so hard to believe?"

"I just figured with you running around, jumping brooms, you wasn't worried about me."

I let out a small sigh. "Whatever."

"What's up, baby girl? You sound like something's wrong."

I shifted around on the couch; then I stood up and paced across my living room floor. "It's just Grammie's really sick and this wedding, it's a lot you know?"

"Come on Idalis," he said, sounding disappointed. "Why didn't you tell me about her when we were together?"

"I don't know. I was just happy to see you, I just didn't . . ." I said, my voice trailing off.

I knew that was a lame ass reason but that's all I could come up with.

Silence fell across the line. I didn't know if I had made a mistake calling him or not. A lot of time had passed maybe our friendship was never gonna be what it used to be.

Finally he spoke. "Idalis?"

I answered, "Yes."

"Can you get out?"

"Yeah. Cameron is with India."

"Meet me at my mom's."

An hour later, I stepped into the house and it felt like I'd been sucked back in time. One of the last times I was in his mom's house was the night of the high school prom. My date canceled on me because he wanted to go with Rainey Johnson, the one chick in school that was guaranteed to put out. Trip hadn't planned on going at all so it wasn't a big deal to him, but my mother got so sick of my crying that she and his mom put him up to taking me. So my mother tossed me and my taffeta laden body in the car and we ended up over here where I found Trip in a tuxedo and his mom waiting with camera in hand. An hour later we were dancing to SWV's *Weak* and wondering when they were gonna feed us. Even in our prom picture he had a look of agitation and my eyes were still puffy from crying.

Trip was seated across from me in the middle of his mother's living room. I couldn't help but feel like we were teenagers cutting class again. My eyes kept going to the front door. It was as if we were expecting at any moment for one of our parents to come in and ask why we weren't in school.

Trinity wasn't home and his mother was asleep, so we were sitting half in the dark, trying to keep our voices down so we didn't disturb her.

I took a drink out of the bottle of water, which I had in my hand. "I never expected things to be this hard, you know?"

"Your Gram's is a strong woman. She'll pull through."

"I pray you're right."

"Trinity told me to tell you she's praying for her."

"Tell her I said thank you."

I smiled at the memories of hanging out with her. She was always good for a laugh, whether she meant to be or not.

"I hate I missed her."

"Be careful." He chuckled. "She may try to turn you into one of her social work cases. She got me twice already."

"I'm not surprised. She was always such a tree hugger."

We laughed.

"Remember when she cried when your mom called animal control on that stray cat that was always in your backyard."

He laughed a little harder. "Oh! Damn. Yeah. She called my mother—"

"A coldhearted human being who wasn't capable of loving God's creatures!" I finished his sentence with a chuckle.

"Yup, and Mama showed Trinity that she was capable of getting her ass whooped for getting smart with her."

Our laughs subsided and we both got quiet. The silence hovered like a huge, wet wool blanket. It felt very heavy and very cumbersome.

I finally broke the silence before my head exploded. "With Grammie being sick, and Mom and Lincoln not getting along, everything is just a mess."

He gave me a crooked smile. "Well, I can't blame your mother."

I tossed a pillow at him. "I'm serious. And you never liked Linc, anyway."

He threw the pillow back. "'Cause he's an asshole."

I chuckled to myself because he had no idea how true that statement was.

"And now India's talking about taking a job in California."

He looked up at me wide-eyed. "Are you serious?"

Heart heavy, I nodded. "I don't want her to go, but I know that's being selfish."

"Have you told her you want her to stay?"

"No."

"Why?"

He kept his eyes on me, giving me his full attention.

"Because I know India. She'd end up staying, just because I asked her to, and enrolling in some clown college just to get another degree."

He laughed.

His laughter filled in every hole that filled my spirit at that point. It was what I needed and didn't even realize it.

"And this job may be just what she needs," I reasoned.

He stretched and I couldn't help but watch as the muscles in his arms flexed against his black DEA tee.

"Man, I'm tired. I can't wait to get back home. Atlanta is taking it out of me," he said.

I smiled a little. "Wow, you hate it that much?"

"This place is heavy. Nothing here for me."

"Don't say that. Your family is here."

He looked at me. "Yeah, that's true. But I like what I got going on over there."

"I can't believe it's been almost six years since you left," I said.

"Yeah, time is flying." He smiled. "You gettin' old."

We sat there for a second, stillness settling between us. In the back of my mind I always wondered if Linc proposing had anything to do with him leaving the way he did. His move was so sudden—almost out of nowhere—but I never brought it up and I knew he wasn't going to do it either. Even when he had come home for his father's funeral he was different, he was a shell of the person he used to be. He kept telling everyone how much he loved New Orleans but there was something in his eyes that only I could see that let me know that was the farthest thing from the truth.

"I heard about what happened with you and your ex," I finally said, dropping my eyes and picking at the tag on the pillow I was holding.

He leaned back. "And what would that be?"

I looked up into his eyes. "Camille's miscarriage."

He sat forward and dropped his head. "Wow. Hundreds of miles away and I still can't have my life to myself."

"Yeah, Trinity called me after it happened."

"Trinity called and told you?" his tone was heavy with disbelief.

"Don't be like that, Trip. She was just worried about you."

"Considering the example I had for a father, fatherhood definitely ain't something that I'm rushing toward anyway, you feel me?" He looked toward the mantel, which held pictures of him and Trinity at various stages. Some included his mother, but I noticed there were no pictures of his father.

Anywhere.

I rubbed my sweaty palms on my jeans. "Yeah, I remember you always saying that you didn't want kids, so that call actually surprised me."

"It wasn't something we planned, trust me," he said. He stood up and took a deep breath. "They say that you learn how to be a father from your father."

I stood up and walked toward him. "You know you're not him, right?"

"I know."

We stood there for a second, not saying anything. In that moment we were little kids again. But this wasn't something that a pack of Now and Laters and an episode of *Transformers* could fix.

He stepped closer, so close that I could see the flecks of gold in his hazel eyes. His locs hung loose, falling down around his back and shoulders. I wanted to reach up and touch them, be there for him, like I'd always been before, be his best friend again.

He finally spoke. "You know I wanted to call you."

"You should have."

He reached up and let his hand brush against my cheek. The same cheek Linc had hit days before. "You're the only thing I miss about this place. You know that, right?"

I touched his hand, never taking my eyes from his. The tenderness of his touch against my cheek caused the blood to warm in my veins. "I miss you too."

"I will always love you for being there for me when my pops died."

When his dad died, Trip wouldn't talk to or see anyone but me. His father sent messages to him from the hospital but he wouldn't take his calls or go see him. And once he died he refused to go to the funeral or the gravesite.

"That's what friends are for, right?" I asked.

He nodded. "I guess so."

He looked around the living room.

I pretended to check my phone. There were no messages, but I played with the screen, anyway.

Anything to keep from looking at him.

Just when I was about to come up with a reason to have to go, his phone rang.

"Spencer," he answered.

His eyes locked on mine. I don't think I could've broken our stare, even if I wanted.

"A'ight, man, just relax. I'm on my way."

He disconnected the call and slid his Black-Berry into its holder. "I gotta go."

"Is everything okay?"

"Yeah, that was Phil. I was supposed to be at J.R. Crickets an hour ago."

"Why didn't you say something?" I tapped his arm. "You didn't have to entertain my pity party."

He started walking toward the front door; I took his cue and followed.

Once on the porch he turned to face me. "You know I'd do anything for you."

I smiled. "I know."

We both headed down the walkway to our cars, and I called out his name. When he turned around, I didn't know what to say, so I just said, "Thank you."

"Anytime, baby girl."

Before I knew it, I was headed back home, with the feeling my life was never going to be the same again.

Chapter Eleven

Trip

"What the fuck you mean he's in the wind?"

Phil slumped back, seated on the conference room chair. "Man, I can't find him. I have been trying to track him down since yesterday."

I paced the floor in the small room. There was no way this was happening. The informant had vanished, and three months worth of work was about to fly out the window.

"Word is, someone from his crew was found tied to a chair with a bullet in his knee, and ain't nobody seen Darius."

I looked at him. "Please tell me you're joking."

"Wish I was."

There was a tap on the door and Lenny walked in, followed by Commander Harris, of the APD.

"Good morning, gentlemen. You both look like shit," he said.

I stood there and waited for whatever it was he was about to say that was gonna fuck up the rest of my day.

"Found an expended round at that scene from the other night," he said.

"What type?" I asked.

"Nine millimeter."

"Hopefully, they can pull a print or something from it."

"That's what you called us in here for?" Phil asked.

"No, but I'm glad you asked, my large friend." Lenny held up an evidence bag. "This is why I called you in here."

I tilted my head a little to make sure I was seeing what I thought I was seeing.

Phil shook his head. "I *know* that's not what I think it is."

I said, "That's weight from the Four Horseman bust. Wasn't that supply destroyed?"

The silver wrapping mixed in with the white powdery substance was unmistakable. Any agent worth his weight knew what the bricks from that bust looked like. It was over 500 kilos and $23 million in cash. That was a huge bust for the agency and for the state of Georgia. We messed up a lot of dealers' payrolls and took a huge chunk out of the drugs on the streets.

I turned my back to all of them and directed my anger out the window.

Phil let out a disgusted laugh. "Wow, y'all are a bunch of clowns."

The commander spoke. "We're checking chain of command and trying to find out what happened."

I turned around and directed my anger at its source. "I can tell you what happened. Your whole setup is a joke."

"Look, Agent Spencer, we are already accommodating you and Agent Porter running around my city playing cops and robbers. I'm not gonna let you piss on all the hard work my officers have put in up to this point."

Lenny barked back at Harris. "Obviously, someone has slipped one of your desk clerk's a couple hundred dollars and has breached our security, putting agents at risk. I don't know how many agents, here or nationwide, have been compromised, Commander. I think my agents have a right to be upset."

Commander Harris scratched the top of his balding head. "I have officers out there too."

Lenny looked at me. "Until we can figure out how to move forward, this piece of information doesn't leave this room."

With that, he led the clearly frazzled commander out of the room. They were gone, along with any progress that had been made on this case so far.

I scratched my temple. "This shit is falling apart from the inside out."

Phil shook his head. "Nah, man. I refuse to let this shit go just like that."

I turned and slammed my fist into the wall behind me, causing Sheetrock to fly out and land on the floor around my feet.

Phil stood up. "Yo! What the fuck is up with you?"

A few seconds later an officer stuck his head into the conference room. "Everything okay?"

I glared at him. "Go find someone to fix this wall, *desk cop!*"

"Man, you need to calm down." Phil looked at the officer who was standing in the doorway. "We cool, man. Just find someone to fix the wall before Lenny finds out, okay?"

The agitated dude standing in the door eyed me. He probably wanted to knock me out, but, instead, he just nodded and closed the door.

"Man, what's going on with you? You trying to get tossed off this case?"

I slid onto a chair at the conference table and put my head in my hands. "This case is just getting to me."

Phil let out a frustrated sigh. "You sure that's all it is?"

I looked up. "Yeah. That's all it is."

Phil leaned against the wall. "So old girl ain't got nothing to do with this?"

I frowned up at him for a second. Part of me wanted to drop his ass too, but I knew he was just looking out for me. So I let his little fucked-up comment go. "You know what? Let's just figure out a way to fix this case so I can get the hell out of town." I stood up.

Phil blew out some air. "Come on, man, this is some bullshit."

"What?" I snapped.

"You just gon' let this chick throw you off your game over some juvenile shit. She's been fucking with your head for years. Let that shit *go*, man." Phil stepped in my path. "Look, I know that's your girl and all, but I need your head in this game right now. Focus on *this*, not on the extra shit you seem hell-bent on getting involved with."

"I already told you it ain't like that."

"Then why don't you tell me what it is so we can squash this shit and move on? Cause if you supposed to be the eyes in the back of my head I need you focused. You feel me?" he argued.

I took a deep breath and brushed past Phil, heading out of the office. "Look, man, I said I'm fine."

I left the station and rode the span of I-285, sunroof open and windows cracked, with no direction or destination in sight. Any Atlanta native knew that it took an hour to ride the concrete circle the encapsulated the city and so far I was half way into my second lap. I kept hearing Phil in my head telling me what I knew what the truth; I was losing focus.

There were so many times I had been in the city and hadn't even let her know and I made Trinity swear she wouldn't tell her. At first my argument was that I was doing it for her, to keep the peace between her and Linc, but now I didn't know if it was more for Idalis or for my sake. One thing I did know was that each trip across the state line was becoming harder and harder.

If I was honest with myself, the miscarriage gave me the perfect excuse to end a relationship that my heart was never in to begin with. She probably knew that and that's why she started acting foolish when I told her that we needed some time apart. I never meant to hurt her, or any of the other women I'd ran through, but none of them understood me the way Idalis did and I would rather be alone than make myself or anyone else unhappy.

My phone vibrated on my hip. I hit the button on my steering wheel and answered.

"Spencer."

"Where you at partner?" It was Phil.

"Spaghetti Junction, headed downtown."

"You straight?" he asked.

"Yeah. I just needed some air. I'm good."

"I'm just worried about you man, that's all. You're like my brother, man," he said.

I blew out some air. "I know."

"You wasn't this fucked up in the head when Camille lost that baby, man. And that was your seed."

"I wish I could explain it, man, I really do."

"I understand, but I ain't trying to have to make that trip to your mom's crib and apologize for some dumb shit and hand her some folded up flag, you feel me?"

"I feel you."

"I don't think you do bruh, you all over the place right now and this shit is real. Your head not being in this game right *here* is the equivalent of you swallowing your gun and I ain't letting that shit happen."

"I hear you. I'm good. I just needed to get my head right," I reassured.

"If there's anything I need to know, you need to tell me now," he said.

"Nah, we straight."

"A'ight, man. Now take your ass to the hotel and get some sleep so we can do some cop work tomorrow."

I let out a short laugh. "A'ight partner. Later."

Chapter Twelve

Idalis

The club hadn't started picking up and I was actually happy about that because I didn't plan on staying long. My head was pounding and I hadn't had a good night's sleep since I talked to Trip a few nights ago. I felt heavy and worn.

I caught a glimpse of myself in the mirror behind the bar. My long hair was pulled back into a lazy ponytail and I barely put on any makeup. In my opinion I looked the way I felt, tired.

"You a'ight, girl?"

I looked in Dionne's direction. She was placing orders on a tray. "Yeah, I'm good."

"You seem preoccupied. What's on your mind?"

I smiled. "Okay, let's skip the cliché 'bartender who doubles as a psychologist' role?"

"Oh, you got jokes," she laughed. "What's going on with you?"

"Just got a lot on my mind."

"Anything I can help with?"

I twisted the top off a bottle of water. "Only if you can tell me how to make the skeletons in my closet stop rattling."

She gave me a look that let me know she understood but had no answers for me. I gave a half-hearted smile and headed toward the back office.

Linc had been scarce the past few days. He kept telling me he was spending so much time away from home because of the case. Part of me believed him and the other part didn't care. I had learned over the years not to ask too much about his cases because all he would ever tell me was he didn't like bringing his work home.

Funny, how quickly things had changed.

I stopped by the table where Mr. Lewis was sitting and asked if he was okay.

"Yes, I'm fine, but you look like you could use a pick-me-up."

I forced a smile. "I'm good. I just wanted to stop by and check on you."

I turned to walk away and he stopped me.

"Miss Idalis."

I turned around. "Yes, sweetie?"

"You look down. Are you okay?"

"Yes, I'm fine, Mr. Lewis."

"Nothing is worth your happiness. Get rid of it before it eats you up inside."

That statement got my attention, especially coming from him. I started to ask him where it came from when I felt a hand on my shoulder.

"How long you been here?"

I turned to face Lincoln.

"I came in around six," I answered.

He was still in his Kevlar vest which meant he was still working. He looked at Mr. Lewis and smiled. "You tryin' to take my woman?"

Mr. Lewis gave a hearty laugh. "No, young blood, but I wouldn't mind if you let me borrow her."

"How much money you got?" Linc laughed.

My eyes met Mr. Lewis's and he gave me a gentle, caring smile before he spoke. "Officer, Miss Idalis is priceless."

Lincoln's smile faded and he looked at me. "Everyone has a price. Even Miss Idalis."

My face grew hot as he nudged me toward the office.

He was silent until we were isolated behind the wooden door.

"So what you been up to, Idalis?" He sat down on the edge of the desk.

I leaned against the door. "Working. Taking care of our son. Planning a wedding. If you were at home, you'd know that."

"You know I been workin' this case. How'd your appointment go at the dress shop?"

That question wouldn't have bothered me so much if I had told him I was going. I closed my eyes and rubbed the bridge of my nose. "You having me followed now, Lincoln?"

He stood up. "Of course not. But you know I got eyes everywhere."

"If that's the case, why are you here?"

"I just wanted to stop by and, you know, make sure you wasn't runnin' your mouth."

I blew out some air and shook my head. "Don't worry, Linc. I haven't told anyone that you like to hit women," I snapped.

"You talked to Trip?" he asked, ignoring my pot shot.

I shook my head slowly. "Nope. Have you."

He let out a slight laugh. "I meant what I said Idalis. I'd hate for his homecoming to be a sad one."

I rolled my eyes. "I heard you Linc. Look, what do you want?"

With his change in body language I became tense.

He started toward me and I braced myself. He got close and pressed my body against the door with his, never taking his eyes from mine. Usually the smell of his cologne was an aphrodisiac, but tonight it was making me nauseous.

I felt him reach behind me and heard the soft click of the lock, which caused my heart to flip in my chest. He slid his hand up my back until it reached my hair. I closed my eyes as he pulled the ponytail holder out before running his fingers through my hair. My breathing became shallow when he brushed his lips against my neck, but it was instantly cut short when the grip he had on my hair tightened just a little.

I inhaled sharply. "Stop."

"Stop what?" He continued kissing my neck. "I can't kiss you?"

Before I could say anything else, his mouth was on mine and he was forcing his tongue in my mouth. I reached up and interlocked my hand with his fingers to keep him from tightening his hold on my hair.

He grabbed me and pushed me toward the desk. I had to put my hands out in front of me to keep my thighs from slamming into the side.

"You jus' said I ain't been home, Idalis. So what's the problem?"

"Lincoln, stop."

He ignored me, reached around, undid my jeans, and pushed them down around my ankles. I tried to block out what was happening, but it was all too real. His rough, angry touch was like acid, eroding my skin.

He bent me over the desk and began pushing his way inside of me, even though I was bone dry. The pain of that alone made my head spin, but that didn't stop him.

"What's wrong, Idalis?" he hissed in my ear. "You ain't wet? You don't want me?"

He continued to force his way into me. I tried hard not to cry out in pain.

"Or maybe you ain't wet 'cause I ain't Trip," he growled, angrily.

The fact that Trip was what this was all about was more than I could handle. He held me by my neck and pressed me down into the scratchy wood of the desk. At that point I would have pissed on myself just to give him any kind of wetness and get him off me.

Head spinning, mind racing, my voice softened as I tried to relax my body. "No, baby. You know I love you. You don't have to do this. Not like this."

I tried to give the impression that I was getting into what was happening to me. With that small gesture I felt his body relax. I spread my legs a little wider, started grinding my hips into him. I silently thanked God that in spite of what I was going through mentally, my body started doing what it was innately programmed to do: produce fluids. I wasn't running a river, but I was wet enough to encourage him to develop a rhythm and loosen the grip he had on my neck.

He grabbed me by my hips and continued moving in and out of me. With each thrust a new tear made its way down my face and landed on the desk, mixing with the other transgressions that I'm sure the worn wood held.

His movements became quicker, letting me know he was close to cumming. I felt his body tense and he let out a low growl with his release. He bent down and pressed his lips against my ear.

"You belong to me, Idalis. You hear me?"

I nodded slowly.

As I was fixing my clothes, there was a tap on the door. Without even checking to make sure I was fully covered, Lincoln opened the door. I was relieved when I saw Dionne standing there and not some drunken-ass pervert.

She sucked her teeth. "Is Idalis in here?"

"Yeah." He shot me a look and walked out of the room.

She rushed over to me. "Girl, are you okay? Do I need to call the police?"

I tucked my shirt into my pants and fixed my ponytail.

"He is the police."

Chapter Thirteen

Trip

"Mama, please stop bringing me stuff to eat."

I was sitting at my mother's kitchen table trying to force down the last of the sweet potato pie, which she'd placed in front of me. When she saw that I was just about done, she walked off, mentioning more pie and something about ice cream.

"Let me feed you. It's bad enough you don't come to visit much, and when you're here, I barely get to see you. Heck, you won't even tell your own mother where you're laying your head at night."

"That's 'cause he's shady, Mama!" my sister, Trinity, yelled from the living room.

"Shut up before I frame you for something," I shot back.

I got up and carried my empty plate to the kitchen. "Come on now, Mama. You know why I do that. I never know who could be following me. If anything ever happened to you, I don't know what I would do." I bent down and kissed her on her cheek.

"What about me?" my sister yelled.

"Trin, they can have you."

"You'd miss me."

"Doubt it." I laughed.

"I understand," Mama said. "But that don't mean I gotta like it. You're too far away from home as it is, then when you come home you don't even stay in the house you were raised in."

Mama started to run water in the sink to wash the dinner dishes. It didn't matter that she had a barely used dishwasher in the kitchen; she was old school and washed her dishes by hand. I rolled up my sleeves, ready to help. She looked up and smiled.

"I remember when you were barely tall enough to reach this old sink, Orlando. And now look at you."

Tears filled her eyes and she quickly looked away. I instinctively knew those tears were brought on by the unwelcome memories that had hitched a ride on the happy one she'd just shared. I hugged her close and told her it was okay. She buried her face in my midsection and I absorbed every tear she wanted to get rid of.

"I'm sorry, baby," she said.

"You have nothing to be sorry for."

She took a step back and turned the water off in the sink before settling onto one of the chairs at the kitchen table. I took the seat across from her, eyes fixed on her tear-moistened face.

"Mama, don't cry."

"Baby, I am truly blessed. These are tears of joy." She looked at me and smiled. "There were so many times that I didn't think I would live to see you two grow up—let alone have my son turn out to be one of the bigwigs for the DEA. God had plans for us, and even in the midst of that chaos, He kept us. He kept you. You suffered sometimes more than me." Her voice cracked and she dropped her head. "But, baby, you didn't let it break you. Every day I thank God for that."

I reached across the table and took her hand. "I'm fine, Mama."

"I'm not so sure, baby. Trinity is worried. Worried you're carrying around a lot of anger, which you can't shake. You need to let go, baby."

I looked down at the floral-printed tablecloth, then back up to her. "I have let go, Mama. And Trinity wouldn't be Trinity if she wasn't worried about something or someone."

"Letting go and running aren't the same thing. You know part of letting go requires forgiveness."

I let her hand go and stood up. "I think you forgave him enough for the both of us."

Our heart-to-heart was cut short when my phone vibrated against my hip. I looked at the number. It wasn't one I recognized, which made the hair on my arms stand up. I got up and went into the hall before answering.

"Spencer," I stated.

"Trip?"

"Yeah, who is this?"

"This is Dionne, Dionne Evans, from Clark."

I let out a laugh. "Yeah, I remember you. How'd you get my number?"

"I got it out of Idalis's phone."

I gripped my phone. "Is she okay?"

"That's why I'm calling. I need to talk to you. Can you meet me somewhere?"

I looked at the clock above the mantel. "Meet me at the Murphy's in Virginia Highland in about thirty minutes."

"Okay."

I went back in the kitchen and wrapped my arms around my mother. "Mama, I gotta make a run."

She squeezed me tightly. "When are you coming back?"

"I'll be back tomorrow for dinner."

She looked up at me. "Don't lie to me, boy."

I smiled. "I promise. And for the record, I'm staying at the W on Peachtree."

I gave her another quick squeeze before cutting through the living room, tapping my sister upside the head, and heading out the door.

In the Tahoe I picked up my phone and hit speed dial for Phil. I was supposed to be meeting him for a beer and wanted to let him know I was running behind. I listened to the phone ring in my Bluetooth before it finally rolled to his voice mail. I left him a message and told him I had to make a stop, but I'd be there as soon as I was done.

My mother's voice resonated in my ears.

"Letting go and running aren't the same thing. You know part of letting go requires forgiveness."

My mind went to Westview Cemetery, off Ralph David Abernathy, my father's final resting place.

I had no idea where his plot was, or what his headstone read, because I didn't go to the funeral. I just knew his body was rotting underneath six feet of dirt, and that's all I cared about.

I remembered growing up and how I used to lay at night and listen to him beating my mom. Whenever I could, I would use my scrawny body as a shield to try to protect her.

Sometimes he would lock the door and I couldn't get in to help her or take the beating for her. Those nights I would huddle in a corner, comforting my sister, planning his death, while she cried into my shoulder. Sometimes I imagined it would be slow; other times it would be as easy as me taking a gun and blowing his head off. Many nights that's what fueled my drive, knowing that one day I was going to stop him.

However, as much as I used to want to be the one to end his useless life, lung cancer beat me to it. He tried reaching out to me on his deathbed, but there was no way I was giving that son of a bitch absolution for what he'd put us through. I guess he figured a few tears and a hug from me, while death hovered in the room waiting to take his sorry ass, would make all those beatings and trips to the hospital go away.

So my mother was wrong.

I did forgive him.

I forgave him for sparing me from serving a life sentence for blowing off his fucking head.

I walked into Murphy's thirty minutes later and took a seat at the bar; I ordered a Corona. The small restaurant was tucked away in a neighborhood where I didn't have to worry about anyone running into me, or vice versa. The bartender asked if I wanted to put in an order.

"No, I'm waiting for someone. I'm good."

I put the Corona to my lips and took a sip. I looked around, taking in my surroundings. Even when I didn't want to be, I was in surveillance mode, looking around for things that were out of place or seemed to be in a place they shouldn't be. They called that a "cop's eye."

I called it OCD.

"Trip?"

I turned around at the sound of my name.

Dionne was standing there. Other than being older than she was in college, she looked the same.

"What's up, Dionne?" I got down off my stool and hugged her. "I see you never did get any height, shorty."

She laughed. "Shut up. Welcome home."

I sat back down. "Thank you."

"So I hear you doing big things over there in New Orleans." She smiled. "And you still fine as hell."

I laughed. "Go 'head with that."

"Boy, please. You always were one of the finest things walking around the AU Center. You know how many fights were caused by that smile and those eyes of yours?"

"There you go." I laughed.

"You lucky I like women or Idalis would have competition."

All I could do was laugh at that comment.

The bartender made his way over to us; Dionne ordered a Cosmopolitan and I ordered another Corona.

"So what's up?" I asked. "I know you didn't wanna meet to talk about college or your sexual preference."

The expression on her face changed from nostalgic to concerned, which caused my senses to kick into gear. Especially knowing this had to do with Idalis.

"Trip." She took a deep breath. "Something isn't right with her and Lincoln."

"What do you mean?"

"Friday night he came in to the club when she was working," she started.

I took a sip of my Corona and raised an eyebrow. "And?"

"And they disappeared to the back. She was gone for a long time, so I went looking for her. When I found her, she was coming out of the office and she was upset."

"Upset like what? Like they had just argued?"

She shook her head and took a swallow of her drink. "Upset like he'd just done something to her but I don't know what."

Bombs went off in my head. Images of my mother's bruised and battered face flashed across the screen in my head. Sounds of her screams and cries blasted in my ears.

"Something like what?" I prodded.

She paused. "I don't know. But something definitely happened in that office, Trip."

Questions were firing in my mind so quickly; I couldn't pin one down long enough to try to get an answer for it. My hand went to the phone on my hip and hung there for a second before returning to my bottle of beer.

I stopped for a second then spoke. "Dionne, I'm not sure what you want me to do baby."

"Can you just"—she looked around—"you know, check on her? Don't you have some top-secret clearance or something?"

I laughed. "Nah, they don't trust a brotha that much."

"She's my girl and I'm just worried about her."

I looked toward the front door. "Dionne, honestly, I don't think I should get involved."

She looked at me like I had just insulted her.

"Why not?"

"What's going on with her and Lincoln is between them. They have a family. We haven't been close in years. I can't get in the middle of that."

She sucked her teeth. "But you're still her best friend, Trip."

"I *was* her best friend. She's about to get married and I can't step on that. If she wants my help, she has to come to me herself."

I felt bad as I watched the disappointment wash over her, but what Phil said was right. I had to stay focused on what brought me to Atlanta, and Idalis wasn't it. She had created a life with Lincoln. It was time for me to do the same.

Dionne slid down off the stool. "I understand. I just don't know what else to do."

I pulled a twenty out of my wallet and tossed it onto the bar and followed her out the door.

The warm night air hung heavy over the city, which was now slowing to a crawl. The hustle and bustle of the streets had been replaced with the slow stroll of people in shorts and tee's search of dinner or out walking their dogs winding down for the night.

Dionne wrapped her arms around me. "Well, thanks for coming. At least now I can tell people I got to see the famous Trip Spencer while he was in town."

I gave her a squeeze. "You're so silly. It was good seeing you too."

She turned to walk away and I stopped her. When she turned around, I told her, "Keep an eye on her. If things get too crazy, gimme a call."

A small smile spread across her face as she turned and headed toward the parking lot.

Later that night I met Phil at Dugans on Ponce for Mad Mondays. He was sitting across from me, hunched over a big-ass plate of wings, fussing about the case. As much as I hated it, my mind was on the other side of town.

"Yo," he said between bites. "You hear they pulling some of the undercovers and putting them in safe houses and shit?"

I took a long draw on my Corona. "I'm not surprised. Atlanta fucked this whole investigation up big time."

We both stopped talking and watched as a thick-ass redbone walked by our table, catching both our attention. She smiled and I winked.

"Whoa, I know you ain't trying to get no ass."

"Fuck is that supposed to mean?" I asked, laughing.

He wiped his mouth. "I thought your emotional ass was saving yourself for Idalis."

I shook my head, keeping my eyes on old girl as she made her way to the bar. "Nah, man, we just friends, right? You want a drink?"

He chuckled. "Yeah, get me another Bud."

"Be right back." I got up and made my way to the bar.

She smiled when she saw me moving toward her. Her fat ass was tucked inside a pair of jeans, which looked like they were made just for her, and a tight tee, which was struggling to contain breasts that seemed too big for her small frame. She was perched on top of heels that added at least five inches to her height.

"Hello, Miss Lady."

She leaned back against the bar. "Hey, you."

I bent down next to her ear. "What's your name, baby girl?"

"Onuka."

I motioned for the bartender. "What are you drinking?"

"A Perfect Ten."

I smiled. "Of course you are." I ordered her drink and another round for Phil and me. The bartender popped the caps and set the drinks on the bar. I leaned in close to her and inhaled her fruity perfume before grabbing the drinks off the bar.

"You here by yourself?" I asked.

"Waiting for a friend. You?"

I motioned toward Phil, who gave me a look that let me know he was waiting for his beer.

I turned and headed back toward the table; without me having to say a word, she followed.

It didn't take long for Dugans to fill up with the after-work crowd. The crowd spilled out onto the patio; the waitresses hustled to keep up with the steady flow of wings and fries coming from the kitchen.

It also didn't take long, or very many drinks, before Onuka's friend ended up in Phil's lap. Meanwhile, Onuka was whispering things in my ear that I'm sure she'd whispered in many ears before mine.

"So what do you do?" she asked.

Phil answered, "We catch bad guys."

"Oh, really?" Onuka ran her fingers up and down my arm. "So that means you're a good guy, then."

I don't know if it was the beers, the crowd or just her in general, but she was starting to get on my nerves. Still, I had to give it to her—shorty was fine as hell.

Phil asked, "So where you ladies going after y'all leave here?"

Her nameless friend, nameless because I didn't care to remember it, spoke up. "I thought I was coming with you," she said, smiling and wrapping her arms around Phil's neck.

"Hell yeah, you can come with me," he said, grinning.

Onuka whispered in my ear, "Can I come with you?"

I leaned back and looked at her. I knew her story without having to ask her a single question. The fake hair, painted-on makeup, tight clothes leaving nothing to the imagination and the way she was giving away the ass.

She was fishing.

I asked, "Why should I let you come with me?"

"Because I know you want to."

I cracked a smile. "You think so?"

She pressed closer.

I felt her lips on my neck as her hand moved up my thigh.

"It's that easy, huh?" I asked.

I felt myself swell against my jeans as her tongue snaked its way toward my ear. Her lips brushed my cheek, that's when I tapped her leg and grabbed my keys off the table.

"Let's ride."

I tossed some money onto the table, and Phil did the same. We headed for the door and I had to wrap my arm around Onuka's waist to keep her tipsy ass from falling. She was now wobbling in the high-ass heels she was wearing.

I looked over at my partner. "Phil, you okay to drive?"

"Yeah, I'm good. You a'ight?"

"What about my car?" Onuka asked, checking her hair in her reflection in the window.

"I'll bring you back down here in the morning," I said, putting my hand on the door pushing it open.

"That's real nice of you, Agent Spencer," a voice came from behind me.

I turned around.

Idalis was standing behind us with India.

The disgusted look she wore on her face spoke volumes.

"Hey, Trip," India said, barely above a whisper.

"Hey India," I spoke, keeping my eyes on Idalis.

"Who is she?" Onuka asked, everyone ignoring her.

Phil walked up and stood next to me. "Hi, how you doin'?" He extended his hand. "I'm Phil, Trip's partner."

Idalis shook his hand, keeping her eyes on me. "Nice to meet you."

She turned and headed back into the crowd with India on her heels.

I went after her. "Idalis, wait."

She stopped and turned around. "What?"

"What the hell is your problem?"

She looked at me, daggers shooting from her eyes. "Go finish what you started with that bitch at your table, Trip."

She turned around again and walked away.

I was about to go after her again, when Phil grabbed my arm. "Let her go, man. Just let her go."

Chapter Fourteen

Idalis

"You can't seriously be mad at him, Idalis."

Tuesday afternoon Dionne dragged me out of the house, trying to cheer me up.

The only reason I agreed to go was because I didn't want to sit around the house, thinking about it all day. That and the fact that she promised me a massage along with a mani-pedi at Spa Sydell.

When India and I first got there and saw Trip at the table with that girl, I wasn't going to say anything because, in all fairness, I didn't have a right to. At first I was gonna go over to the table and speak, maybe introduce myself to his partner and leave, that's it. But when I saw that chick hanging all over him and then them heading for the door, it was like my body was on remote control and I got up and followed. India tried to stop me, but I told her either to stay there or shut up and come with me. Seeing him with his arm around that girl's waist, knowing they were leaving together was more than I wanted to deal with after what I had just went through with Linc and I just lost it. India tried to stop me, but it was too late. And now I was pretty sure his partner probably thought I crazy.

"Idalis, stop beating yourself up," Dionne said.

"I'm not."

She lifted her head from the massage table and looked over at me. "I would've probably done the same thing."

"I can't believe he was leaving with her," I finally admitted.

"What did you expect? He's single. He deserves a life too."

At the sound of that, I placed my face back in the little hole in the massage table, hiding the hurt that had crept up on it. "Yeah, I know."

She kept talking as the masseuse worked on my back. Every area of stress she kneaded out with her strong hands and warm oil was quickly replaced with a new wave of stress as I remembered seeing that chick kissing on Trip's neck. At this rate this masseuse was definitely about to earn her money.

"Maybe it's not what you think," Dionne continued.

"Dionne, the way she was hanging all over him, I'm pretty sure they weren't on their way to Bible Study."

As the massage therapist worked my legs, Dionne asked, "What do you want from him?"

"I don't want anything from him."

"If that were true, then you wouldn't be upset about some hoodrat he was about to take back to his room and bang."

I lifted my head and looked at her with wide eyes.

She laughed. "What? You know it's true. You and I both know he wasn't trying to wife her up. His dick was just hard."

I heard the masseuses laugh a little.

"Don't laugh at her. It just encourages her," I told them, laughing.

"I'm serious. He's a man. What do you expect? He's fine as hell. She was probably pitching him pussy all night."

"That don't mean he had to catch it."

"Why do you care?"

I turned my head and faced the wall. I didn't have an answer for that. Or maybe I didn't want to answer that.

"Idalis, you're torturing yourself for nothing. If you're gonna be with Linc, then you need to let Trip go, completely."

After our massages we wrapped fluffy white robes around our bodies and headed to the manicure and pedicure room. We climbed up onto the huge leather chairs and let the technicians go to work on our hands and feet. I chose OPI's Chick Flick Cherry for my fingers and toes. Dionne went with O'Hare & Nails Look Great.

During lunch I tried hard not to let my gloomy mood hang over the table, but it was hard. I pushed my salad around on my plate with my fork and let Dionne do most of the talking.

"Has India mentioned anything else about California?" she asked.

I shook my head. "No, but I think she's probably scared to say anything."

"Has she told your mom?"

"Knowing her, no." I took a sip of my water. "I wouldn't be surprised if she waited until she was on the plane to tell her."

"Don't be like that, Idalis. She has a right to live her own life."

I leaned back. "I know, I know. Why can't she live it in some loft downtown like the rest of the single women in Atlanta?"

"Well, I can't really blame her. You're getting married and have a family. She needs to spread her wings. Find out who she is, independent of you."

I rolled my eyes. I wasn't trying to hear anything she was saying. And judging from the look on her face, she knew that.

"Just talk to her. Give the idea a chance before you disown her," she laughed, trying to lighten the mood.

I gave her a side-eyed glance. "Whatever."

"Well, all I know is you can't disown me."

"True. So what's up with you and your girl Stephanie?" I asked. "She hasn't been by 404 in a while."

She paused for a second, like she wasn't sure how to answer my question.

"We're taking a break from each other."

"A break?" I asked.

"Yeah, she was getting too clingy for me, and I really ain't ready for all that."

Stephanie was usually at the club almost every weekend, typically posted up at the bar keeping Dionne company. Dionne claimed she was cool with it, but I knew it irked the shit out of her. If I knew anything about Dionne, it was that she didn't sit still for long, and she definitely didn't like to be crowded, so her cutting that girl loose didn't surprise me.

"Was she mad?" I shoved a forkful of lettuce into my mouth.

She laughed. "She didn't seem to like it. But she won't return my texts either."

"I'll take that as a yes."

She nodded. "Yeah, me too."

After lunch Dionne dropped me back at my mom's. India's car was in the driveway and I could hear Cameron playing in the front room.

I opened the door and Cameron immediately latched onto me. I couldn't help but laugh as I sank to my knees under a barrage of hugs and kisses.

"Where's Mama?" I asked.

India pointed toward the kitchen, never taking her eyes off the paper she was reading.

"What's that?" I asked.

"Offer letter from that company in California."

I stood there and looked at her in disbelief. "So you're serious about this?"

"Why wouldn't I be serious about my career? Did I say anything about you leaving the Four Seasons to run 404?"

"Whatever, India. I left the Four Seasons to own my own business."

"No you left to own a business that Linc *wanted* you to own."

I started to walk to the kitchen, when she stopped me.

"You know what, Idalis. Believe it or not, the world doesn't revolve around you."

I whipped around and looked at her. "What are you talking about? I never said it did."

"You don't have to. Look at how you're acting. You can't even be happy for me."

I tossed my purse onto the couch. "Why would I be happy about my sister moving across the country India?"

"Maybe because *I'm* happy."

"You're happy *now*. What's gonna happen when this little stunt gets old and you're ready to move on to the next thing? Who's gonna have to come bring you back home? Me!"

She stood up from the couch. "*Stunt?* That's what you think this is?"

I folded my arms across my chest. "Come on, India. California? You mean to tell me you couldn't find *one* company in the entire state of Georgia to hire you? You jump from one thing to another. You collect degrees like it's a hobby."

"That's not the point, Idalis, and you know it. Would you be happier if I was being some puppet for a man like you're doing with Linc?"

"Whatever India. So what is the point then?"

"You hate the fact that it's not all about you, Twin, admit it."

"I never said it had to be about me!"

"You don't have to! You got everybody on edge about this wedding. You got Trip chasing his tail.

One minute you want him, and then the next you mad 'cause he with some girl—"

I cut her off. "Whoa. I tell you what. Since it's such a problem, you don't have to be in the wedding. Then you won't have to worry about it! And as far as Trip is concerned, he's none of your damn business!"

She stood there and glared at me. Her eyes were glassy with tears, and hot with anger. Before she could say anything else, my mother appeared in the doorway to the living room.

"Now, I've listened to just about all that I'm gonna listen to of this foolishness. Stop it. Both of you. Right now!" she fussed.

We stood there, with tears streaming down both of our faces.

Before I could say another word, India grabbed her purse and stormed out the front door. I heard her car start and her pulling out of the driveway.

"Idalis, what is going on?"

"Nothing, Mama," I said, wiping my face and scooping up Cameron.

"It didn't sound like nothing."

I looked at my mom. She was a short woman, barely registering five feet. Her jet-black hair was pulled back in a tight bun, the same hairstyle she had worn for the last twenty years. When it hung loose, it was long enough to reach her pudgy waist. Her skin was as smooth as the day she was born, not a blemish anywhere. I always admired that about her. Time, however, had etched a road map of wrinkles around her eyes and at the corners of her mouth.

"I don't want to talk about it," I said, making my way into the kitchen. Mama followed me and poured a cup of tea before she took a seat at the kitchen table. She motioned for me to sit across from her. I knew what this was about, but I didn't dare say no.

I slid onto the chair and braced myself for my lecture.

"That wasn't *nothing,* Idalis. What is going on with you and your sister?"

My voice was shaky. "Did she tell you about California?"

"Yes."

"And you didn't say anything?"

"Idalis, I don't want her to go any more than you do, but India is grown."

I got an attitude and pushed my chair back, standing to my feet. That was not what I wanted to hear.

"Sit. Down. Idalis." Her voice was stern.

I was probably one of the few women alive who was almost forty and still scared of her mother. So I did as I was told. "Yes, ma'am."

"You need to apologize to your sister."

A look of surprise came over my face. "Why do I have to apologize?"

"You were wrong."

I let out a heavy sigh.

"When all this dust settles, she's all you're gonna have, Idalis. Whether she's three miles away or three thousand, you need to make this right. I am not gonna be here forever, and men come and go, but your sister is forever.

"You are twins, rare gifts from God with a bond that is impenetrable when you're at your strongest and right now you're not. You need each other Idalis, you needed each other to thrive in the womb and you need each other now."

With that, she got up and headed back toward the hall, where Cameron was playing.

There was no point in trying to argue with her because there was no argument. She was right. But I didn't have the energy to deal with India, or anything else for that matter right now.

I went upstairs to check on my grandmother. When I got to her room, I pushed the door open a little. She looked so peaceful, lying in the bed. I walked over and sat on the edge of the bed. Her face was soft, and her striking Indian features stood out—the high cheekbones and the deep-set eyes.

Mama had braided her hair into two braids, which were resting on her shoulders. I touched her hand and she stirred, but she didn't open her eyes. I could really use some of her words of wisdom right now, but I didn't want to wake her. I knew how precious sleep was to her.

The bone cancer kept her in a lot of pain and she didn't get much sleep. I tucked a stray hair in place and planted a kiss on her forehead before heading back downstairs.

My mother had cleaned up Cameron and his mess and was setting him up in his high chair for dinner.

I heard a car pulling into the driveway. I looked out the window, expecting India and her stank attitude to be coming back, prepared to continue arguing. My heart stopped when I saw Trip's truck pulling up behind mine, instead.

I opened the door and stepped outside before he had a chance to knock.

"Trip, what are you doing here?"

"Looking for you."

"Why didn't you just call?"

"Because I knew you wouldn't answer."

I looked back toward the house, then back to him. "Probably not."

"Don't you think we need to talk?"

"Nothing to talk about. You're single. You can fuck whoever you want to fuck."

He shook his head. "Come on, Idalis. I sent that drunk bitch home in a cab."

"Sorry to hear that."

His tone changed to frustration. "What do you want from me?"

"I don't want anything from you."

He took a step toward me but stopped.

"Idalis, what's going on with you? You're not the same person I grew up with," he said.

"Maybe because I grew up," I snapped.

He snapped back, "So, are you trying to tell me you pissed about some ho whose name I probably wouldn't have remembered the next day?"

I crossed my arms against my chest. "Like I said, you can fuck whoever you want to fuck."

He let out a sigh. "This is ridiculous. You're getting married but you want to check me. You acting real out of pocket right now, not mention you got people worried about you."

"Worried about what?"

"What's up with you and Lincoln?" he asked.

I turned and headed toward the house; then I stopped and went back and got in his face.

"There's nothing going on with me and Lincoln. It sounds like somebody is just jealous."

He shook his head slowly. "Idalis, it's not like that, and you know it."

"Oh, it's not?"

He asked, "If nothing is going on, what happened a few nights ago at 404?"

My mouth opened slightly, but nothing came out. Tears burned my eyes, but I dared them to come out. "What goes on between me and my fiancé is none of your business. I'm not a little girl anymore. I don't need you protecting me."

"I guess that's Lincoln's job now."

"Exactly."

"Well, who's gonna protect you from him?"

Trip kept his eyes on me for a moment before heading toward his truck.

I called out to him, but he ignored me, got in, and drove off.

Chapter Fifteen

Idalis

My mom and I ate dinner in silence.

Other than the sound of Cameron crashing his cars on the table and singing songs, which only he understood, there was no interaction. I knew what she was going to say if I tried to spark up a conversation, and I didn't feel like expending the energy right now.

Trip and India had taken all the emotional energy I had for the night.

After I finished helping my mother clean the kitchen, I headed upstairs to visit my grandmother. I walked into the room and found her seated on her rocking chair, watching television. As always, my heart ached a little seeing how frail she had become. Her brown eyes lit up and a smile spread across her thinning face when she saw me come into the room.

I sank down onto the bed across from her. "Hi, Grammie."

"Hey, baby. Why do you look so sad?"

"I got into an argument with India, Grammie."

Her voice was stern. "That's your sister, baby, you don't push her away you need her."

"I know Grammie, but I don't want her to go."

She turned her head and looked at me. "Listen, baby. Whenever you're in conflict, you figure out whatever the hardest thing is to do, and you do it, because that's usually the right choice."

"So you also think she should go?"

"I think India needs to do what's gonna make her happy. She can't live for you or anyone else."

I tried hard to stop it, but the tears flowed. I slid onto the floor next to her, laying my head in my grandmother's lap, and cried as she stroked my hair. She started humming and the song soothed me. I wanted so bad for her to be proud of me, and I felt like I was blowing it, big-time.

I sat up and hugged her, inhaling her scent: the smell of her hair, the scent of her soap, everything. I wanted to take in her strength.

Before I left, she said, "You do what you have to do to be happy too, baby. You hear me? But don't do it at the expense of anyone else."

"Yes, ma'am."

I kissed her and told her mama would be up with her dinner.

After putting away most of Cameron's toys and picking out the ones he wanted to bring home with him, we headed home. My mother didn't have a lot to say before I left, but I didn't think she would. I knew she wanted what was in the best interest of both India and me, so I couldn't be mad at her.

At home, after Cameron succeeded in damn near flooding my bathroom with his over-the-top bath play, he fell asleep before I could finish getting his pajamas on. The later it got, the better I felt. I slowly allowed myself to relax into my evening. By nine o'clock I had washed my hair, showered, pulled on a pair of Lincoln's APD sweats, and was relaxing on my couch in front of a rerun of *Criminal Minds*. Trip called around nine-thirty, but I let his call go to voice mail. I was almost relieved when there was no follow-up beep alerting me of a message.

"Good," I said, aloud to the empty room.

I got up and started turning off the lights and checking the locks. I already knew that Lincoln wasn't coming home because he'd sent me a text earlier saying something about working late because of the case. Honestly, I didn't even read the whole thing. I just deleted it.

Once I made sure the doors leading to the deck were locked, I turned the lights off in the kitchen, causing the night lights to dimly illuminate the room. I was just about to set the alarm for the night, but I noticed a light coming from underneath the door that led to the garage. I rolled my eyes because Lincoln was always forgetting to turn the light off whenever he left.

In my socks I padded out into the garage. The first thing I noticed was how dirty my car was. I had to remember to have Lincoln take it to get it washed. I skirted around my car and reached for the light switch on the wall; but before I could touch it, I damn near tripped and broke my neck. My foot got caught on the strap of a black duffel bag. I reached down to untangle myself. As I pulled the strap free, the bag tipped over, exposing its contents.

For a moment I stood there staring at what was laying on the concrete floor next to my feet. I stepped over the pile, never taking my eyes off it, as if it would disappear if I did.

I stooped down and picked up one of the stacks of money. I held it in my hand and stared at it like the intruder it had just become in my life. I dropped it back to where it had been resting. Just as I was about to reach down and touch a brick of cocaine, Linc's voice echoed through the garage.

"What you doin' out here?"

I stood up and looked at him, but he was staring at me as if I were in the wrong.

I could barely speak. "Wh—what am I doing?" I motioned to the stack on my garage floor. "What the hell is this?"

He walked down the steps and came toward me. "I asked you a question. Why are you in here?"

I motioned toward the light switch. "You left the light on again and . . ." I could barely finish my sentence.

"And what?"

I felt light-headed. My hands were trembling. "Lincoln, why is this in my garage?"

"I'm keepin' you with this big-ass roof over your head and clothes on Cameron's back. Keepin' that club runnin'. That's all you need to be worried about."

I looked at him in disbelief. "You're joking, right?"

"Does it look like I'm joking?"

My eyes cut to the bag on the floor. "Lincoln, where did you get this from?"

"Why you out here goin' through my shit, Idalis?"

"I wasn't going through your shit! I tripped over the bag and—"

Before I could finish my sentence, he reached up and grabbed my face, squeezing my cheeks in his hand, cutting me off. "And what?"

He shoved me backward so hard that my body slammed into the trunk of my car—thankfully keeping me from hitting the concrete ground of the garage. It took all I had in me not to let out the scream that swelled in my throat out of fear of waking Cameron.

A sinister smile spread across his face. "I told you about questionin' me, Idalis."

I was frantic. Anger and fear shared space in my chest; each fighting and clawing to take over. "What if Cameron had come in here and found this?"

I watched, stunned, as he resituated everything back into the bag and zipped it up.

Totally ignoring me.

He stood up and glared at me. Defiant and angry. "Go to bed, Idalis."

I followed him as he made his way back into the house, closing the door to the garage behind us. He made his way to the front door, and I headed toward the steps to go upstairs and check on Cameron.

"I'm on my way back out," he spoke to my back.

Just as my foot touched the bottom step, he called out my name.

"Idalis."

I kept my hand on the railing and my back to him. "What?" I answered matter-of-factly.

"I hope you ain't plannin' on doin' nothin' stupid."

I turned around and shot him a look. "Meaning?"

"Meaning, opening your mouth."

I was in complete disbelief, not sure how to respond. In my opinion there was no response. I flinched, gripping the railing even tighter when he walked toward me.

He leaned in and planted a kiss on my lips. "And if you're thinkin' about runnin' your mouth, I would think long and hard first."

"Why?" I asked. "You gonna slap me around some more?"

He let out a laugh. "Nah, I'd just hate for you to get pulled over"—he started walking toward the door — "and have your car searched. It would be a shame if they were to find drugs in your possession. 'Cause you know if they do, you're going straight downtown, right? And by the time you fuck Trip to get out of holdin', Cameron will be so deep in the system, you'll never see him again."

Nausea washed over me as I stood there and glaring at him, my mouth was hanging open in disbelief.

He winked at me. "Sleep tight."

The front door closed and the soft click of the lock set off a bomb inside me. I fell to the steps and sobbed. I wanted to scream, to break things, to scoop up my son and run. But I knew that no matter where I ended up, he'd find me.

At some point I managed to pull myself up off the steps and made it to the living room. I didn't know how much time had passed. I just remembered waking up on the couch with my phone in my hand.

I looked down at the display and saw that I had found Trip's number in my contacts, but I didn't hit send.

My head and my ribcage were pounding, so I got up and grabbed some Advil out of the medicine cabinet in the downstairs bathroom. I popped two in my mouth and washed them down with a handful of water.

I looked at my reflection in the oval-shaped mirror. *At least this time it wasn't my face,* I thought. I lifted the oversized tee and spied the large purplish red bruise on my side from where

I slammed into my car. That little souvenir was unmistakable, and to call it painful wasn't doing it justice.

I pulled my shirt back down and went upstairs to Cameron's room. I stood in his doorway and watched his little chest rise and fall under his *Cars* comforter. I moved closer and stood over him, watching him sleep. His face was so angelic; it always made me smile. But what broke my heart more than anything . . .

What bothered me the most . . .

Was how much he looked like his father.

*"It is a man's own mind, not his enemy or foe
that lures him to evil ways"*

— Siddhartha Buddha

Linc's truck rolled to a stop in front of the address that Twist texted him. "This is it," he said.

Nate leaned forward and looked across Linc and out the window.

"All right, let's see what this dude is talkin' about."

"You think we need to trust Twist?"

Linc rubbed his goatee. "He's been good up to this point. Moved a lot of shit for me. If he says this cat is one hundred, then I believe him."

"I know, but this was supposed to be a hit and run type deal. When we started this a while back we were gonna hit these dealers up hard and get out the game. There's a lot going on," Nate argued. "Shit's getting to hot out here."

"Once we move the weight we got things will start running smooth again. You let me worry 'bout that the heat, you just keep banking the money."

Nate put his hand on his arm. "Yo, is this about that shit with Idalis and Trip?"

Linc pulled his arm away. "Man if you don't get the fuck outta my truck with that bullshit. This is about my money and my reputation. These fools won't hesitate to wipe me out if I get caught slippin', ya dig."

"A'ight I hear you," Nate said.

"I feel where you comin' from. Trust me, I'm on top of this shit, believe me."

"That's all I wanted to know," Nate responded.

They got out and headed toward the huge double doors situated at the top of the steps. This was supposed to be a quick exchange and Linc hoped it went down the way it was supposed to.

He was out of his comfort zone and he was on edge. The only reason he'd agreed to meet this dude was because he needed the stacks to flip the weight he was sitting on.

Nate hit the door three hard times as Linc looked over his shoulder, half expecting someone to rush up on him at any moment. Shit was getting hectic and he was losing his grip, not to mention he was out of his element. But if this dude could deliver like Twist said, then it just might be worth the risk.

A few moments later the door swung open and a big dude, who had to weigh no less than 250, was standing there. He didn't look happy. Instinctively, Linc put his hand on his gun, but he didn't pull it out.

"Yo, playa, fuck y'all want?" he barked.

"Whoa! Whoa!" Linc answered, hand still on his gun. "Damn, you need to calm the fuck down. Where Twist?"

Twist ran up behind the dude, laughing. "They cool; they cool." He pushed by the dude and ushered them inside. "It's about damn time."

Twist led them down a long hall and into a room where a tall brown-skinned guy was waiting. Linc began sizing up the dude immediately: a black Yankees cap rested on top of his head; an oversized black tee hung loosely on his muscular frame. Linc was sure he had more than muscles under that shirt. He was in the small room with two other dudes; one was situated near the window, where he was setting up scales. Linc couldn't help but notice how big he was, and the fact that the dude looked like Charlie Murphy on steroids. There was a little light-skinned dude sitting on the couch playing Xbox; Linc didn't even bother to acknowledge him. The other guy, the one who opened the door, made his way into the room and stood in the corner.

"Linc, this is Geech, the guy I was telling you about."

Geech looked up from that briefcase opened in front of him. "Y'all late. Let's get this over with."

Twist looked around the room. "What's the hurry?"

Geech looked at Linc. "I don't like cops," he said, looking at Linc. "All this heat in the room can only start a fire."

Linc looked at him. "I didn't come here to be your Facebook friend, ya dig. You got my money, pot'na?"

"Everything is in here." Geech turned the open briefcase around, showcasing its contents.

Linc eyed the neat stacks of fifties tucked inside the black case. He motioned for Nate to check the contents. He watched intently as Nate pulled stacks out of the case and studied them closely.

"Looks like it's all here," Nate finally said.

Linc picked up the duffel bag on the floor next to him and in one switch motion tossed it to the man who had been lurking in the corner. The bag flying in his direction made him put up his hands to catch it, taking away any chance he had of going for whatever heat he was carrying.

"Y'all got your shit; we out." Linc turned to walk out of the room and he heard the sound of guns being cocked.

He pulled his Glock from his holster and turned around. "Oh, it's like that?" he taunted. "You blaze. We blaze. What's up?"

His heart was pounding hard in his chest; he could hear it in his ears. Sweat popped up on his brow as his eyes scanned the room. He didn't come over here for this shit. From the corner of his eye he could she Nate's gun pointed at the dude standing by the table.

Geech cracked a crooked smile. "Yo, where you going playboy? I know you in a hurry to supply your merry elves, but this shit needs to be checked."

Linc gave a nod and Nate lowered his heat, but he didn't put it away.

Everyone stood around in silence, watching intently as one of Geech's boys pulled each silver-coated brick out of the small duffel bag and weighed it before meticulously examining each bag of pills. He then pulled a small pocketknife from his back pocket, flicked the blade open and cut a small slit in the top of each brick, revealing the powder hidden inside. A small amount of the light, airy powder settled on top. He moistened the tip of his finger, collected a sample on the tip and rubbed it in his mouth on his gums. Moments later, he gave an approving head nod.

Tension slowly lifted as Geech turned his attention back to Linc. "Yo, big man. What a brotha gotta do to get his weight up?"

Linc holstered his gun. "How much weight you talking?"

"Let me be clear, I'm not just talking weight— I'm talking insulation."

Linc answered, "I'm listening. . . ."

He knew what Geech wanted. But Linc wanted to hear him say it. That way he stayed in control. He wasn't just gonna put his shit out there like that. He'd run interference for dealers numerous times for a cut of their books, so it wasn't like it was something new. But he didn't know this dude, so Geech was gonna have to ask for it. And it definitely was gonna come with a price.

"I need some breathing room to get my payroll back up, and the streets are hot right now."

"And?"

Geech walked around and leaned back against the table. "I know you got some people on the inside who ain't real happy about their supply being held up."

It made Linc uneasy that Geech seemed to know about what he had going on, but he had to respect the man and his hustle.

"So what are you sayin'?"

"I think we can both stand to benefit from this, but I need help keeping the bad boys in blue off my back."

"What kind of weight you looking for?"

"I'm ready to flip high six figures. For starters."

Linc looked over at Nate and smiled. "I can handle that. But what you gon' do for me?"

Geech motioned toward a sitting area, with two oversized armchairs on the other side of the room. "Let's talk."

After almost two hours of back and forth they came to an agreement that made both Linc and Geech very happy and promised to make them both extremely rich if they played their cards right.

With the weight Linc was about to supply Geech he could stop rolling low-level dealers and focus most of his attention on working Geech. He could leave the petty street level shit to Nate if he wanted it. This was exactly what he needed, he'd be so far removed from what was going on they'd need a surgeon to figure out his connection, because realistically he'd be right in the heart of it all.

Linc handed Geech the paper he'd been writing on.

Geech scanned it for a moment then looked up. "You sure about this?"

"You want somethin' from me pot'na, that's my price. Take it or leave it."

Geech glanced over to the other side of the room where Twist was drinking and playing Xbox and where Nate and the other dude were talking, before folding the paper and putting it in his pocket.

"So this agent on this list, what's up with him? He may not be that easy to get to."

Linc stood up. "He's my problem, not yours. You just need to get rid of him. Along with everyone else on that list."

Chapter Sixteen

Idalis

I rode around I-285 and tried to find answers in the intermittent traffic and asphalt that encapsulated the city. I kept replaying the threat from Linc. At this point I wouldn't put anything past him, including planting something either in my car or on me just to get me locked up. I couldn't live my life searching my car every time I pulled out of the driveway, or checking my pockets and purse whenever I left the house.

That was just crazy.

Things were falling apart at the seams and I couldn't get a grip on them: India, with this California mess, and Linc flipping the script the way he had. I felt like I was dealing with a bunch of doppelgängers. One thing I did know, with both of them losing their minds, only Trip seemed to be making sense to me right now.

I picked up my phone and tried Trip's number.

It went to voice mail, so I left him a message.

"Hey, it's Idalis. When you get this message, can you call me? There's something going on, and I don't know who else to talk to."

I tossed my phone onto the passenger seat and saw the exit for I-20 coming into view. I hit the gas, exited, and sped west.

Fifteen minutes later, yet again, I was standing in the middle of my past. Only this time it was broad daylight and all secrets were on display. The rickety porch made me feel like I was a little girl standing there in ripped jeans and ponytails, about to ask if Trip could come out to play.

I heard the locks click; then the door opened and his mom was standing there, smiling. I couldn't help but smile. She was so tiny and much older than the last time I saw her when her husband died.

Her hand shot up and covered her mouth in surprise. "Oh my Jesus, Idalis Arrington." She pushed back the old screen door, welcoming me into her home. "It's been so long."

She hugged me tightly, causing me to wince from the pain in my side, but I didn't pull away.

"How are you, Miss Myrtle?"

She turned and pushed the door up. "I'm good. I'm good. Come on in and have a seat. When's the wedding?"

"It's in a couple months." I said.

"Wow, coming up fast." She busied herself re-arranging pillows on the couch; then she moved a throw blanket from one side of the couch to the other. She was just as nervous about me being in her space as I was about being there.

I smiled, no real comeback for that. I made my way to the couch and took a seat.

"How's your grandmother?" she asked.

"She's okay," I responded. "She's been up moving around."

She nodded her approval. "Praise God. I saw your mom at church the other Sunday and she said she seemed to be doing much better."

"Uhm . . . I can't stay long, I was actually"— I looked around nervously—"I was, uh, looking for Trinity. That her Acura parked in the driveway?"

She looked back toward the bedrooms. "Yes, she's back in her room."

A few moments after that, I heard her coming down the hall. "Mama, who was at the door?" She stopped when she saw me sitting on the couch. "Oh my goodness! Hi, Idalis!" she squealed, rushing over to hug me.

She was sporting twists she didn't have the last time I'd seen her. They were in their beginning stages but I knew if she followed in her brother's footsteps her locs would be long and beautiful in no time.

When she smiled, her cheeks smiled back with matching dimples.

"Wow, Idalis, you look great."

"Thank you, so do you. You're hair is cute!"

"Thank you," she said, playing with her twists. "How's India?"

"She's doing well. Talking about moving to California."

Trinity dropped her head a little and laughed. "That's India."

We sat down on the couch as her mother placed two glasses of lemonade in front of us and disappeared down the hall.

"So what's going on?" she asked. "Trip told me you came by the other night. I hate I wasn't here."

"I know. He said I had just missed you," I said. "Have you talked to him today? I'm trying to get in touch with him. I called but I got voice mail and he didn't respond to my text."

She looked confused. "That's odd. He must be busy. But he's been coming by here a lot before he goes to his hotel in the evening sometimes."

I let out a sigh.

She gave a worried look. "You okay?"

"Yeah, I just really need to talk to him that's all. And I think he's mad and avoiding me."

Her eyes got big. "Why?"

I filled her in real quick on what happened at Dugans and when he came by my mother's. I tried my best not to sound as pathetic as I really was. But the more I talked and listened to myself I couldn't help but feel a little childish.

She waved her hand, dismissing what I had just said.

"Girl please, he I'm sure he ain't mad at you. And whoever she was she was just something to do."

"I know, I just been dealing with a lot. My grandmother isn't doing so well and planning this wedding is taking its toll on me." I stared at the glass of yellow liquid sitting in front of me, but I had no desire to drink it.

"I know. Mama told me about your grandmother. I'm sorry."

"Thanks." I stood up and grabbed my purse. "Do you know where Trip is staying?"

"At the W on Peachtree."

Her phone chimed with the sound of a text message. She read it and put the phone back down.

"Okay, maybe I'll try to catch him down there."

She stood up and walked me to the door. "I really hope you two can work through this. I know he misses you a lot."

"So much time has passed and things are just . . . complicated now, Trin."

"I know. But it's nothing that can't be fixed. Y'all been through too much. You're family, Idalis." Her phone rang and she checked the display. "It's work. I gotta take this."

After a quick hug I stepped out onto the porch.

I stood there for a second, trying to figure out what I was doing, or, for that matter, what I was trying to do. I knew beyond a shadow of a doubt that Lincoln would carry through with his threat of setting me up. But after the way I acted, I wasn't even sure if Trip would *want* to help me.

But at this point I had to do something. My son's life depended on it.

I checked my watch, then my phone. I had two missed calls from India and a text.

You need to come home.

I guess Trip would have to wait.

I jumped into my car and sped across town to my mother's house.

When I pulled into the driveway, my body went numb when I saw an ambulance in the driveway. My mind went to my grandmother and I couldn't breathe. I jumped out without turning the car off and ran through the front door. My mother was

standing in the foyer, talking to a medic; she saw
the frantic look on my face and immediately came
to me.

"Mama, what's going on?"

"It's your grandmother."

"Is she—"

"No, no," she reassured. "She's being transported to the hospital."

"For what?" I asked, looking toward the steps.

"Her doctor wants to do some tests on her.
She's in a lot of pain," she said. "The ambulance
is just a precaution, just transportation."

India came rushing through the front door.
When I saw her, my eyes filled with tears. Her
face was soaking wet, covered with panic.

Standing there, I felt like we were thirteen
years old again and my father had just had
his second heart attack. The first one merely
scared all of us, giving us a cold dose of reality;
the second one played for keeps, taking my
father one afternoon while we were unknowingly
playing at school. I remember us standing on the
same porch, watching my grandmother drive off
to the funeral home to make arrangements with
my mother.

Moments later two medics appeared on the steps
carrying my small grandmother on a stretcher and
the present flooded back to me, slamming into my
body like a huge tidal wave.

She appeared to be asleep, undoubtedly induced, but she looked so peaceful. I walked over and touched her hand, wishing I could rewind time for her. I felt my mother's hand on my shoulder and I turned around.

"I am going to ride with them. Cameron is taking a nap on the couch."

I nodded and stepped aside, letting them pass. My mother put her purse on her shoulder and followed them out the door and down the steps. My heart wrenched and a lump formed in my throat.

"God, please. Not now. I need her," I whispered. "Not now."

I cried into India's shoulder and she did the same into mine.

"It's gonna be okay, Twin. She's a fighter, right?"

My sister, younger by mere minutes, was looking to me for strength. Right now, though, I had nothing to give her but promises and reassurances—and I wasn't sure about any of these anymore.

"Yes, she is, India."

She broke our hug and placed my car keys in my hand. She must've turned my car off for me. "I need to make some calls."

I wiped my face with my hand. "Okay. I'm gonna check on my baby."

Tears flowed as I made my way to the living room, where Cameron was sleeping, oblivious to what was happening around him—the way a child's life should be.

I pulled out my cell and dialed Lincoln.

It went to voice mail, so I left him a message.

India and I sat at the kitchen table for hours, mostly in silence, waiting for the phone to ring. She made us something to eat; afterward, she munched on the salad she had in front of her, while I pushed mine around my plate.

"You need to eat, Idalis."

"You're not the boss of me."

I looked at her and we shared identical weak smiles.

India gravitated toward my mother after our father died, and I found comfort in my grandmother. I didn't feel that the love was any less or any different, but I found solace in the long talks that I had with my grandmother.

I got up and found myself pacing the kitchen floor.

Restless energy propelled me upstairs where I found some Motrin in the medicine cabinet. My side was aching worse than a toothache. I swallowed the tablets dry as I made my way back downstairs. I looked in the kitchen and India was texting someone.

I ended up in the living room looking out the window, then back in the kitchen again.

I couldn't sit still.

She put her phone down. "You want me to go to your house and get y'all some clothes?"

I stopped in my tracks and processed what she had just said.

"No, I need some air. Can you stay here with Cameron?"

She nodded.

Chapter Seventeen

Trip

"So that's what you came up with?"

"This might be our best chance," Lenny argued.

I sank back on my chair. "You know this is gonna blow up in our faces, right? I grew up here. What makes you think that I can just blend in and throw some cuffs on somebody without somebody recognizing me?"

Commander Harris spoke. "Agent Spencer, Atlanta has changed in ways you can only imagine."

I mean-mugged him. "So what is that supposed to mean? They gon' spot me a mile away and won't hesitate to put a bullet in my head just for bragging rights." I jumped up and got in his face. "And as sloppy as APD is, y'all punk asses prepared to make that trip to my mother's house and explain to her how y'all fucked up?"

Phil stepped in between us. "Man, calm down."

I turned and walked toward the window situated on the other side of the conference room. My blood was on fire. When this meeting was called tonight, I knew that it was gonna be a bullshit session. We hadn't gotten any further with this case than we were a week ago. They were grasping at straws, and it was getting us nowhere.

"Come on, Lenny, let's be real. You can't seriously want me to put my life in their hands? After the way these clowns been fucking up?"

Commander spoke again, "This is the best option we have."

I shot him a look. "Man, was I talking to you? I'm talking to *my* motherfuckin' boss!"

Phil finally spoke up. It was about time because I was starting to think his ass had lost the ability to speak. "Look, I'll do it. I didn't grow up here so it makes better sense but we hand-picking backup on this one Lenny, no bullshit," Phil pointed out. "We ain't trusting nobody."

Lenny nodded in agreement. "Make it happen," he instructed, the commander.

"The fact that we even have to do this shit is what's pissing me off," I barked. "They should've been on top of this from the beginning."

Lenny scratched the crown of his head. "It's too late for that now. Let's figure out the best way to handle this and get it done."

I knew from Lenny's tone that was the end of the discussion. He wanted it to happen so we had to make it do just that.

Commander Harris picked up a stack of manila folders, which were on the table. "We'll be in touch." He turned and headed out the door.

"Yo, y'all got anything on that round that was found at the last scene, or y'all fucked that up too?"

He shot me a look but rather than respond, he just kept walking.

"Why do you always have to piss them off?" Lenny asked, heaving out a deep sigh.

I walked toward the door. "'Cause I don't like them."

"Well, maybe they don't like you either," he called to my back.

"Good," I responded.

Phil and I stood in the hallway, waiting for the elevators. "Man, you love getting under his skin." He laughed, shaking his head.

I shrugged. "Hey, it's what I do best." The doors to the elevator hissed open and we stepped on. "So where you off to?" I asked.

He pulled a Hershey's bar out of his pocket. "Still chasing that asshole, Darius. Got a lead on him over near Bowen Homes."

"You need me to ride?"

"Nah, I'm good. I'm just gonna slide through and see if I can get a lock on him and try to get some things in motion for this bust. Then I'm headed out to meet up with this female CO for dinner."

"You loving Atlanta I see."

He smiled. "And Atlanta's loving me. What you about to get into?"

"My bed. May swing by my mom's for a second."

"I can make a call. I'll see if she got a friend, if you trying to hang out."

I laughed. "Nah, man, I'm good."

The door opened and we headed toward the front lobby.

"I'ma let you have that. I'm out. Call me if you need me," I said.

"Will do, partner."

I slid behind the wheel of the Tahoe and stuck the key in the ignition, but I didn't crank the engine. I leaned back and let out a heavy sigh. I closed my eyes for a moment, tried to clear my head; then I remembered where I was, and snapped them back open. I chuckled a little and shook my head as I looked across the street at the jail.

I cranked the engine, pulled out onto Peachtree, and headed toward my rented castle. I would have to catch up with my mom tomorrow. I was in desperate need of a hot shower and a good night's sleep.

I hoped the concierge at the hotel could find some Tylenol or Goody's Powder to squash the tension, which was now riding my neck, preparing to settle in my head. I sent Trinity a text earlier and asked if she'd tighten up my locs for me, but she didn't hit me back.

I checked my dash: 9:36.

Yeah, it was too late to stop by my mom's, anyway.

I settled in behind the tinted windows of my truck and rolled up Peachtree. I hit the button on the radio. I flipped through the stations until I heard the smooth voice of Si-Man Baby coming through my speakers. I smiled and thought about how much play his *Blue Lights in the Basement* radio show had gotten me back in high school.

Once I reached the hotel, I grabbed my bag out of the passenger seat, hopped out and gave the keys to the valet, along with a ten-dollar bill.

I tossed the bag over my shoulder and headed into the building maneuvering around people rushing out, just getting their nights started. They couldn't wait to hit the streets and all I could think about was a hot shower and climbing into bed.

In the dimly lit corridor, my eyes focused on the lobby situated at the end. The upscale hotel's lobby was more like a living room on steroids, expensive steroids at that. It was a little too uptight for my taste, but it was the department's dime, so I wasn't complaining too loud. But it wasn't the relaxed atmosphere, or even the music coming from the lobby, that had my attention. Hell it wasn't even the drunk ass White chick giggling and kissing all over another chick in the hall that had my attention.

It was the figure sitting on the couch.

For a minute I thought my eyes were playing tricks on me, causing my stride to slow just a little. But the closer I got, the more in focus the image became—especially when she spotted me and stood up.

Idalis.

She moved in my direction, meeting me at the end of the corridor. I could tell she was nervous. I hoped she didn't know that my stomach was doing all kinds of somersaults too.

"What are you doing here?" I asked.

She looked at me and didn't say anything for a moment. Finally she said, "I don't know."

"How long have you been here?"

She shrugged her shoulders. "An hour maybe."

We rode the elevator to my floor in silence. And once we made it to my door, I slid the key into the slot and unlocked my suite. I stepped aside and let her into the room.

I followed behind her, making sure the door was locked, and tossed my bag onto the couch. It was full of workout gear that I had planned on using if I couldn't wind down for the night.

Guess that plan just went out the window.

The bag hit the couch with a thud, causing her to flinch and finally turn and face me. We stood there for a moment, just looking at each other, not saying anything.

I spoke first, "You didn't answer me, Idalis. What are you doing here?"

She sank down on the edge of the bed; the bed barely giving under her small five foot four frame. "I just needed my best friend. Is that okay?"

I sat on the edge of the coffee table and leaned forward, resting my arms on my legs. "That's always okay. What's going on?"

She sighed deeply and looked at me. Her eyes were rimmed red, she'd been crying. "It's my grandmother."

I searched her face for answers. "Is she okay?"

She blinked causing tears to stream down her face.

I reached up and wiped one away with my thumb.

"An ambulance took her to the hospital today. She's not doing as good as we all thought."

"I'm sorry."

She stood up, shaking her head slowly. "This is too much. So much is going on. I don't know if I can handle all of this."

"What else is wrong?"

I watched her move from the bed to the over-sized window. She pushed back the heavy curtain and stared out into the darkness. She stood there for a moment, not saying a word and I just watched her. I didn't want to force her or upset her more by making her talk.

She started speaking; her soft voice was barely above a whisper.

"I think India really is gonna leave and go to California," she said, her voice wavering even more. "And my mother is okay with it, can you believe that? My grandmother is in the hospital," she said, keeping her eyes on the street below. "Everyone is changing. Everyone is leaving me. I don't know what to do," she said, finally looking at me.

"What do you want to do?" I asked. The question was open-ended but we both knew who and what I was referring to, but she sidestepped my question.

Her expression softened. "Do you have anything to eat in here?"

I shook my head and motioned to the desk. "There's a menu for room service over there."

I watched her for another moment as she picked up the plastic bound menu and started to flip through it. Slowly I stood up and tried to regain some control and comfort in my own space.

I pulled off my Kevlar vest and tossed it onto the couch, next to my gym bag. I took my SIG-Sauer P226 .9 mm out of its holster and locked it away in the table next to the bed, along with my day.

She looked up at me. "Split a burger and fries with me?"

I smiled, becoming aware that she had given to me all of the information she wanted to share for now. Right now, we were just Idalis and Trip, and nothing else existed for her.

Considering everything she was going through, I'd take what I could get.

"Yeah, I'll split one with you. But can I shower first?"

She nodded. "Just be quick about it. I'm hungry."

For some reason I didn't want to leave her alone. I watched her for a moment, sitting with her legs crossed in the middle of the bed, her eyes scanning the laminated pages of the menu.

In that moment she was twelve years old again, with two Pocahontas braids draped over her shoulders, trying to help me with my math homework while I played video games across the room. She always ended up doing it for me rather than deal with my complaining about how I would never use it in life.

In the bathroom I opened the glass door to the shower and started the water running to let it heat up. As steam filled the room, I got undressed. I wrapped a towel around my waist, secured my locs, and brushed my teeth. Just as I turned the water off in the sink, I heard a tap on the door.

"What's up?"

"Can I order dessert too?"

I laughed. "You inquiring about your meal spread is leading me to believe that I'ma get stuck with the bill."

"Of course. It's all getting charged to the room, Mr. Big Time," she retorted, giggling.

"Yeah, whatever. The department's picking up the tab, so yeah, go 'head and get what you want, baby girl. I'm outta here as soon as this case is over." I chuckled.

"Thank you, Trip."

I smiled and stepped into the shower and pulled the glass door closed.

I positioned my body under the water and the sheer heat of it coming in contact with my skin caused my muscles to relax. I leaned forward and pressed my hands against the stone tiled wall and let the water cascade down across my back and shoulders.

I tried hard to stop my mind from replaying the day and the details of the case, but it was all over the place: the fact that Phil's informant had vanished, and evidence tampering was making my stay in the Peach State longer than I wanted it to be. There was too much going on. Phil was right, Atlanta had problems deeper than they realized.

I reached up and rubbed at the stress knot in my shoulder, letting the hot water soothe my tense muscles.

I stepped back and tilted my head up, letting the water rush against my face, neck and chest.

That's when I noticed it.

Hands massaging their way up my back, reaching around to my chest.

I was so deep in thought.

Caught up in my own world.

I didn't even hear Idalis get in the shower.

Chapter Eighteen

Idalis

My head was spinning as I undressed in the steam-filled bathroom.

For a split second I stood in the foggy room and watched Trip through the steam-covered glass. I admired the contrast of the tattoos, covering his arms and shoulders, against his fair complexion; the sheer perfection of his body was amazing, to say the least. His arms were huge, cut. Knowing Trip the way I did, I was sure he put in many hours in the gym sculpting them. Water ran down his back, kissing the natural curve of his body, around to his toned abs, eventually finding its way down to his muscular thighs. As I opened the door to the shower, my heart was in my throat.

I stepped in and instinctively my hands massaged their way up his back around to his chest.

I could tell I startled him.

He spun around and grabbed my shoulders. "What are you doing, Idalis?"

I stared up at him, thankful that the water from the shower was masking the tears saturating my face. "Taking a shower."

His grip loosened and his hands slid down my arms.

He kept his eyes on me as he interlocked his fingers with mine. I stepped closer, moving us backward directly under the stream of water. I closed my eyes as he reached up and smoothed my hair back with the flow of water causing it to slick back resting on my back.

My body caught fire when I felt his lips on my neck. His mouth opened and his tongue danced on that spot where my neck and shoulder met, and the heart between my legs throbbed pushing a moan up and out of my throat. I slid my arms around his neck and pulled him closer as his mouth left a trail of kisses on my neck before planting soft ones on my cheek, then capturing my mouth with his.

The kiss was soft at first, held back by hesitation and uncertainty. He gently sucked on my tongue as my hands caressed his face and neck, bringing on more intensity. He began to swell against my stomach as I felt his hands on my hips, causing my core to throb. His touch moved to my waist; his tight grip, coupled with our bodies pressing together, caused my bruised side to scream out in pain making me wince in pain, flinch and pull away.

He looked at me. Confusion and concern filled his eyes. He reached behind him and turned off the flow of water, signaling the end of our escape.

"Idalis, what's that about?"

I pushed the glass door to the shower open and stepped out. I grabbed one of the huge, fluffy white towels and wrapped it around my body before leaving the bathroom.

"Nothing," I said, using a towel to squeeze the extra water from my hair.

He stood in the door of the bathroom, water running off his body pooling at his feet. He grabbed a towel and wrapped it around his waist and came in the room. The weight of the water had freed his locs and they rested long and heavy down back. He reached down and tightened the makeshift knot holding the towel in place.

"Come here, Idalis."

I sat on the edge of the bed.

I was a little kid. Defiant.

Not moving.

He spoke again. "Baby girl, please come here."

Keeping my eyes on the floor, I stood up and walked in his direction.

When I got to him, he placed his hand under my chin and lifted my face to look at him. He looked into my eyes, and when I saw what looked like tears filling his, I felt like my heart was going to explode.

He spoke, "No matter what, don't take your eyes off mine. Do you hear me?"

I nodded slowly and did what he told me. As he slowly reached up and released my body from the confines of the towel, I kept my eyes fixed on his. I felt the fluffy white towel puddle at my feet as it slid from my body. His eyes stayed on mine as he ran his hands along the contour of my body, starting with my thighs. My breathing increased as his fingers gently trailed up the sides of my body until he reached my rib cage, where his touch lingered a moment before he gently pressed. With that action I flinched, closing my eyes to the pain.

"Look at me, Idalis."

I opened my eyes, releasing the tears and the truth they held. I looked up into his eyes, and the fire in them threatened to turn me into a pile of ashes where I stood. I opened my mouth, not even sure of what I was going to say, but slowly he shook his head silencing me.

"He put his hands on you, baby girl?"

I bent down and picked up the towel and wrapped it around my body. "I didn't come here to be judged."

His phone vibrated against the table, taking our attention for a brief moment, but he kept his eyes on me. He reached up and tucked my hair behind my ear. "Is that what you thought I would do?"

"Honestly, I don't know what I thought." I felt my face warm. In all of this, that was probably the one thing I *did* know. I didn't know what I was doing, why a troubled heart led me to a hotel downtown. Maybe I was running on autopilot. Emotionally, my switch had been reset and I was only doing what came naturally.

I reverted to doing what I always did when I couldn't deal.

I found him.

He stepped a little closer, examining me with his eyes. The piercing color of them was almost intimidating, powerful. Growing up, we used to pretend his eyes were that color because he was a superhero waiting for his powers to develop. One week the power would be lasers the next week it might be him seeing through walls. I remembered how one time India and I got into a fight and I ran to his house. For the rest of the afternoon, we sat around watching cartoons, eating Sour Patch Kids, and trying to get lasers to shoot out of his eyes so he could go zap her for me.

Even with all he dealt with on a daily basis in his own house, he was always there for me. Ready to zap anyone who wronged me. I was just as much an escape for him as he was for me. I always ended up staying later than I was supposed to, and he usually had to sneak me out. That typically involved me hiding behind the couch his living room until his mom and dad were out of sight. So we came up with a signal, a wink, to let me know it was safe for me to make a break for the door and not be seen, ensuring we didn't get in trouble.

Unfortunately, it didn't always work and one night he got a beating for having me in his house while his mom was at work, but he didn't complain or blame me for anything. That time the beating wasn't that bad. But when he came to school the next day in a long-sleeved shirt, I knew what was hidden beneath the material. But lucky for both of us, that wink worked more times than it didn't.

"You know what I thought, Trip?"

He tilted his head to the side a little. "Tell me."

I spoke, trying to steady my voice. "That you'd use your superpowers. And make it all go away."

For a split second I thought my legs had given out, but Trip had picked me up and his mouth was on mine. This time there was no hesitation in his kiss. I wrapped my arms around his neck as he carried me to the bed.

He gently laid me down and slid the towel away from my body. He covered it with a kiss each portion of flesh he exposed. He kissed his way to my bruised side and lingered there for a moment—placing gentle, healing kisses on the spot that needed it the most.

I sucked in a breath and exhaled my appreciation.

His tongue teased my belly button as his hands massaged my thighs, coaxing them apart. He kissed his way to my inner thigh before running his tongue along my bikini line, sending shock waves through my entire body. He stopped, only to nibble gently on the crease where my thigh connected to my body.

He ran his tongue along my folds, letting his tongue quickly slide between for a taste, only to take back the pleasure, setting me on edge. His hands gripped my thighs, pushing them apart, exposing me on every level of what made me who I was. I felt his mouth on me and my head started to spin.

His tongue worked rhythmically and deliberately until he found what was hidden inside. I felt his fingers spreading me, exposing what was buried underneath. He tenderly sucked it into his mouth, driving me over the edge when he began to run his tongue across my sensitive spot at the same time. I reached down and tangled my fingers in his locs, holding him in place as I lightly rotated my hips and released all over his tongue.

When I opened my eyes, he was over me. Looking down at me. The fire in his eyes had been replaced with something else. Something that made my heart cry out in a way it hadn't in a long time.

I felt him between my legs, throbbing, blindly searching for what I was willing to give.

He kissed me, sucking in my bottom lip.

I reciprocated, tasting myself on him. The taste was intoxicating.

"Are you sure?" he asked.

I answered by sliding my hand between us and guiding him into me. I felt his body tense as my warmth drew him inside. Slowly, inch by inch, I spread open for him. He slid into me, and I moaned my approval. Once he was buried inside, he froze. I felt him twitching and swelling inside me.

"Your side . . ." he started to say. "I don't want to hurt you," he finished saying as he began to move in and out of me slowly.

"Then don't," I breathed.

His mouth found mine again as he slowly pushed deeper inside me. Our connection held a level of healing for both of us, at that point, that was otherworldly. He kissed me as his stroke took on a slow and deliberate, mind-blowing rhythm, causing beads of sweat to pop up all over my body. Tears escaped my eyes and rolled back toward my ears. He kissed his way to each one, willing the pain and anger to leave my body.

He slid his hands under my body, cupping my bottom with his hands and raising me slightly off the bed as he buried himself deeper inside, hitting spots that caused me to cry out. My nails dug into his back as he rotated his hips, stirring up every feeling for him that I had fought so hard to bury. A low growl escaped his throat and he buried his face in my neck, gently sucking as his grip tightened and his thrusting became more intense, and his release took control. My own orgasm rode my body in waves and I got lost in the pleasure, letting it numb my pain and replace my worry.

Together, exhausted and spent, we fell into a deep sleep.

Hours passed.

I opened my eyes and blinked against dried-out contacts.

The sound of the rain against the window stimulated my senses. When I was finally able to focus, the clock on the table let me know it was almost midnight.

I untangled myself from Trip's grasp and slid out of bed. I dug around in the dark until I felt my phone. I grabbed his T-shirt off the couch, pulled it over my head, and slipped into the bathroom. I took a deep breath and tapped my screen. I had five missed calls and three texts from Lincoln. I didn't even open them. Instead I read the one text message from India asking if I was okay and where I was.

I texted her back: With Trip. I'm okay.

My phone immediately lit up: Lincoln called.

Those two words stopped my heart. I typed: And?

She responded: Told him about Grammie and that you were asleep. Didn't feel good.

I answered: My car?

I asked that because I knew he had driven by, or, at the very least, had someone else ride by to make sure that I was there.

She answered: Garage. Didn't want to carry Cameron in the rain.

I took a deep breath and said a small prayer of thanks for having a sister who, even when she was mad, would still look out for me.

I asked: Any word on Grammie?

She typed back: No. Mama said she's sleeping.

That made me feel better. I typed back and thanked her, and then I told her I'd be back in the morning.

After sliding my phone back into my purse, I climbed back into bed. When he felt me next to him, he gently wrapped his arms around me.

"You a'ight?"

I nodded into his chest. "I'm good."

"Are you ready to tell me what's really going on?"

"Not now. Just let me have tonight. I promise I will tell you everything in the morning."

He kissed me on my forehead. A few moments later, I heard his breathing change and I knew he was asleep again.

I took comfort in the fact that all of this was about to be over.

I was finally taking control of my situation.

I had no idea how wrong I was.

On both counts.

*"The face of the enemy frightens me, only when
I see how much it resembles me."*

-*Oscar Wilde*

Geech popped the latches on three black briefcases on the table in front of him and spun them
around. Neatly bound stacks of cash rested inside.
Each held case held 250 grand.

"Where's your boy?" Geech asked.

Linc looked up. "He'll be here. Chill out."

"He better be." Geech slammed the cases
closed.

"Where you at with that assignment I gave
you?" Linc asked.

Geech laugh a little. "Already got wheels in
motion on that playa. Don't worry."

Linc just nodded. He didn't ask because he
didn't need details. He just wanted to know
when it was done.

"You buried that shit right?"

"Oh you so far removed from the whole thing,
people gon' be offering you condolences."

Linc nodded his approval.

"Oh and I know it's you leaving all these dealers laid out around the city, pot'na" Linc said. "You need to slow your roll."

Geech smiled. "Collateral damage homeboy. I told you, I'm taking this city over. They ain't ready for me."

"Look here, I understand where you comin' from and what you tryin' to do, but you getting some attention you don't want."

"That's what I got you for, right?"

"Yeah, a'ight. My insurance don't cover stupidity, ya dig," he said, pulling his phone from his hip. He scrolled through the messages of the bitches that he didn't want to hear from, asking why he didn't call back or if he was coming over, looking for the one he did want to hear from and didn't see one.

That pissed him off.

He shoved his phone back in it's holder on his hip. Linc turned and walked around the coffee table and moved toward the kitchen of the tiny apartment. He checked his watch. It was getting late and this place would be filling up soon with people looking for a fix or trying to settle up with what they had scored on the street. He needed to be long gone by then. He had managed to get Geech out in the open but he didn't know how much longer he was gonna stay before he dipped out.

"How long you gon' be here, Linc?"

Linc looked over at Niecey, the chick that was renting the spot. She was sitting on one of the run-down chairs at the kitchen table, shooting up some heroin he sold her in exchange for using her spot for this meet. The sight of her disgusted him, but she was a necessary evil. Her hair was tangled on one side and the clothes she was wearing looked like they'd seen at least a couple weeks' worth of activity.

He figured she couldn't weigh more than a hundred pounds wet, but somehow she managed to keep her cute face, which she used to her advantage when working the corners. He dated her off and on in high school, back when she was fine as hell and was pitching him ass on the regular because he was a star quarterback. He broke up with her when he went off to college and met Idalis and he never thought twice about her.

She carried her hurt into adulthood and turned to drugs for comfort. The love she never lost for him worked in his favor. That, plus her addiction, enabled him to work his way back into her life through her veins.

He never had to lay a hand on her.

Part of him felt bad, but he had learned that life ain't fair. If he was gonna hurt, then everyone around him was gonna pay. No one was exempt, as far as he was concerned. And the fact that he'd been running drugs through her spot for a couple years now was proof of that. All it took was keeping her high out of her mind, and a compliment every once in a while, to give him complete control of her and her spot.

"I'm leaving after I handle this business. Why?" he snapped.

She pulled the needle from her skinny arm and closed her eyes. Her eyelids trembled as the poison soothed her inner demons. Slowly she opened her eyes and focused on him. "'Cause you being here is bad for business."

"Just chill out. I'll be gone soon."

He headed back to the living room. Nate was sitting on the couch, rolling a blunt. Geech and his boy were standing by the door, talking. He was just about to pull his phone out, when there was a knock at the door. Linc walked up and Nate prepared to open the door.

Linc placed his hand on his gun. He nodded and Nate opened the door.

Twist entered the room, followed by Darius, who was carrying two big black duffel bags. But it was the one who entered behind Darius that got Linc's attention.

He was the largest of the three and was eating a bag of Lay's.

Their eyes met and they had a hate-filled, wordless exchange as Geech's boy checked him for wires. The sound of the door closing snapped him out of his trance.

Linc stepped from behind the table, body tense with anger; he tried hard to hold it together as Darius set one of the bags next to his briefcase.

Darius spoke directly to Linc. "It's all there."

"Open it," Linc ordered, never taking his eyes off the big dude with the potato chips.

He did as he was told. Unzipping the bag, he tilted it toward Geech, revealing multiple stacks of silver bricks of coke and clear bags full of multi-colored X pills.

Geech smiled big. "That's what I'm talking about." He slid the briefcases to the end of the table one by one. "It's all there. Seven hundred and fifty large."

When Geech made a motion toward the bags, Linc snatched his Beretta out of his waistband, setting off a chain reaction of guns being pulled out and cocked.

Still, Linc never took his eyes off the big dude; instead, he pointed his gun at Twist.

"I told you, don't fuck up didn't I?"

Twist held up his hands, eyes wide. "Yo, what the fuck I do?!"

Geech pointed his gun at Darius. "What the fuck is going on?"

Linc nodded in the direction of Darius, but spoke to Twist, "You brought this trouble to me?"

He watched as Darius's eyes jumped from him to the guy and back again.

Darius shook his head. "Nah, man, I don't know what he's talking about, Twist, man."

Linc cocked his gun. "You created this mess and you gon' clean it up, Twist."

"Yo, what you mean?"

He could see the heat and anger coming from big dude's body. It wasn't the agent he wanted, but it was a start. "You're gonna put a bullet in Agent Porter and make this right."

Phil's had his .9 mm SIG trained on Linc. "If I don't walk out that door real soon, it's gonna get kicked in and you are gonna have agents attached to every inch of your ass."

Darius broke for the back door, but Geech fired, catching him in the leg. That didn't stop him from hobbling his way down the hall and disappearing out the back patio doors.

"Kill that fucking cop!" Linc yelled.

Linc pumped two rounds into Twist's chest as he moved quickly in order to avoid the hail of bullets. Taking a hit in the vest, Linc spun around and managed to squeeze off two rounds in Phil's direction. Nate took a bullet in the back, but not before pumping two rounds into Geech, hitting him in the chest and neck. Phil caught both of Geech's boys before he went down and they collapsed at the door.

In an instant Linc snatched one of the duffel bags and threw it over his shoulder. He stuffed as much of the contents back inside the other duffel bag as he could before tossing that over his other shoulder, and grabbing two of the three briefcases.

His adrenaline was pumping and all his senses were on high.

He eyed the pool of blood spreading around Phil's lifeless body.

He heard the sirens and the sound of footsteps running down the hall.

"Agent down!"

The last thing he heard as he sprinted through the back patio doors toward his car parked two streets over.

Chapter Nineteen

Trip

Inside the emergency room I pushed through the dense crowd of agents and officers huddled in the already crowded waiting room. Some faces were familiar to me; others I had never seen before. All of them might as well have been on the same force at this point. An "officer down" was a call no one in law enforcement wanted to hear come across his radio. When you did hear it, no matter who you reported to, you responded.

As I brushed past them, I read their eyes.

Some held pity.

Others question marks.

"Trip!"

I stopped and looked in the direction that the voice had just come from. I saw Lenny waving me in his direction. I headed toward him; my senses were on high. He ended a conversation he was having with a nurse and got in my face.

"Where the hell have you been?" he barked.

"Lenny—"

"You know what? I don't care where you were, but I bet Phil is gonna wanna know if he makes it out of surgery."

His yelling got the attention of everyone in the room, but I didn't care, because that tiny bit of information caused some of the tension to leave my body in knowing that Phil wasn't dead.

"If?"

Lenny placed his hands on his hips and dropped his head. His voice softened a little. "Yeah, *if.*"

"Where'd he get hit?"

"Right side. Collapsed his lung."

I stood there, hands resting on my waist. My mind going a mile a minute. My thoughts went to Idalis, whom I'd left asleep in my room. I looked toward the ceiling and blew out some air.

My eyes went to the clock hanging over the nurses' station: 2:30.

How the hell did shit get so fucked up, so fast? Less than an hour ago, I was in the middle of the best sleep I'd had in months, only to be awakened by the phone on my hotel nightstand ringing. I jumped up to stop the ringing before it woke Idalis.

"Phil's been shot. He's in surgery."

Those were the last words I remembered hearing. Next thing I knew, I was standing in the ER at Grady Memorial, and my partner was fighting for his life.

According to Lenny, when he got the call about the bust, he tried to call me but didn't get an answer. He didn't want to miss the opportunity, so he went ahead with the sting with the agents we'd picked, without me.

That was confirmed by the voice mail he'd left on my phone.

"Partner, call me. No sweet dreams for either of us. I just got a lock on Darius. We gotta move now. It's going down tonight."

I leaned against the wall. "Lenny, I'm sorry."

"Save it for Phil." He turned and disappeared into the crowd of agents.

I leaned back against the wall and closed my eyes. There was no way this was happening.

Moments later I felt a presence standing in front of me, but I didn't open my eyes.

"Yo, man, sorry about your pot'na."

I lowered my head and his face came into focus, setting me off.

The next thing I knew, people were screaming and yelling, and I was going at it with Lincoln in the middle of the hospital waiting room. Nurses and patients waiting in the small area were shrieking and scattering like roaches.

Lenny and two other agents pulled me off him. Lenny was yelling, trying to snap me out of my rage. "What the hell is wrong with you?"

I looked down at Lincoln, who actually had a smirk on his face as he touched the trickle of blood running down the corner of his mouth. I tried to break free and get at him again. By then, however, a sea of dark blue APD was between us. Lincoln stood to his feet and shrugged off the officers who had come to his aid.

Agents now stood on one side of the hall. APD on the other.

"It's cool. It's cool," he said, keeping his eyes on me. "He's upset. His boy just got shot." He looked me square in the eyes. "I'd be upset too, if I wasn't there for my pot'na."

"Man, y'all better get his bitch ass the fuck outta here before I shoot him!" I yelled.

"Trip, you need to calm down," Lenny ordered.

I snatched away from them and stormed out the ER doors.

Behind the wheel of the Tahoe, I splashed out onto the streets of Atlanta, no real destination in my mind. The rain had stopped, but my head felt like it was full of thunder and lightning.

I called Trinity. She didn't answer.

I thought about going back to the hotel, but I decided against it.

My mind went to Phil lying on that operating table.

Thought about the fact that I wasn't there for him.

Thought about the bruise on Idalis's side.

I wasn't there for her either.

That made me hit the gas. The next thing I knew, I was on I-20, heading west.

I dialed Trinity again.

This time she answered. Her voice heavy with sleep and confusion.

Twenty minutes later I pulled up into West-view Cemetery. When I pulled up the drive, my headlights illuminated Trinity's Acura TL. She was in jeans and an oversized, long-sleeved Spelman T-shirt. She was standing outside her car, with tears streaming down her face.

I slammed the truck into park and jumped out into the damp night air.

I walked up to her. "Where?"

Tears ran down her face. "Trip, I'm so sorry."

"Where, Trin?" My voice boomed through the night air, causing my baby sister to jump. She turned around and started walking.

"Over here," she said. "This is crazy! It's dark and muddy, Trip."

I pulled my department-issued flashlight off my hip, giving us light. Anger propelled me forward. I followed her through the wet grass until she came to a stop.

She turned and looked at me. Eyes pleading.

"Which one?" I snapped.

She pointed to the headstone situated to my left.

I shone the light on it.

Orlando Eugene Spencer II 1945-2007
Beloved Husband and Father.

My sister's voice sounded like she was a mile away. "Trip, let's go! This is crazy!"

Rage caused my legs to move.

I paced the small patch of grass in front of the grave site.

So much hate. So much anger.

Phil took a bullet, was fighting for his life and his ass got off easy.

"Son of a biiiiitch!"

My voice echoed through the cemetery as I snatched my 9 mm from its holster, cocked it, spun around, and started firing rounds into his grave.

My gun roared angrily into the night air.

As each round pierced the ground, it carried with it a different level of rage and hatred. With each flash of my barrel, I saw my mother's bruised and battered face, heard the sobs of my baby sister crying because of a beating I took in her place or my mother's. But with each casing that the 9 mm expelled, I also felt a release.

"Trip, please stop. *Please,*" my sister sobbed, clinging to my arm.

I stopped shooting and looked at her; the terror in her eyes snapped me back to reality. She was looking at me the way I'd seen my mother look at my father many times—eyes wide with fear and panic.

I lowered my gun to my side and took a step back. My breathing was ragged as my chest rose and fell against the confines of my vest. My face was wet from tears, which I didn't realize had fallen.

"Please, Trip," she begged.

I holstered my gun and she wrapped her arms around my body and sobbed into my chest. Her crying shook my frame. I held her tightly, trying to soothe her. I could feel her heart beating.

"I'm sorry, Trin. I'm so sorry."

My phone gave two short vibrations to my hip. A text message.

I pulled my phone from my hip and read it: Phil is out of surgery.

"I gotta go, Trinity."

She reached up and wiped her face with her sleeve. "Are you gonna be okay?"

I nodded. "Phil just came out of surgery."

"Trip, I'm sorry about Phil."

I hugged her tighter. "Not your fault, baby girl."

"You know it's not your fault either, right?"

I let that question hang between us. I kissed her on her forehead.

"I'll call you later."

I walked her back to her car and made sure she pulled off okay before I jumped into my truck and sped off into the night toward the hospital.

When I made it back to the hospital, the halls were just as crowded as when I'd left. Everyone was standing around, waiting for news of Phil.

I found Lenny. "Where is he?"

He nodded toward the window to my partner's room. "Doctor says all we can do now is wait."

I stood and looked at my partner laid out in the bed. Tubes were snaking their way around his large body, giving him support.

Support I wasn't there to give.

"I have a call in to his mother and his brother," I heard Lenny say.

My heart ached at the thought of his mother and younger brother having to see him like this. And explaining that I wasn't there when it happened.

I stood there and watched his huge chest rise and fall. There were two nurses tending to him, and a doctor stood over him, scribbling notes in a chart. The scene was too surreal, too much for me to handle.

This wasn't supposed to happen.

How did this happen?

Lenny grabbed my arm and steered me down the dimly lit hallway, away from the agents and the officers who were still hovering around.

"If there is anything going on with you and Briscoe you need to tell me now Spencer?"

I let out a sigh. "Lenny—"

"No bullshit, Spencer. What's the deal?"

"It's nothing."

"Well, it sure as hell didn't look like nothing to me. Not the way you laid into him."

"Look, I'm fine. I'm just on edge."

He stepped up to me and lowered his voice. "I need you at one hundred percent, Spencer. I can't afford to have you flipping out and losing focus. What happened tonight is a direct result of what can happen when you're not on your game."

"I know."

"Do you?" His tone was stern but caring. "Because I don't think you do. Your partner is fighting for his life right now. Does that sound like *focus* to you?"

"No, sir, it doesn't."

Lenny looked down the hall, then back to me again. "Don't make me pull you off this case, because, God help me, I will."

"Yes, sir, I understand."

"Whatever crap you and Briscoe are dealing with, I suggest you table it, Trip, before I do it for you."

He turned and headed back toward the crowd.

It was almost six in the morning.

It wouldn't be long before the sun would be coming up.

Shedding light on things that were best meant to be kept in the dark.

Chapter Twenty

Idalis

"Trip, this is Idalis. Can you please call me when you get this message?"

I left Trip a second message before hanging up. When I finally woke up and rolled over he was gone, no note or anything. I was a little disappointed because I didn't get a chance to talk to him about what was going on with Linc. I knew if anybody would be able to tell me what to do, he would.

I stood in front of the huge bay window, which had my mother's front yard on display. The colorful flowers we'd planted for Mama were struggling to take their rightful place in the garden in spite of the heat. I guess that was the approach I had to take. No matter what my environment was, I had to make the choice to wither or to bloom.

My cell phone rang; it was Lincoln. I thought about letting him roll to voice mail, but changed my mind. His temper was the last thing I needed right now.

"Hello."

"How's your grandmother?"

"No word yet." I sank down onto the couch.

"Anyone there with you?"

"No. I don't know where India is."

Linc got quiet for a moment. Cameron was playing in the hallway rolling cars back and forth on the hardwood. Somehow that simple playful act seemed much louder now than it had in the past.

"You hear about ya boy's pot'na."

I stood to my feet. "No. What about him?"

"He got popped last night."

My hand shot up and covered my mouth. "Oh my God."

He let out a small chuckle. "Yeah. He over at Grady. Don't look good."

My heart dropped.

I wasn't sure what time he'd left, but I figured he'd gotten a call at some point and didn't want to wake me. That had to be why he wasn't answering his phone.

He asked, "So you haven't talked to him?"

"No, Linc"—I walked to the front door and peered out—"I haven't."

"What's Cameron doing?"

"He's right here playing. Where are you?"

"Getting ready to leave the house."

I asked, "You stayed there last night?"

"Yeah. It was weird not havin' you here."

I swallowed hard. For a moment he seemed "normal." There was no anger or hatred in his voice. For a brief moment I thought I might have wanted things to go back to the way they were, but I knew they would never be the same.

His voice cut into my thoughts. "When you plan on comin' home?"

"I'm not sure. I may try to get by there tonight."

Again. More silence.

I cleared my throat. "I really would like to sit down and talk. We have a lot going on that we need to sort out."

"Idalis, I already told you. We're not canceling the wedding."

"I know what you said, but—"

"I gotta go," he said, cutting me off. "We'll talk later."

He hung up without giving me a chance to say anything else.

I stared at my phone for a moment before placing it on the table.

A couple hours later, India made it back. She looked refreshed, like she'd had a hot shower and something good to eat. Her hair was slicked back in a ponytail and her face was fresh, no makeup, just a thin shiny layer of lip gloss. She'd obviously stopped by a friend's house and got herself together.

She was wearing a pair of Capri pants and a T-shirt with a picture of Tweety Bird on the front and a caption that read: *Chick With Brains.*

We were the textbook version of a before-and-after picture.

"You need to go take a shower. You look a mess; and when you look a mess, you make me look bad," India remarked.

She placed a couple bags of groceries on the kitchen table alongside a bag of takeout. The kitchen filled with the smell of Chinese food; my stomach rumbled to life.

She pulled plates down from the cabinets without saying anything.

I sat pushing apps around on my phone, pretending she wasn't there. You would've thought that we would've put our differences aside, but it seemed like this was an even bigger wedge between us.

I heard her keys hit the table. "Did Mama call?"

"No."

I stood up and started pulling groceries out of the bags. I had to do something or I was gonna go crazy. I was overwhelmed with more emotions than any one person should have to deal with at one time or in one lifetime for that matter.

"Have you slept?" she asked.

I shook my head.

"Come on, eat something, Idalis. Then you need to lay down."

"I'm not hungry."

I heard plates hitting the wooden table behind me. "You need to eat something."

She scooped Cameron up and set him up at the table with a sandwich, fruit, and a juice box. I sat in a daze as she scooped shrimp fried rice onto my plate.

"Lincoln called. Trip's partner was shot last night."

"What?" The spoon she was using hit the table with a loud clang.

I put a forkful of rice into my mouth. It nauseated me, but I chewed and swallowed it, anyway.

She picked at the edges of her egg roll. Not saying anything.

I pushed my plate away from me and headed to the front porch. I stood there for a moment and let the wind swirl around my body. The sky was on fire, with various shades of red and orange. The weight of the day was slowly forcing the sun down in the western sky. It was much cooler than it had been earlier.

My mind was with my grandmother. I imagined her lying in her hospital bed, fighting for her life. When my father died, she had made it a point to help my mother with raising us and keeping us on the right track. Mama never did remarry, so it was never easy for her raising twin girls and trying to keep food on the table.

My grandmother filled in the gaps whenever she could, whether it was letting us spend the weekend so our mom could get some rest, or making sure we ate dinner after school, before we headed home. I spent many hot summer nights on this porch, getting my hair braided and complaining to her about everything from boys to the fact that I believed India had to be adopted, regardless of the fact that we were twins.

"Grammie, something's wrong with her," I used to argue.

As I got older, our conversations went from schoolgirl complaints to a woman in search of the answers to life's lessons. She would always give me the same advice: *"Figure out whatever the hardest thing is to do, and you do it, because that's usually the right choice."*

I returned a call from Dionne and updated her on what was going on. She told me that everything was going okay with the club and that everyone was praying for my grandmother. After I thank her, I hung up and tried Trip again.

The phone rang twice before his voice came across the line.

"What's up, baby girl?"

"I heard about Phil. I'm so sorry."

"Not your fault."

"I know, but I know how close you two are."

We talked about how terrible it was that his partner and my grandmother were both hospitalized, battling for their lives.

He asked, "You need me to stop by?"

I chewed my bottom lip. My mind said no, but my heart was screaming yes. "If it's not out of your way," I finally said.

"Gimme about an hour, and I'll be by there."

He hung up, and just like that, he was on his way.

By the time Trip made it to my mother's house, India was sprawled out on the living room floor, playing with Cameron, and I was on the couch, waiting for the phone to ring. Part of me didn't want the call to come from the hospital, but a bigger part of me needed to know what was going on with my grandmother. I thought about calling, but I didn't want to worry my mother. My grandmother needed her attention right now more than I did. I was sure she would call as soon as she heard something.

When I heard the knock on the door, a sense of relief washed over me when I opened it and saw Trip standing there. I could tell he was tired. He was in his DEA T-shirt and black jeans. He wrapped his arms around me and I breathed him.

"Are you okay?"

I nodded into his chest. "Are you? How's Phil?"

He stepped into the foyer. "He's still unconscious."

"I'm sorry."

"Hey, Trip," India's voice came from behind him.

A smile spread across his face as he hugged her. "Hey, girl."

"Sorry about your partner."

"Thanks. I'm sorry about your grandmother."

We all stood in the foyer for a moment as a hole in time began to fill with a common bond of family and love.

We headed down the hall toward the kitchen.

I pulled a plate out of the cabinet and grabbed the leftover Chinese from the fridge. "Hungry?"

He laughed a little. "I guess I am, since you're already fixing my plate."

"I'm going into the living room," India announced, heading out of the kitchen.

I felt Trip's eyes on me as I spooned the cooling food onto his plate.

"You look tired, Idalis."

"I'm fine." I forced a smile. The microwave beeped and I retrieved his plate, placing it in front of him. "Now eat your food."

He laughed. "Yes, ma'am."

"I need to get out. I'm about to go sit with Dionne at 404 for a little while." India was standing in the doorway with her Coach bag tucked under her shoulder. "I'll be back a little later. Cameron is playing in the living room."

With that, she was gone.

"You two still on the outs?"

I rubbed my forehead and shrugged. "I guess we just don't have much to talk about these days."

"Now is not the time for y'all to be beefing."

"Yea, tell me about it."

I went into the living room to check on Cameron. He was munching on some Goldfish my sister had given him and running a truck back and forth on the coffee table. He stopped me before I could make it back to the kitchen.

"Mommy?"

"Yes, baby."

"What are you doing?"

"Talking to my friend."

"Can I talk?"

I looked toward the doorway that led to the kitchen. Trip was standing in the doorway. "Not right now, sweetie. Finish eating first."

"Okay." He smiled big, and I started back to the kitchen. "Mommy?"

"Yes."

"Where's Nana?"

I stopped in my tracks and felt the lump expand in my throat. I opened my mouth to answer him, but nothing would come out. My legs got weak and I felt like they were going to give out on me.

"Your nana will be back in a little while." Trip appeared in the hallway.

"Oh," Cameron said. That explanation satisfied his question. He studied Trip for a second, then said, "Hi!"

"Hey, little man." Trip smiled.

Cameron held up his truck to show him. "I have a truck."

"I see," Trip said, moving toward the makeshift racetrack. "That's a nice truck l'il man."

Cameron smiled and continued to play. I leaned against the wall and tried to regain my composure. I watched them for a second, seeing how my baby was so easy about sharing his toys with this man, and how Trip quickly became wrapped around his finger as well.

The house phone rang and I jumped out of my skin. I looked at the caller ID display; it was Piedmont Hospital.

My mouth went dry. It was my mother.

"Hey, sweetie."

"How's Grammie?"

"She's comfortable. The doctors are running another bone scan on her."

"Why?" I asked.

"They think the cancer may have spread." Her voice cracked just a bit. Tears once again flowed from my already swollen eyes. I did my best to hide the fact that I was crying. I didn't need my mother worrying about me too.

"Mama, do you need me to come to the hospital?"

"No. Cameron doesn't need to be around all this death. You stay put. I will be okay."

"Are you sure?"

"Yes. They are going to keep her, baby."

"No, Mama."

"Baby, this is the best place for her right now. Where is your sister?"

I swallowed the lump in my throat. "She left a little while ago."

"Okay, let her know I called."

"Call if you need anything."

"I will."

I let out a sigh, rubbed the knot in my shoulder, and tried to figure out what to do. I felt so helpless—or worse, I felt useless. My grandmother was fighting for her life, a life that had meaning. I had nothing to show for mine right now, except a bunch of deception and conflict.

When our call ended, something inside me snapped. I made my way down the hall to the kitchen and sank onto one of the kitchen chairs and cried. My mind was all over the place. I needed to call India and some other family members. I reached for a tissue, and Trip was there, wrapping me in his arms and trying to calm me down. I cried into his shoulder.

"Baby, let it out," he encouraged. "It's okay."

"Why her? Why *my* grandmother?" I cried. I felt so selfish. I would never wish anyone's grandmother sick or dead; I just wanted mine a little longer. I needed her.

The sound of Cameron's playing stopped my pity party. I lifted my head from Trip's shoulder and looked toward the hall. He cupped my chin and looked into my eyes.

"I should be comforting you. Your partner is in the hospital."

He smiled. "I'm okay. Go lie down. I can keep an eye on him. You need some rest."

I shook my head. "I can't let you do that."

"Why not?"

I raised my eyebrow. "Have you ever watched kids before?"

He gave me a look like he was offended, then he smiled. "I'm a DEA agent. I catch hardcore criminals for a living. I think I can handle a toddler."

That made me smile. "You don't know Cameron."

He hugged me close again. "We'll be fine."

I was wary of leaving him alone with Cameron, but I was mentally exhausted. I was no good to my son right now, anyway, so I agreed and made my way to my grandmother's room. The embroidered blanket was still disheveled from them coming to get her. My heart ached when I noticed her slippers still resting beside her bed, waiting for her to slide her feet into them. I bent down, picked them up, and placed them on the chair. I would take them to the hospital tomorrow.

I curled up in her bed and hugged her pillow. I didn't want to cry, but I did. I wanted her back, wanted her here. My issues were insignificant right now. Nothing else mattered right now. I called work and told them what was going on, and that I had no idea when I would be back. Family really did come first, I realized. Luckily, the club owners were understanding and told me to take my time.

I wasn't sure how to fix this, but I knew I had to do something.

And God had even met me halfway.

The hardest thing to do . . . was right downstairs.

I don't know how long I'd been asleep. I thought I was dreaming when I heard my sister's voice. She sounded stressed as she shook my sleeping body.

"Idalis!" Her voice was a harsh whisper. "Get up!"

I looked around the room and blinked my reality back into focus. My grandmother's world came rushing back to me, a cruel reminder of what I was doing there.

"What is your problem?" I struggled to sit up. "And why are you whispering?"

She had a panicked look on her face, which caused my heart to jump.

"Uh, we have a"—she stopped and took a deep breath—"no, *you* have a problem."

"What are you—"

That's when I heard the voices. Their tone was calm and monotonic, but I could sense a growing intensity. Then, as if I had been zapped with a stun gun, I jumped up and ran to the window. The all black Dodge Charger police cruiser parked out front behind the black Tahoe confirmed my worst nightmare.

Linc was here.

"How long has he been here?"

She shook her head and shrugged her shoulders. "I just got here."

My first thought was Cameron; my second thought involved an ambulance and body bags.

I heard Lincoln ask, "How long has she been sleep?"

Trip answered, "About an hour."

Then Lincoln spoke again, "Yo, why are you even here, pot'na?"

"I came to check on my friend and her grandmother, just like this case, doing your job for you."

"Well, I'm here now, so you can go."

I looked at India. "Where's Cameron?"

"Playing downstairs."

I grabbed a pillow and threw it at her. "You *left* him!" I fussed.

She just sat there, wide-eyed, like she was totally clueless on what to do.

I took a deep breath, prayed to God, then headed downstairs. As I walked toward the living room, I noticed Cameron playing in the middle of the floor. Lincoln was standing by the doorway and Trip was across the room, both facing each other, with my son in the middle. I brushed past Lincoln and picked up Cameron, joining him in the middle of all the madness. He smiled and hugged my neck.

I returned his smile. "It's way past your bedtime, little man."

Both Lincoln and Trip made a move toward me, but I quickly gave both of them a look that said: *Don't even try it.* I took Cameron and sat on the couch with him. My mind was racing. I was more nervous than a hooker in church during altar call, but I didn't want them to know. Somehow I had to regain control of what was going on, and now was going to be the time.

I spoke in a soft, controlled tone, which forced them to listen. "This is how this is going to go"—I looked at both of them, then continued—"and neither of you is going to raise your voice in front of Cameron."

"Idalis—" Lincoln tried to interject, but I just held up my hand and silenced him.

My sister appeared in the doorway. "Leave her alone, Lincoln," she snapped. "I called him and asked him to come."

I was shaking so bad that I thought I was going to drop my son to the floor. Lincoln looked at both of us as anger rode his body, hardening him. I scanned him, trying to ignore the gun on his hip.

I knew how people could get crazy in situations like this, and he had definitely proven he wasn't the same man I'd fallen in love with. His eyes went from Trip to me, and back again. They did that dance a couple more times before he locked eyes with me.

"I'm going back to work." He turned and walked toward the front door. "His ass better not be here when I get back."

I handed Cameron to my sister. "Can you take him upstairs?"

She glared at Lincoln before heading up the steps.

I followed him to the front door. He opened the door slightly before turning to face me. "Fuck is he doing here, Idalis?" he asked.

I let out a sigh and ran my fingers through the many tangles in my hair. He had no idea how close to the edge I actually was.

"Lincoln, you know he's my best friend," I said.

He slammed the door shut, making me jump and causing the small mirror on the wall next to it to shake. Before I knew it, he was in my face. "You think I give a damn about some bullshit high school friendship?"

"Lincoln, keep your voice down." My voice was weak and I felt like my throat was closing up.

"I'm only gon' ask you one more time, Idalis. Why is he here?"

I co-signed on India's lie. "My sister told you. She called him. My mother and grandmother practically raised him. He's just concerned, that's all."

"That's bullshit, and you know it."

I closed my eyes and rubbed the bridge of my nose.

He let out a sigh, then backed off a little. "You need to take your ass home."

"Lincoln, I can't just—"

Fire rose in his eyes and I saw his jaw tighten.

He snatched the door open and it slammed against the wall behind it, causing me to step back a little. Before it could bounce back, Trip was in the foyer and Lincoln was standing in the doorway.

Lincoln directed his fire at him. "What?" His anger caused his voice to boom in the small foyer. He frowned at Trip. "Oh, now you wanna play protector? Shouldn't you be at the hospital on deathwatch pot'na?"

I lowered my head. My heart sank when he said that.

When I looked up again the look in Trip's eyes scared me. It was a look I'd never seen before.

"Stop it"—I stepped in the middle—"Cameron is upstairs."

At that moment my sister came running down the steps, ready to jump in and fight, if necessary.

India spoke up. "Since my sister won't say it, I will. I want *both* of you to leave. We are dealing with too much, and this is uncalled for. And I don't want it in my mama's house," she argued. "So, please, just leave my sister alone."

Trip walked over to the steps and placed a kiss on India's cheek before giving me a weak hug. "Call me if you need anything."

He ignored Linc and headed out to his truck. A few moments later the engine turned over and he sped off.

Lincoln stared at me for a brief second before following the same path Trip had just taken.

I stood in the doorway and watched him slide behind the wheel of his police cruiser and take off. I wanted to shout things at him, throw things at his car, but my arms were heavy. I took a deep breath and closed the door.

My sister came over and asked, "Are you okay?"

"I'm fine."

"I'm going back upstairs with my nephew. You better fix this before Mama and Grammie come home."

All could do was stand there as she disappeared up the steps, taking my sanity with her.

Chapter Twenty-one

Trip

I shifted my body around on the small, uncomfortable chair situated in the corner of my partner's hospital room. The fake leather whined under the weight of my body. The hiss of the machine helping Phil breathe was loud and intrusive. I felt like it was mocking me, trying to prove that it could do something I couldn't. I made that chair into my bed as I sat and prayed my partner would open his eyes. I reached up and slid the blinds back, allowing the new day to fill the sterile room.

"You been here all night?"

I looked up and saw Lenny standing in the door. He looked as bad as I felt.

I stood up. "Yeah, I keep staring at him, expecting him to wake up."

He walked over to the bed. "He will."

"He better." I stood to my feet. "What's up? What you doin' here?"

"Forensics called. They came up empty on that shell casing. Heat from the round being fired burned off any print."

"Damn. I was really hoping that would've given us a solid lead."

Just then, a tall female doctor walked in; two nurses were on her heels. One of the nurses began to tend to the machines connected to Phil; the other started checking his IV lines and breathing tube.

The thin black lady extended her hand. Her white lab coat was a stark contrast to her beautiful dark chocolate complexion. Her jet-black hair was secured in a neat bun at the base of her head.

"Hello, I'm Dr. Patterson. I operated on your partner."

I took her cold, scrawny hand in mine and gently shook it. "Is he okay?"

"Yes, he's doing well. The first bullet cut through his right shoulder, slicing through muscle. It was a through-and-through."

"Okay."

"The second pierced his lung before exiting his lower back. We were able to stop his internal bleeding and repair the damage. He's stable now."

Lenny spoke up. "When do you expect him to wake up?"

The doctor looked at Phil, then back to us. "When he wakes up is going to be up to him."

"But he will wake up, right?" I asked.

She nodded a thin veil of reassurance. "I don't see any reason why not. The breathing tube is more of a precaution than anything. I ordered his breathing tube out today."

I felt like the weight of the world had been lifted off my shoulders. I eyed the nurses as they finished up and left the room.

"Thank you very much." I shook her tiny hand again.

"Don't thank me. Your friend is a fighter. He's a very strong man, and he's as healthy as an ox." She headed toward the door. "He made my job easy."

I looked at Lenny and smiled. "She's never seen him eat."

That got a small laugh from Lenny.

I made my way to the door. "I need some air. Call me if anything changes," I insisted. "I'm going to get something to eat and see if I can get ahead of this."

Lenny took over my post on the noisy chair, and I set out in search of something to put in my stomach. My first thought was the cafeteria, but I really did need fresh air. I headed for the parking deck.

I drove the streets of downtown Atlanta with the windows halfway down. The crisp early-morning air filled the truck and cleared my head a little. It was almost eight, but my mind was all over the place. I needed to get something to eat and soon. I jumped on I-20 and headed toward my mother's house. I knew that I could get something there and possibly catch a nap before heading down to headquarters. I wasn't gonna stop until I found out who shot Phil. In more ways than one, this case just got personal.

At my mom's I took a shower and changed clothes before settling in over a mountain of eggs, turkey bacon, and grits. I was reading a story in the newspaper about a local cardiologist who was in the middle of a standoff the night before. It caught my attention because the dude, Sean Morris, had seen my pops a couple times in the ER before he died. According to the story, he was in some love triangle ended up taking his own life.

Guess everyone was having issues.

I heard someone come into the kitchen, but I didn't look up from my paper.

"Trinity, can you get me some orange juice?"

"She's in the shower."

My mother's voice made me look up. "Mama, what are you doing out of bed?"

"I'm not handicapped, boy."

I swallowed a mouthful of grits. "I know you're not. How's your hip doing?"

"It's better. That doctor Trinity took me too gave me something for the pain. He ordered a bunch of tests too."

"Good."

Her eyes were sad when she spoke. "Trinity told me what happened."

I reached up and secured my locs behind my head before picking up my fork again. "Phil is gonna be fine."

"I've been praying for him." She went to the sink and, true to form, began making dishwater. "She also told me about the grave site."

I stopped eating, but I didn't look at her. I kept my eyes fixed on the food in front of me. "Mama—"

"I'm not gonna fuss. But from the sounds of it, you got a lot of anger inside."

"Mama, I'm fine."

She poured me a glass of orange juice and set it in front of me. "No, you're not."

"What do you want me to do, mama?"

"I want you to let it go. It's time, baby."

I would never disrespect my mother, but right now she was pissing me off with all this for-give-and-forget bullshit. I just wanted to get full and catch a quick nap before heading out. I didn't come by here to be lectured. I looked up and saw Trinity sneak past the kitchen. She gave me a look that let me know she agreed with my mother. She didn't stop and kept moving toward the living room.

"Don't you have somewhere to be, you little snitch?" I called to her.

"It's Saturday, grumpy," she called back.

"Now, don't you go blaming her," Mama took her seat across from me. "Baby, I'm worried about you. We both are. You're shutting us out. Have been for years."

"I understand what you're saying, Mama, but I'm not shutting anyone out."

"Well, I don't know what else to call what you did. It's almost like when we put your dad in the ground, we buried you too."

I leaned back and let out a sigh. "Come on, Mama. I didn't do anything. I took a job that happened to be in another state. That's all."

"And I also know that Idalis needs her best friend—now more than ever."

"Idalis is fine." I pushed back in my chair and stood up. "Can we drop it, please?"

"I'm scared, baby, that's all. That could be you in that hospital bed."

"But it's not." I bent down and kissed her cheek. "I'm going to lie down for a little bit."

She didn't respond; instead, she busied herself by clearing the table.

I made my way down the hall to the bedroom that I used to call mine. I pushed back the door and it creaked and squealed, yielding to my intrusion. I couldn't help but laugh to myself at how huge I used to think the room was when I was growing up.

The large bed, situated under the window at the far end of the tiny room, had been there from the day I started high school, when it replaced my old bunk beds. The worn wood of the dresser and chest of drawers told all thirty-eight of my years.

I opened the small closet door.

My mother had filled it with extra blankets and sheets, but the ghosts of my sister and me huddled in the corner would always live there.

I closed the door and stretched out on the bed, which strained under the weight of my body. I balled a pillow up and tucked it under my head.

Lying in the bed, I watched the ceiling fan circulate the stale air around the room. I ran through every bit of the case in my head, tried to think of anything I'd missed, anything that didn't make sense, any piece that stood out. Up until now, everything had been done by the book, at least on our end. Phil must've felt really good about the lead to go without me.

That's when it hit me; I sat up on the bed.

Darius!

I kissed my mom and slapped my sister upside her head on my way out; then I bolted out the front door. I needed to get downtown. I didn't know much about Darius, but I was hoping that since he was a logged informant, I could find something in the system that would lead me to him.

Back in the office, I sat in front of the twenty-inch flat-screen monitor, scanning the database for anything that might lead me to Darius. The original UC that had linked Phil with the informant had been snatched off the street and put in hiding so I was on my own. I didn't know much about him, but I was hoping to come across something. During my search I became both amazed and frustrated at how many people had given that name to their sons, and even more so at the fact that so many had been in some sort of legal trouble at some point.

After two hours of searching and cross-referencing, I finally got a hit. I scribbled down the address and headed for the elevators.

Agent Roberts passed me in the hall. "What you got, Trip?"

"Going to check out an address. If Lenny needs me, tell him to call my cell."

"Any word on Phil?"

"He's still hasn't woken up," I called out as the elevator door closed.

I maneuvered my truck around the bowels of southwest Atlanta. This time of morning everyone who laid claim to the streets was either just getting to bed, or already asleep, resting up for the night shift. I had learned over time that runners who took the early-morning or day shifts weren't exactly a wealth of information. They were more like placeholders, keeping the porch light on, so to speak, for the ones who handled the real weight at night.

The address I had led me to Center Hill, off Bankhead, or rather Donald Lee Hollowell Parkway. After all these years, that name still didn't register. No matter how they packaged it, Bankhead would always be Bankhead.

I pulled up in front of the shabby house that displayed the address from my paper. The rundown property squatted right in the middle of the block and was surrounded by a messy yard. The two corners where the house sat were decorated with guys standing watch.

I could hear whistling popping off in the air, the hood version of a siren. Even at this time of the morning, eyes were watching and runners were alerting everyone that heat was in their midst. I stepped out and made my way through the maze of trash and overturned toys to the front porch.

The rickety screen door squeaked when I pulled it open. I rapped on the door two hard times. When no one answered, I reluctantly pressed the doorbell, in spite of the exposed wires. That must've gotten someone's attention. Shortly afterward, I heard the soft click of locks being released.

A stout dark-skinned woman, dressed in a ratty robe and nightgown, opened the door. Her hair was up in rollers, with a scarf wrapped tightly around the sides of her small head. Her deep-set, glassy eyes and dark lips told her story without her opening her mouth. She looked like a woman who'd just gotten to sleep, only to have me interrupt it with my visit.

"Can I help you?" her tone angry.

I flashed my badge. "I'm looking for Darius Grey."

"He ain't here."

"Do you know where he is?" I pushed.

She heaved her huge, braless breasts and let out a heavy sigh. "What is this about?"

"I need to ask him some questions about a shooting that took place a couple nights ago."

I watched as she fidgeted and adjusted her nightgown. "Well, he not here."

I looked over her shoulder and scanned her messy living conditions. There were piles of clothes all over the floor, like she had started to wash clothes and suddenly changed her mind. The dirty floor and toys scattered everywhere let me know there was a child close by.

I glanced over my shoulder and took inventory on how quickly the landscape had changed. Corners were now empty, but my eye caught the lookouts in the windows across the street and the house next door.

I reached in my pocket and pulled out one of my cards and held it out for her to take. "If he shows up, tell him to call me."

She sucked her teeth. "Why? So y'all can just throw him up in jail again? He just got out a couple months ago."

"Ma'am, I just wanna ask him a few questions. If he hasn't done anything, then there's no need to lock him up, is there?"

She snatched the card out of my hand and slammed the door.

Chapter Twenty-two

Idalis

I hated hospitals. My mother always said that death roamed the halls, which fueled my distaste for them. There was no medium emotion when it came to hospitals: you were either elated, usually due to a birth, or devastated, usually because of death or not-so-good test results. All the nurses smiled at me as I made my way toward my grandmother's room. I forced a smile, but my stomach was churning enough acid to eat through rock.

I dreaded what was on the other side of the door labeled 406. I took a deep breath, and then pushed the cracked door fully open. My mother was sitting on a chair at the foot of the bed, flipping through a magazine. I didn't need to see my grandmother to know she was on a machine that was helping her breathe. I could hear it hissing, taunting me, letting me know that death was roaming the hallway, waiting.

I fought tears as I turned the small corner and saw her.

My mother looked up, but she didn't move in my direction.

Instead she sat silently, letting me digest what I was seeing.

I took a deep breath and moved to her bedside. Her eyes were closed. Mama had braided her hair into two long, shiny braids, which rested on each shoulder. I tried to fight my tears, but they came in waves. My mother came and led me to a chair next to the bed.

"Mama, is she okay?"

"No, baby, she's not."

I looked up at my mom, feeling like I was five years old. I wanted her to make it all better, but I knew she couldn't. I looked to my grandmother. I wanted her to get up, help me, help me clean up my mess, but she didn't. She lay there, a shell of the woman I had known all of my life. Not many women my age could say they had their grandparents all their lives, but I was lucky. God had blessed me with her for almost forty years, and I wasn't ready to let her go.

"Isn't there something they can do?"

"Now it's just about making her comfortable."

I wiped my eyes, "I don't understand. I thought that her doctor wanted her here as a precaution, to help manage pain."

Mama nodded; then she sat on the edge of the bed, never letting go of my hand. "They did the scan, and the cancer has spread to her organs."

"Oh my God!" I said, shaking my head and trying to control my sobs, which were shaking my body.

Mama hugged me and tried to console me. "Baby, she's comfortable. That's all we can ask for, for right now. The tube is helping her breathe."

I wiped my face for what seemed like the thousandth time and took a deep breath. I thought about Cameron and how he kept asking for her. I didn't know what to tell him. He was with India. She was taking him to the zoo and out to eat.

That freed up my morning to run some errands, stop by my house and check on things as well as swing by 404 and show my face. I had been leaving the Barnes & Noble at Camp Creek Marketplace when my mother called me.

I stepped into the hospital corridor and called to check on my twin.

"Hey, you okay?" she asked.

"Yeah. Mama called you?"

"Yeah."

"You on your way to the hospital?"

Her voice was shaky. I could hear Cameron in the background. "Yeah. We're just leaving McDonald's. Um . . . let me see if I can get Ms.

Walker from next door to come sit with him and I'll be right there."

The lump in my throat grew bigger. "Hurry up, Twin."

Back in the room I took my post in a chair across from the bed. My mother was sitting in a chair next to my grandmother's bed.

"India is going to get Ms. Walker to keep Cameron; then she'll be on her way."

She nodded, never taking her eyes off her mother.

The door to the room hissed open and Lincoln stepped inside, getting my mother's and my attention. I got up and hugged him.

"Are you okay?" he asked.

I shook my head into his chest. "No."

He walked over and hugged my mother. "Hey, Mrs. Arrington."

She smiled. "Hello, Lincoln."

"Do you need anything?"

"No, I'm fine."

He gave me a look that let me know he wanted to talk to me.

"Mama, I'll be right back."

We stepped into the hall and for a second he stood with his back to me.

I asked, "What's wrong?"

"I need to take care of some business right quick, but I'll be back in a little bit."

My body grew rigid and I crossed my arms against my chest. "Lincoln, I need you *here*."

"Idalis I will be right back, just let me handle this."

I turned to walk away, but I stopped and turned back around. "Does this have anything to do with what I found in the garage?"

Anger flashed across his face as he shook his head. "You worryin' about the wrong thing."

My eyes went to the closed hospital room door, then back to him. "Then what is it?"

"Let it go, Idalis." His voice was rising, causing the nurses to peek up from the counter at the nurses' station.

"Lower your voice," I hissed.

He stared at me for a moment, like he was reading me, examining my body language. I felt my face warm and my stomach started to churn.

"I really wish you would knock off this innocent act you have goin' on."

Then I was stunned. "So just like that, huh? You gon' treat me like shit, and my grandmother is lying in there, dying?"

"Treat *you* like shit, Idalis?" He let out a slight chuckle. "Wow. You got life fucked up—you really do."

I turned to go back into the room and he grabbed my arm. "Where are you going?"

"You know what? I don't really care what you do anymore," I said through clenched teeth. "Just go." I snatched my arm free.

He stared at me for a moment before turning and heading down the hall. I stood there and watched him leave. I could feel the nurses' eyes on me. I could even hear their whispers, but I didn't care at this point.

I checked on my mother before leaving to clear my head. I ended up leaving the hospital and making my way to Chick-fil-A and getting a chicken sandwich and some lemonade. There were too many people in the restaurant, so I decided to eat in my car in the parking lot. I backed my car into the space so I could people watch and try to take my mind off my grandmother.

Every so often I would check my cell phone: nothing but the time and that stupid signal tower were staring back at me. The small restaurant was overrun with hospital visitors, who probably all felt the same way I did about the food they served up in the cafeteria.

Most were getting their dinners to go; some were staying to escape the heavy atmosphere that awaited them up the street, but they all were linked in a way that far exceeded the chicken sandwiches that they carried.

I sipped my lemonade and picked at my sandwich as I stared out my car window at the people going about their day. The proverbial traffic jam that was Piedmont Avenue was holding true to that today. I looked down at the engagement ring resting on my all-important left ring finger and thought about the history that Lincoln and I were supposed to be in the middle of making. So much had changed in less than a week. My life was turning into a train wreck right in front of my eyes; there was nothing I could do to stop the fallout.

I dialed Trip.

Relief washed over me when I heard his voice come across the line.

"Hey, are you okay?" he asked.

I pressed my phone against my ear, my sad attempt to feel closer to him. "She's bad, Trip."

"I'm so sorry, baby girl. Do you need anything?"

"Yes, I need my grandmother not to be dying," I said, wiping away a stray tear.

"I know."

"How's Phil?"

It was his turn to carry the weight. "He's doing good. Still unconscious. Breathing tube is coming out today."

"Wow. That's good news."

"Yeah, it is."

I swallowed, rearranged the words in my head and hoped they made sense when they exited my mouth. "Trip, I'm really sorry."

"For what?"

"For everything."

"What are you talking about, Idalis?"

"For pretty much all my life, you've been there for me, no matter what the cost." I took a deep breath and tried to steady my voice. "I mean, when we were little, you would make sure I was okay, even when you knew you were going to get in trouble . . ."

"Idalis—"

I cut him off. "Let me finish. If it wasn't for me, you would've gotten that call from Phil and you would've been there for him. It's my fault. It's always my fault."

"No, it's not, Idalis."

"Yes, it is!" I sobbed into the phone. "And now, being the selfish person that I am . . . I was calling you . . . again . . . to get you to save me again. To make this hurt go away."

"Don't do this, Idalis. Not now."

"Why? Why not? It's true. I'm getting what I deserve."

His voice, calm and steady, held so much love. "You think you deserve to have your grandmother die baby girl?"

I grabbed a napkin and wiped my face. "Yes. No. I don't know."

"Idalis, if you try to make what's happening to your grandmother about you, then yes, that is selfish, but that's not you. That's not the Idalis I know."

"I don't even know who I am anymore."

"What do you mean?"

"I'm just not the same Idalis Arrington that you grew up with."

My phone beeped in my ear and I looked at the screen. It was India.

"Trip, I have to go. It's India. I'll call you back."

"Make sure you do."

I didn't even remember driving back to the hospital.

India called and told me that Grammie was asking for me. Fresh tears spilled from my already swollen eyelids in waves as I navigated my way back up Piedmont to the hospital. I brushed past a group of people huddled in the lobby; they were cooing over a woman who was holding a newborn. As I made my way onto the elevator, I ignored a nurse who asked if I was okay. I stood perfectly still in the elevator, promising God things that didn't even make sense if He'd just spare my grandmother. The doors hissed open and I stood frozen.

A voice came from behind me. "Is this the floor you wanted?"

I turned around in a haze of grief and looked into the distinguished white man's face standing behind me. His dark hair was starting to gray around the temples and he was freshly shaven. His dark suit and stark blue tie brought out the color in his piercing blue eyes.

Not sure why I noticed that, but I did.

He reached around and pushed the button to hold the door open, causing his cologne to swirl around me.

He repeated himself. "Is this your floor?"

"Uh . . . I'm sorry. Yes, this is my floor." I turned and stepped off the elevator.

When I got to my grandmother's room, my mother was staring out the window and India was standing next to the bed, trying to hide her tears. I walked toward her and touched my mother's shoulder.

Without turning around she spoke. "They took the tube out. She's asking for you."

Mama hugged me before leaving with India, leaving me alone in the room with my grandmother.

Grammie was so fragile and so small.

I moved to her bedside and touched her hand.

The coolness of her skin caught me off guard. Her eyes opened slowly and she smiled when she saw me. I tried to will the tears to stop, but they wouldn't. Her gaze moved to the chair, motioning for me to sit down. On shaky legs I did as I was told, never taking my eyes from her face.

"Grammie, are you in pain?"

Her voice was raspy and low. "No, baby, but you are."

That caused me to cry harder; my shoulders shook, but I kept hold of her hand.

"I can't handle this."

"Yes, you can, baby. You need to make things right with your sister. You hear me, child?"

I slowly shook my head. "I don't know if I can. I need you Grammie."

"Yes, you can, baby." She cleared her throat. "I will always be with you, watching over you all. You know that. It's time, baby. My soul is tired."

"But I need you. We need you." I sobbed.

"Idalis," her voice was stern, causing me to sit up a little straighter. "You make things right, for you and that baby. You hear me? Make it right."

My heart shattered.

I nodded. "Yes, ma'am."

"I love you, baby."

"I love you too, Grammie."

I leaned over onto her bed and hugged her, willing death to go away and find someone else's grandmother. I wasn't strong enough to go on without mine.

Minutes slipped by, taking a piece of my grandmother with it each time. I laid my head on her chest and she stroked my hair, calming me, humming a song, which only she knew. After a while I finally sat up and hit the buzzer for the nurse. The thin white lady appeared almost instantly, wearing a comforting smile.

"Can I help you?"

I wiped my face and took a deep breath. "I haven't heard my grandmother take a breath in the last few minutes."

She gave me a small sympathetic nod and left the room.

Almost two hours later, I was stuck on autopilot.

I drove I-285 in a tear-induced haze with no real direction in mind. I knew India had taken Mama with her, but I didn't remember leaving the hospital. I had a Tazo Green Tea Latte from Starbucks in my cup holder, but didn't remember getting off on Camp Creek and going through the drive-through. I pulled into a parking space and called a few relatives and told them what had happened. In between talking to relatives and calling the house to check on my mother and sister, I called and talked to Lincoln. I wasn't ready to go home and deal with the emotions that were waiting there for me, so I merged back onto I-285 and headed toward Greenbriar.

On my way to 404, I tried to imagine burying my grandmother. I conjured up images of a church filled with grief. An atmosphere so thick with sadness that it threatened to choke everyone in its midst. My mind conjured images of a packed church, wall to wall flowers, the coffin; all of it was there, everything except my grandmother.

I parked my car near the door and headed inside. It was early and the DJ was just setting up. Dionne smiled when she saw me.

"Can I get a Heineken?" I slid onto one of the stools.

She popped the cap off the green bottle and slid it toward me. "How you doing? How's your grandmother?"

I stared at the tiny white napkin that my bottle rested on; then I looked up at her. "She passed this afternoon."

Dionne made her way around the bar and wrapped her arms around me. "I'm so sorry, Idalis."

"Thank you."

She took the stool next to me. "How's your mom and sister?"

"They're okay. India is at my mom's with her and Cameron."

"Do you need anything?"

I shook my head. "I just wasn't ready to go home yet, needed to clear my head."

"I understand."

Dionne had lost her mother about a year ago, so I knew if anyone could understand what I was going through, it would be her.

I looked around the club. "I hope it picks up."

"It will." She looked at her watch. "It's still early, Si-Man isn't even here yet."

I let out a sigh and took a long draw of my beer. "I can't believe this is happening. It just amazes me how quickly sugar can go to shit."

"That's true, but your grandmother lived a full life. She was in a lot of pain too. She's definitely better off."

I nodded in agreement. "Yeah, I just wish I could've had her a little while longer."

"Idalis, you're stronger than you give yourself credit for."

"Sometimes I'm not too sure about that."

"What do you mean?"

"I've made some mistakes—mistakes that I'm not sure I am strong enough to correct. And when I looked at her, I always seemed to find the strength I needed to push forward." I swallowed the lump in my throat. "And now . . . she's gone. I don't know what to do."

Dionne touched my hand. "No, she's not gone, Idalis." She took my hand and placed it over my heart. "She's right here."

We both had matching sets of tears rolling down our faces.

She continued speaking. "There is nothing that you could've done that would've made her love you any less or that you can't fix. You just have to believe you can."

I slid down off my stool. "It's not that simple."

"Don't do this to yourself, Idalis."

I hugged her. "I'll call you tomorrow. I need to stop by my house and grab some things before I head back to Mama's."

"Okay. Call me if you need anything, I mean it. Idalis, you do know that sometimes people complicate things much more than they need to be."

I threw a ten-dollar bill on the bar.

"Yeah, and sometimes people get what they deserve."

Chapter Twenty-three

Trip

"Any word on the missing informant?"

I shoved my BlackBerry back in its holster and turned to Lenny.

"No. I got a couple agents watching his house. Hopefully, he'll turn up soon."

We were all at the station going over what had been found at the scene where Phil had been shot. My blood boiled as I looked at the pictures hanging up on the corkboard.

Lenny sat down on the corner of one of the empty desks. "We got another call this morning."

"From where?"

"Fulton Industrial."

I asked, "Related?"

"Not sure right now," he said, voice heavy with frustration. Lenny stood up and looked around the room at the agents. "I need you fellas to wrap this up, and do it fast."

I cut my eyes at him. "What do you think we're trying to do?"

"I understand, but this is getting out of control. Phil's in the hospital and informants are disappearing."

Ever since the doctors had taken Phil's breathing tube out, we were waiting for him to wake up and tell us something, anything that might give a clue into what had happened during that bust. But more than anything, I wanted to get my hands on whoever had put my partner in a hospital bed. We'd been partners for over five years, and neither one of us had been so much as grazed by a bullet. Something we both were damn proud of up until now.

I walked over to the board and scanned the pictures of the deceased men. Out of all the dead bodies at the scene, we were only able to ID two so far. Both were small-time dealers, one went by the name of Twist. We were still waiting on IDs for the others. My eyes locked on one in particular. His face was twisted in pain. The last thing he felt before he died. His large white tee was soaked with blood from the rounds that Phil managed to pump into his chest before he went down.

"What did they find?" I asked one of the agents taking notes.

"Got a cell off one of the guys in the living room, but it's busted. Hopefully, the lab can pull something from it. Couple bags of X, some bricks that are being processed to see if they match the original bust."

"Whose apartment was it?" I asked, sitting on the corner of a desk.

The reason I asked was because I knew that "dead and deader" on the floor probably weren't listed on the lease.

"Some woman named Denise Chambers. Witnesses are saying she was a crackhead who sold and used out of her apartment."

I looked around. "Anyone know where she is?"

"Nobody knows," he said, shrugging his shoulders.

"Of course not." The phone on the desk I was leaning against rang. I picked it up. "This isn't my desk," I said before hanging it up again.

"We got some officers tracking her down now," one of the officers said.

I nodded. "Good."

This case was all over the place, and it didn't seem like there was an end in sight. It seemed like one simple drug bust had opened up an enormous can of worms, which none of us had been prepared for. But there was no way I was gonna let Phil's ending up in the hospital be for nothing.

Lenny stood up, signaling the end of our meeting.

"All right, gentlemen, I need you to do what you do, but I need you to do it faster. Let's get Phil home."

We all filed out of the room. My body was heavy as I made my way back to the truck.

I rolled the driver's-side window down and stared out into the parking lot, watching the people moving up and down Spring Street. Some were on their cells; others were rushing to and from work. They were all oblivious to what was going on in the dark corners of the city that no one dared to go in.

No one but us.

Before heading to the hospital, I decided to stop by the scene from the call that came in this morning. When I pulled up, there was still a crowd of people standing around. Some were hugging each other; others were snapping pictures with their cell phones.

I scanned the crowd and saw two women who were crying relentlessly. Judging from their ages, and the fact that one was pregnant and had a small child clinging to her leg, I figured they were girlfriends of the victims. I couldn't help but feel sorry for them and the kids. The dead bodies in that apartment were probably their only source of support.

Sadly, this was the only life some of them would ever know.

I took a deep breath and realized I didn't have the energy for this.

Not today.

I would never admit it, but it was like we were fighting a losing battle.

It wasn't the war on drugs. It seemed more like the war against us. No faster than we would kick in a door, another one would go up. Phil would always just laugh and say, "Guess we gotta make sure we keep a good supply of boots."

Atlanta would have to actually do some work for once. I made a U-turn out of the parking lot. If they found anything worth anything, they would let us know. I hadn't heard from Idalis, and as much as I hated to admit it, it bothered me.

Just as I pulled out onto Fulton Industrial, my phone rang. My mother's number came across the display.

"Hey, Mama, what's up?"

"Hey, baby. I got some bad news."

"What's wrong?"

"It's Idalis." My mother's voice wavered. "Her grandmother passed this afternoon."

I slumped back in my seat. "What?"

"It was sudden."

I merged onto I-20. "I'm on my way over there."

Even though the streets were calm, I was barely maintaining the speed limit. The dark sky was tiled with rain clouds, mimicking how I felt. They all looked on the verge of bursting and raining down, saturating the city with bottled-up frustration. The highway raced by me, miles at a time. I felt my tires lose a little bit of traction on the damp pavement, but that didn't slow my momentum.

Ever since I had crossed the state line, this place had held nothing but frustration. I was ready to get the hell out of town.

I pulled out my phone and dialed her mother's home number. I figured she would be there. My heart rate doubled when the phone started ringing. Just when I was about to hang up, she answered.

"Idalis?"

"No, this is India. She's asleep."

"This is Trip, India. Is she okay?"

"She's doing better."

"How are you?" I asked.

"I'm hanging in there. I'm watching TV with Cameron."

"Okay."

"How's your mom? Do you guys need anything?"

"No, we're good. My mother is taking a nap. Are you gonna stop by? I know they would like to see you."

"I'm on my way."

"Thanks, Trip."

Twenty minutes later I was sitting in their mother's living room with Idalis. She and India had swapped places, and now she was upstairs taking a nap. Their mother had come down briefly for something to eat and to have some tea, and I was able to see her and offer my condolences.

For the first time since I'd known the family, I felt uncomfortable sitting in their house. I watched as her son played in the middle of the living room floor. Every so often, he would bring me one of his cars or trucks in an attempt to maintain our friendship.

I looked at Idalis. A mirror image of India. Her eyes were rimmed in red. She fidgeted with the seam on the side of her Capri jeans. She was sitting with one leg folded under her, and her sockless foot was bouncing up and down.

"Are you sure you're okay?"

She shook her head and wiped a stray tear from her cheek. "No, but I have to be right?"

"I wish there were something I could do."

She gave me a weak smile. "Yeah, me too."

I took a deep breath. "Look, I'm really sorry about the other day."

"It's okay. I wouldn't have expected anything less out of both of y'all being in the same room," she said. The whole time she spoke, she never took her eyes off Cameron, who was now coloring.

"You wanna talk?"

"Not really. Not now."

I watched as her leg bounced up and down. She was unraveling right before my eyes, and I felt helpless to stop it.

"Idalis, it's me. You can talk to me. You know that, right?"

She got up and started picking up toys from the middle of the floor. "I said I'm okay. Please, let's not do this now. Ok?"

"I'm just worried about you. Everyone is."

She stopped what she was doing and glared at me. "Everyone? Who is *everyone,* Trip?"

"Wait. What are you getting upset about?" I asked.

She stood up, hands on her hips. "So what are you saying? You and *everyone* have been having conversations about me behind my back?"

"Come on now, it's not like that, and you know it."

"Then what is it?" She stood there and looked at me as if I had two heads. I didn't want to upset her. I knew she was dealing with a lot, but I couldn't help what my gut was telling me.

"You know what, Trip. Can you please just go?"

"Idalis, I didn't come over here to argue with you."

"I can't tell. And you can tell Dionne she needs to mind her own business."

I let out a short laugh. "Oh, so now you mad at her? She just came to me out of concern. If you wanna be mad at anyone, you should be mad at—"

She cut me off. "Myself!"

"What?"

"That's what you were going to say, right?"

I took a step toward her. "What are you talking about? Nobody is blaming you for anything."

Her eyes filled with tears. "Just go, Trip."

I stood there for a second. "Are you serious?"

"Yes I am. I'm about to bury my grandmother, and you come at me with this?"

"This is crazy."

"I can't do this. You come back into town and turn my world upside down and . . . and it's too much."

"Wait a minute! You showed up at *my* hotel room, or did you forget that?"

She bit her bottom lip as I watched anger flash across her face. "Wow, you had to go there."

"Yes, I did. You been pushing and pulling me ever since—"

"You know what"—she bent down and picked up Cameron—"just go."

Part of me wanted to stay and try to figure out where all this was coming from, but I was too tired both emotionally and physically to argue with her. And she was right; she was about to bury her grandmother and I didn't want to make it any harder for her.

I headed toward the door. I grabbed the knob, but I didn't turn it. She walked up behind me, ready to usher me out of her life.

"When is the funeral?" I asked.

When she didn't answer me, I turned around and looked at her. The cold look in her eyes spoke volumes.

She didn't want me there.

I shook my head and stepped out onto the porch.

Before I could say anything, I heard the door close behind me.

Chapter Twenty-four

Idalis

I had been in a fog for the better part of a week.

And when I wasn't feeling my way through the day, I was riding some sleeping aid to dreamland. I vaguely remembered Dionne picking up Cameron and taking him to her house so we could get ready for the funeral. The funeral itself was surreal. I felt like a shell of myself as I navigated the mourners who flooded the church. I was completely numb through the whole thing. I could feel the squeeze of the hugs and barely focused on the words of encouragement being offered up. It was a good thing that India was standing next to me or I would've toppled over. I was even less clear on how I ended up sitting at my mom's kitchen table, trying to decide what to do about my grandmother's stuff.

I watched my mother interact with the people who had gathered at the house, all bearing a different covered dish. As much as she tried to hide it, I could tell she was tired. I was happy when she was finally able to go and lie down. After the repast my mother went to her room and closed her door. I made sure she ate before she retreated into her own personal grief. India had ended up falling asleep on the couch.

Trip respected my wishes and didn't come to the funeral. I knew I couldn't have handled him and Linc being in the same room again. After what had happened the last time they were together, I needed space to figure out how to right my wrongs.

However, no matter what my self-serving reasons were, I still couldn't shake the look that his mother and sister kept giving me during the service. It wasn't anger as much as it was pity. But the look that my mother gave me after finding out that I'd asked Trip not to come was anything but sympathetic. It was a look that would've made me pee my pants when I was kid.

I made my way to the living room and threw a blanket over my sleeping sister before heading upstairs to check on my mother. I pushed the door back and saw her sleeping peacefully, which made me feel a little better. It was coming up on eight and I needed to call and check on Cameron. Lincoln left the repast and said he was heading to the station. I was actually thankful that he was gone. I didn't need his attitude around me either.

After putting away the food, I sat down and called Dionne. I didn't think Cameron needed to be at the funeral, around all the crying and sadness. He was too little to understand, and Dionne was sweet enough to keep him for me.

"Hey, are you okay?" she asked when she answered.

I sank onto one of the chairs in the kitchen. "Yeah. I'm good. Mom is asleep and India is taking a nap on the couch."

"Have you slept?"

"Not yet. How's Cameron?"

"He's fine. He just finished eating. He's watching *Wonder Pets.*"

I laughed a little. "You're gonna get the song stuck in your head."

"Already there."

We both laughed a little.

"I think I'm gonna head to my house tonight and drop off our dirty clothes and get some clean ones. I can come and get Cameron in the morning."

"That's fine."

"Thank you so much."

As much as I wanted to be mad at her for talking to Trip behind my back, I knew it was coming from a place of genuine concern, so I couldn't be mad. I appreciated all she did for me, so I decided not to even bring it up.

"I'm surprised that Trip and Lincoln made it through the funeral without choking each other," she said.

I swallowed hard. "Trip wasn't there."

"What? Why?"

"I asked him not to come."

She let out a sigh and got quiet.

"Don't do that, Dionne."

"Do what?"

"I did what I thought was best for me and my family."

"No, you did what you thought was best for you and Lincoln."

"You know what. Since you wanna open that door, I would appreciate it if you'd stop going behind my back and telling Trip on me. I'm grown."

"Grown? Idalis that man had you in your office in tears. And I don't care what you say I know he did something to you that night. I was just worried about you," she countered.

"Well you can stop worrying, I'm fine."

She didn't say anything. I knew she was mad, but no one was as angry as I was. I wasn't going to let anyone make me feel bad for doing what I believed in my heart to be the best thing.

"Look, once this is over Trip's going back to Louisiana. That's the one point everyone seems to keep overlooking," I pointed out.

"So that's what your problem is? You don't want to open up because he's gonna leave?"

"That's what he does. He bails."

"And what do you think you're doing?"

"Trying to be happy and build a stable home life for my son."

"With Lincoln?" She let out a sound of disgust. "You've got to be kidding me."

"Don't do that, please."

"Idalis, you really need to snap out from whatever it is you're going through. Lincoln isn't right for you, and you know it. You've known it longer than you want to admit. Your relationship hasn't been right for a long time."

"We're just going through something, that's all."

"Dealing with things for a few weeks is going through something—y'all have been going at it off and on for the last few years."

"So what I guess you think that Trip is the answer?"

"That's not what I'm saying. But, honestly, I definitely know that Linc isn't."

I got up and started pacing the small area in front of the kitchen sink. "You just don't understand, Dionne."

"Well, help me understand."

I stopped dead in my tracks and focused on the tiny clock hanging above the door leading to the hallway. I watched the second hand sweep around the face of the clock. I wanted to help her understand, felt like maybe I would understand more myself if I talked it out. But I couldn't. The words were stuck in my head, refusing to be put on display and ridiculed.

I let out a heavy sigh. "Look, I appreciate what you're trying to do, but I'm really tired."

"Fine, get some sleep."

"Thank you."

"Okay. Here's Cameron."

I heard some fumbling around as she put my baby on the phone.

"Hi, Mommy."

Hearing his tiny voice brought tears to my eyes. "Hey, baby. Are you having fun with Aunt Dionne?" I smiled.

"Yes."

"Okay, it's almost time for bed. I'll be there to get you in the morning."

"Okay. Bye, Mommy."

There was more fumbling before Dionne's voice came back on the line.

"Thanks again, Dionne. I told him it was time for bed. Don't let him sucker you into staying up all night."

She laughed. "I won't. I'll talk to you tomorrow. Try to get some sleep."

"I will. Good night."

I disconnected the call and did one more check on my sister and mother. They were both still sleeping. I managed to drag a half-asleep India upstairs to bed, and she even seemed coherent when I told her I was gonna go home and I'd be back in the morning.

I stepped into my empty house and felt like I didn't belong. Not because it had been a couple days since I'd slept there, but mainly because everything about my life seemed wrong at this point. If I wanted, I could blame everyone from Trip to my mother for what I was dealing with, but that wouldn't be right or fair.

After I threw some fresh clothes for Cameron and me in a bag, I took a long, hot shower and pulled on an oversized pair of pajama pants and a T-shirt. In the kitchen I pieced together a small salad and warmed up some salmon, which was in the fridge. I had been so focused on my mother eating that I hadn't had anything since breakfast.

Just as I finished eating, my sister called. She barely remembered what I told her before I left.

"Are you okay? When are you coming back over here?"

"Twin, I told you before I left that I'd be back in the morning. I'll probably go get Cameron first."

"Okay."

"Mama still asleep?"

"Yeah." She yawned.

It was contagious.

I did the same.

"What are you doing?" she asked.

I picked up the remote. "Watching TV. Trying to relax. It's too quiet."

"You need to try to get some sleep."

I flipped past a rerun of *The Office,* settling on an even older episode of *Grey's Anatomy.* "Yeah, I guess I do."

"You wanna talk?"

I rubbed my temple. "No."

"Why?"

"Because I've had enough stress for one day."

There was a moment of silence before my sister did what she does best, try to fix everything and everyone around her, forcing her opinion on you even when you didn't ask for it. She'd had that problem forever, and obviously had no intention of trying to break the annoying habit.

"He's like . . . family. And you were wrong for not letting him come to the funeral. Grammie was like a grandmother to him too."

"Are you kidding me?" My defenses shot up like a steel trapdoor.

"You heard me, Twin. You were dead-ass wrong, and you know it."

"The only thing I know is you have no idea what you're talking about."

"Oh, I don't?" she snapped back. "I've been carrying around this weight with you, Idalis! It's a lot on me too. You're being selfish."

I chewed on the inside of my mouth, used that as a counteraction to stop the tears that were stinging my eyes.

"What do you want me to do, Twin? Huh? Since you know everything, tell me what to do!" I got up and grabbed some tissue from the bookcase. "You don't think this is hard for me? You're leaving, anyway, so what do you care?"

"Oh, hell no! You're not putting this shit on me. I have nothing to do with this. You're playing this thing like a game—and, worst of all, you're changing and making up rules to suit you."

"You need to keep your voice down before you wake up my mother."

"Whatever, Idalis."

"So now the girl who can't, or rather *won't*, hold down a job, and who hasn't had a real relationship in years, is gonna tell me how to be a grown-up? Yeah, miss me with that."

She blew out some air. "You know what, Idalis? I may not have a nine-to-five gig, and yeah, I don't have a man. But I know right from wrong, and you're wrong. Trip doesn't deserve this."

"I didn't ask you for your opinion."

"Well, you need to ask somebody, because you are out of control! You can think for yourself, but instead you're letting some dog-ass man dictate your life. That's crazy, Idalis! What happened to the strong, older-by-three-minutes sister I always looked up to?"

"I'm right here."

"No, you're not. You've allowed Lincoln to turn you into some fuckin' Stepford wife, who can't go to the bathroom without checking with him first."

"That's not true."

"Yes, it is. I know it, Mom sees it, and Grammie saw it before she died. You left that cushy job at the Four Seasons just because he bought you a damn club. What kind of shit is that?"

"Did you ever think maybe I liked that club?"

"Yeah, right. He only did that to keep tabs on you Idalis. I'm not stupid and neither are you."

"Well, once you move to California, you won't have to worry about me or my club!"

"You know what? Bye!"

After I hung up, I tossed my phone onto the couch and stared at it for a few seconds. I wanted to call back and make her understand. I wanted to scream at her. I wanted to cry and beg her to stay. She's my twin; she was my best friend, even before Trip.

Why couldn't she see that without her, I just didn't feel I made sense?

Chapter Twenty-five

Trip

My truck was wide open, slicing through traffic on I-20, headed east.

We'd gotten a tip that Darius was hiding out at a cousin's house, out in Decatur. Right now, a lot was hinging on what he could or couldn't tell us. The fact that he was running had pissed me off. Lenny and two other agents were already set up at the house, where another agent on my team and I were headed. They'd been watching it since last night and were sure he was there.

It had been almost a week and I hadn't spoken to Idalis. Phil was intermittently conscious, but he wasn't coherent enough to answer any questions yet. My mere presence in Georgia had ruined two lives so far; I was determined to right at least one wrong, and Darius was going to help me do it.

Whether he wanted to do so or not.

I jumped off at Memorial Drive and sped by the jail. I hooked a right onto Kensington and pulled into Avondale Estates. I stopped at the top of Kingstone.

The streets were quiet. I radioed Lenny to let him know I was in the neighborhood.

"We're watching the address. Two females exited about twenty minutes ago, but no one has left since," he chirped back.

"Any movement in the house?"

"Not yet."

I parked my truck around the corner, and Agent Michaels and I hopped out, making our way toward the address. I noticed another agent alongside the house. He moved closer to the front when he saw us.

"Two pit bulls in the back. Sounds like there is at least one in the house," he said.

We stepped up onto the porch and Michaels hit the door three times, hard, with his fist, causing the dogs to go crazy. A moment later they stopped. I gave a nod and everyone drew guns; Lenny and the two other agents ran around back.

"We got movement," someone yelled from the back of the house.

I began banging on the front door. "Open up! DEA! Search warrant!"

"Front window," Michaels yelled.

Out of the corner of my eye, I saw the curtains flutter.

I gave Michaels a nod. "Take it."

I stepped to the side and he took a step back; with one kick he busted the door off the hinges. We bolted toward the back, with adrenaline on high, guns drawn. I could hear them yelling instructions in the back of the house.

"Get down! Get down!"

We ran up just as Lenny was putting a knee in Darius's back. He had a makeshift tourniquet around his left thigh. Judging from the ratty condition of the bandage, I could tell it definitely wasn't done at a hospital.

I holstered my gun. "What's up, Darius? I've been looking for you."

He twisted his body to look up at me from the floor. "Man, why you looking for me?"

Lenny finished cuffing him and got up off his back. I stepped in and pulled him up off the floor. He cried out in pain, but I didn't give a damn. He needed to be glad I didn't kick him in his leg for what had happened to Phil.

"You know damn well why." I slammed him against the wall, causing the dishes in the china cabinet to rattle. "Who shot my fucking partner?"

"Man! Watch out!" he said, trying to wrestle away. "Dude shot me too!"

I reached for my .9 mm. "If you don't start talking, I'ma shoot you in your other leg!"

Lenny's voice came from behind me. "Trip, let him go."

I ignored Lenny and kept talking to Darius. "I can have a bullet in your other leg before he can get over here to stop me. I suggest you start talking."

"Look, man, all I know is that shit went south fast. I called and told Phil I had a meet set up with Twist and that dude Geech y'all been looking for, but he had to move quick 'cause shit was going down right then. It was on from that point."

"What happened?"

"Yo, dude just started freaking out soon as we got there. Talkin' 'bout Twist set him up and shit."

"And," I pressured.

"And next thing I know, bullets is flying and I'm hit in the leg."

"So just like that, he started blazing?"

He squirmed against the cuffs. "Look, all I know is Phil set dude off and that's when the shooting started."

"Fuck you mean he set him off?" I asked.

"Yo, just what I said."

"You think dude knew Phil was heat?"

"Look, man, I don't know if he knew who he was employed with or not, but he definitely didn't like Phil's ass."

I took a step back and examined Darius's face for anything that would justify me hitting him in the throat before I turned and headed to the front door.

"Man, take his ass to Grady to get his leg looked at, then lock his dumb ass up," I said.

He called out, "Lock me up! For what? What I do?"

"I don't like you," I called back.

"Come on, man! What if he comes looking for me?"

"Not my problem."

I kept walking.

Back downtown, I sat in a conference room alone, going through the files for what seemed like the hundredth time. The fact that Darius said dude was set off by Phil was really bothering me because that meant this shit just got more complicated than any of us could imagine. The fact that the original undercover was buried wasn't helping the situation either.

About an hour later, I got a call telling me that Darius was admitted to Grady. I made sure there were cops posted outside his door. I also told them that when he was released to the jail infirmary, they had to keep an eye on him.

"He gonna need surgery?" I asked Lenny.

"Nah, bullet grazed his thigh. Took out a nice chuck of meat, but he'll be fine."

"Lenny, if he's right and this dude knew Phil, we got problems."

"Yeah, I know. There's no telling how many other agents have been exposed."

"We need to try to get an ID from Darius. The sooner we make a bust and plug this hole, the better."

"Trip, I know how bad you want this guy, but I need you to be careful. Take one of the other agents with you."

"I don't need a partner, Lenny. I have one."

He knew better than to argue with me about my partnership with Phil, so he just let my comment go.

"I'm sending a sketch artist down to the hospital to see what Darius can come up with," I continued.

"Okay. I'll keep you posted," he said.

I disconnected the call and tossed my Black-Berry onto the table.

"Sketch artist?"

I turned around and saw Lincoln standing behind me. I turned back around and kept looking over my case notes. "What do you want, Briscoe?"

He took a seat at the table across from me. "What you need a sketch artist for? Your cocky ass havin' a self-portrait done?"

"Yeah, figured I'd have one done up for you. 'Cause the way you keep popping up, I'm starting to think you got a crush on me."

He laughed. "Yeah, a'ight. So you got somebody who thinks they can finger the shooter."

I frowned up at him. "Man, why are you still talking to me?"

He shifted on the chair and leaned forward. A slick grin spread across his face. "It's just you and me up in here." He looked toward the door then back to me. "Why don't we stop playin' and put this shit out on the table."

I leaned back, giving him my attention. "What's on your mind?"

"Playa, your problem with me isn't professional. Your problem with me is the fact that I'm layin' pipe—on a regular basis, I might add—to the woman you been in love with since grade school."

I let out a laugh. "That's the best you could come up with? Get the fuck out my face with that shit."

"You and your obsession with my fiancée is gettin' old; and truth be told, it's about to get you fucked up, pot'na."

"And your fucked-up attitude toward her is getting old, and *that's* about to get *you* fucked up, again," I said, looking up at him.

He flexed his jaw. "There you go worryin' about shit that ain't got nothin' to do with you."

"Yeah, and if that were true, she wouldn't keep calling me and you wouldn't be sitting here getting on my gotdamn nerves."

I watched as he leaned back from the table. "Stay away from Idalis playa, or a dying pot'na is gon' be the least of your problems."

I stood up. "My partner isn't dying, and if you mention him to me again"—I shoved my phone in its holder—"being Idalis's consolation prize is going to be the least of *your* problems."

He let out a short laugh. "Just admit it. You never got over the fact that she gave me that ass and not you. You been walkin' around with this bullshit since college."

"Man, would you *please* go do some cop work?" I slammed the folder closed. "I don't have time to sit around playing Dr. Phil to your insecure ass."

He stood up, and the hairs on the back of my neck jumped to attention. I kept gathering the paperwork, keeping him in my peripheral.

As bad as I wanted to hit him, I wanted to get whoever had put my partner in the hospital even more. I believed Lenny when he said he'd toss me off this case if I couldn't handle myself with Linc.

I glanced at him. "This conversation is over."

"You sure about that?"

"Positive."

"Nah pot'na this conversation hasn't even started yet," he started. "I got a feeling you think because you tucked behind that agency badge that I won't reach out and touch your punk ass."

Slowly I reached down to my hip, pulled my gold DEA badge and credentials off my hip and tossed them on the table followed by my P226 .9 mm.

"What's up?" I taunted. "But remember, ain't nobody here to pull me off you this time."

He glared at me for a moment before heading to the door. I could tell by his body language that he wasn't really trying to end this, at least not this way.

"Oh, and, Briscoe," I called out to him.

He stopped in the doorway. "Fuck you want?"

"If you put your hands on Idalis again," I glanced up at him. "I'ma shoot you myself."

He gave me a sly grin. "Game on muthafucka."

"What's the supposed to mean?"

"I know you not worried Supercop," he said, walking away. "This is far from over, believe that."

Chapter Twenty-six

Idalis

"I understand the policy and I will try to make it there on Monday."

I tossed my cell onto the passenger seat and sped around I-285 toward Langford Parkway. I was looking forward to going back to work. I loved my son, but I needed some adult interaction. Hell, who was I kidding? I needed a drink.

The past couple weeks had definitely taken its toll on me. With my grandmother's passing and Lincoln flipping out, I managed to miss the final fitting for my gown and still owed them my last payment. And now that same cheerful seamstress, who had been so anxious to help me before, currently saw me as a deadbeat bride who didn't pay her bills. It wasn't that I didn't have the money; I just couldn't bring myself to look at that gown—let alone, put it on and continue with the lie I'd created. It had become exhausting, and it was costing me more than just the four grand I'd put up for that damn dress.

There was a line snaking its way out the door, and the young guys working valet were scrambling around, trying to maintain order in the parking lot. I had them put my car off to the side, instead of the usual spot right up front. I didn't want and unwanted dents from people stumbling in and out of the club.

Once inside the club I absorbed the energy coming from the crowd. I needed all the help I could get tonight. I stopped and spoke to a few people who wanted to offer condolences for my grandmother then pressed my way deeper inside forcing smiles for some pictures for a couple local magazines and websites before I headed to the bathroom.

I wiggled through the crowd to try to wash my hands. I couldn't help but laugh to myself at the females gathered around the tiny sink applying an extra layer of gloss to already shiny lips or finger combing freshly woven hair. Everyone was putting on her best face in hopes of snagging that special someone.

On my way to check the bartenders, I made my way past the DJ booth. Raymond looked up when I made my way by and gave me a wink, causing an involuntary smile to spread across my face. I waved and winked in return.

"Good to have you back," Dionne said, smiling.

I smiled, leaning against the bar. "Thank you so much for holding it down while I was out." I looked around. "It's packed in here."

"I know. I'm glad too. I couldn't take another Saturday night like the last one. It was so slow; Raymond's tip out was horrible last weekend."

"Wow."

"And you know he wasn't happy."

I laughed. "I know he wasn't."

She nodded over her shoulder. "Your friend is waiting for you."

I stood on tiptoes and looked in the direction she'd just nodded. I laughed when I saw Mr. Lewis sitting in the corner. When he saw me, his face lit up with his somewhat toothless smile.

"He's been so lost without you."

"Aw, really? Nobody took care of him?"

She laughed and shook her head. "He didn't want anyone else. He kept coming to the bar for his drinks. He didn't want anyone serving him." She reached under the counter. "He left you this, though."

I took the envelope she held out and opened it. There was a twenty-dollar bill inside. "Oh my goodness. He's so sweet."

"If you say so." She turned and headed to a crowd that was forming on the other end of the bar. "He creeps me out."

I couldn't help but laugh at that.

After hugging and thanking Mr. Lewis, I made my rounds and checked on the bartenders and servers. I ended up helping one server with a birthday party, which was a good thing. I figured the busier I was the less time I had to think about what was or wasn't going on in my life at this point.

I dropped Cameron off with India on my way in to the club and checked on my mother. India didn't have much to say to me, and I wasn't exactly bursting at the seams to talk to her either. So we avoided each other the whole time I was in the house. I knew there was nothing she wouldn't do for Cameron so I knew there was no issue with me leaving him with her.

I was standing near the bar, talking to Si-Man, who was waiting for a radio commercial break to be over, when Dionne came up behind me and whispered in my ear.

"You got a visitor at the bar."

I turned around and checked the bar. From what I could see, the same people who were there a few moments ago were still there.

"Who? I don't see anybody."

She looked toward the bottom level bar. "Not this one, down there."

I looked and spotted him immediately. He was wearing all black, locs pulled back in a ponytail and his beard and goatee freshly shaped-up. Some random chick had already zoned in on him. I could tell from the look on his face that he wasn't interested in hearing what she had to say. And I really couldn't blame him. She had on a pair of too-tight jeans, and her stomach was spilling over the waistband. Her spiked blond hairstyle stood up on her tiny head, making it worse.

I stood there for a moment and contemplated making him suffer through the rest of the conversation.

Dionne nudged me with her shoulder. "Girl, you better go get his fine ass."

I rolled my eyes and made my way down the steps in his direction.

"What are you doing here?" I asked, walking up on him.

"Heard about this spot, and wanted to come check it out."

I leaned against the bar. "You don't strike me as the clubbing type."

He took a sip of the Corona he was holding. "I haven't heard from you. I wanted to check on you."

"Got a lot going on."

"I know. I haven't seen you since—"

I cut him off, "Yeah, I know."

I grabbed his arm and pulled him outside. I didn't need everyone in the club knowing my business. As friendly as they were, I knew they wouldn't hesitate to stand around being nosy, snap a picture and toss me up on some gossip blog the first chance they got.

The humid night clung to my skin and hair as I leaned against the railing, and he stood in front of me.

"I'm sorry about asking you not to come to my grandmother's funeral," I said.

"I understand. I know where you were coming from. But I have a confession."

"What's that?"

He smiled. "I was there."

I let out a laugh. "Where? I didn't see you."

"I'm a DEA agent. Hiding from you really isn't that hard." He laughed. "I had to pay my respects to your grandmother. She damn near raised me."

I nodded; then I looked out into the parking lot and finally fixed my eyes back on his.

"Being with you, spending time with you, has been nice, but . . ."

"But what?" he asked.

"We can't go back. Too much has happened."

"I'm not asking you to go back, Idalis, but we can't keep playing this push-and-pull game. Either we're friends, or we're not."

I rubbed my forehead. "Now you sound like India."

"Sounds like she knows what she's talking about."

I rolled my eyes, then stared off into the adjacent patch of woods next to the club.

"Look, all I'm asking you to do is snap out of whatever trance Lincoln's got you in and see him for what he is. You deserve better, and you know it."

"I guess better would be you?"

He shook his head. "I didn't say that."

"Exactly. I see your mouth moving, but you're not saying anything."

"Neither are you," he shot back.

The door to the club opened and a gush of cold air blew out along with small crowd of partygoers who were stumbling their way to the valet. One girl was clearly drunk and carrying one of her shoes in her hand. Her dress was barely securing her huge breasts, which were fighting against the thin material to get out. She limped around, giggling, as her friends held her up and tried to help her maintain some of her dignity.

"Ooh! He's fine!" she slurred, pointing at Trip. "Look at his eyes."

Her crowd of friends erupted in laughter. "Come on, Tiana, you so crazy!"

I grabbed the handle of the door before it closed.

"Look, I need to get back inside."

He held up his hands in defeat. "Fair enough. But would you please just think about what you're doing?"

"Good night, Trip."

I snatched the door open and made my way through the crowd. I did my best to hold back the tears until I made it to the bathroom stall.

I pushed the door closed and grabbed a wad of tissue from the roll of toilet paper. A few moments later I heard a bunch of "oohs and aahs" coming from the other side of the door.

"Damn! Who is you?" one woman asked.

"Hey, sexy, you looking for me?" another drunken voice asked.

At first the comments didn't register, and then it dawned on me what was going on.

Trip's voice made me cringe. "Idalis!" He knocked on the door to the stall.

"Oh my goodness. Are you kidding me? Get out of here!"

"I'm not leaving until you come out and talk to me."

A slurred voice chimed in. "Yeah, girrrrl. Come out here and talk to his fine ass."

I turned the lock and pushed the door open. The sight of him standing in the ladies' room was both comical and pitiful, all at the same time.

I just shook my head. "You know you got issues right?"

He cracked a smile. "You see what you got me doing? You got me up in the ladies room."

I couldn't help but smile. "Yes, and you're crazy."

His phone lit up and he pulled it from his hip. I watched his expression change from playful to serious.

"I gotta go."

"Everything okay?"

He nodded. "Yeah. It's Lenny. I gotta run. Call me later?"

I nodded, then watched him wade through the crowd of loud females who had gathered in the small bathroom to watch him make a spectacle of himself.

Dionne came in, looking confused. "Idalis, you okay?" She looked over her shoulder. "Did I just see Trip come out of here?"

I chuckled. "I'm fine. And yes, you did."

"You don't look fine."

I nodded my head, grabbed some fresh tissue from the roll of toilet paper, and wiped my eyes. "Yeah, I'm good."

"You sure? You want me to call your sister?"

"God no! I'm good." I flushed the wad of tissues away.

She stared at me for a second, and out of embarrassment I looked away.

"Idalis, seriously, what's going on?"

"Dionne, I wouldn't even know where to begin."

"Why don't you try?"

"The situation with me and Trip is complicated. Way more complicated than us just being best friends with a state's worth of distance between us."

She pulled some more tissue from the roll of toilet paper and passed it to me. "Idalis, I've known you and Trip for way too long, and one thing I can say is that he cares about you, and it's obvious you care about him. No, I take that back. It's obvious y'all are in love with each other. So why all of this back-and-forth?"

"Too much has happened."

Her face softened. "What could possibly have happened?"

I ignored her question. "I need to deal with Lincoln first anyway." I rubbed the bridge of my nose. "I need to end all of this the right way."

"Fuck him! Idalis, you have a supportive family, and you have friends who would be willing to help you get out of that situation."

I shook my head. "I have to think about Cam too, Dionne, not just me."

"That's exactly why you need to get away from him."

I nodded. "Yeah, I know. And I will."

"You sure you don't wanna go home?"

I forced a smile. "I can't. I owe Ray a Heineken. And you know he'll never let me live it down if I don't get him one."

That made her laugh a little, which, in turn, made me smile. "Yeah, you got a point."

After stopping by the crowded sink to clean up, I headed back out to the floor. Dionne slid me a glass of Merlot, which I happily took. I needed all the help I could get to relax and try to focus on how to get this monkey off my back.

I grabbed the glass and headed back to my office.

I called and talked to India and apologized for our mess. She was the last person I wanted to be fighting with. Mama was right; I was much stronger with her than without her. If there was anyone I didn't want to alienate, it was India. I needed her on my side in all of this. If I was gonna right my wrongs and push past this, I was gonna need all of the help and support I could get.

"Twin, I don't wanna fight with you either. I just want what's best for you that's all. And I know that Grammie would want you to be happy."

"I know," I said, as I sorted through purchase orders.

"I'm thinking about splitting with Linc."

She got quiet for a second, then she finally spoke. "If you're serious you know I got you, right?"

"Yeah, I'm serious," I said, fighting tears and trying to steady my voice. "This shit's not right, and I gotta get out. Some of the shit that he's done . . ." my voice trailed off. I didn't want to burden her with that right now.

"Well no worries, okay?" she assured, her shaky voice matching mine.

"No worries," I said.

"You need me to go by your house and grab you and Cam some stuff?"

I scratched my head. "No, I don't wanna do it like that. I'm gonna tell him."

"Idalis, he's a fool. He already hit you once. Do you think he's just gonna roll over and let you walk away."

"And you think he's gonna act any better if he comes home and I've packed up me and his son and left without telling him?"

She let out a sigh. "Yeah you got a point."

I stood up. "I'll see you when I get there and we'll figure this out then."

"Okay, I love you, Twin."

"I love you too, Twin."

The door had finally slowed down and some of my waitresses were starting to cash out and I ran a Heineken to the DJ booth for Raymond.

He took the bottle and smiled. "Thanks, sweetheart. I'm sorry to hear about your grandmother."

"Thanks, she's better off. She was in a lot of pain."

He looked over my shoulder toward the dance floor. "Here comes your boy."

I turned around and saw Linc making his way through the crowd. He stopped and spoke to a few people before making his way to the booth.

"What's up, Ray?"

Raymond gave him a head nod and put his headphones back on. I started toward the bar, with him on my heels. He followed me and ordered a Corona.

"What time you finished?" he asked.

"I don't know. Trying to be out of here by midnight."

His eyes stayed on the crowd, which was now trying to get coordinated enough to wobble all over the dance floor.

Si-Man's laugh-filled instructions poured from the speakers. "What's wrong wit y'all? Your *other* left." He laughed.

Raymond mixed the song back to the beginning, giving everyone a chance to get in sync.

The acid in my stomach was churning so much I thought it would dissolve me from the inside out. Linc was extremely agitated. He kept checking his phone, and his fidgeting was making me uneasy. His eyes kept darting around the crowd. Every once in a while, he'd look at the door. I couldn't tell if he was looking for someone or avoiding someone.

"What are you doing here? I thought you had to work." I finally asked.

He didn't respond. He just checked his phone again.

Now it was my turn to be agitated. "Lincoln, what's going on?"

He looked at me. "Look shawty, we need to go. We need to talk."

I looked at him like he was crazy. "I can't leave now. The radio station isn't done until midnight.

And my car is outside, anyway. You can go, and I'll meet you at the house."

He set his half-empty bottle on the bar and looked me directly in my eyes. "Hurry up, get your shit so we can get the hell outta here."

Before he could say anything else, I turned and headed back to the office. I paced around in the office for a few minutes, wasting time before flipping through a few invoices. They might as well have been in Chinese because I couldn't focus at all. My mind was strictly on trying to figure out how to leave without Lincoln.

Around eleven forty-five, I counted down my pull of the bartenders and tipped out for the DJ and stuck it in the safe before heading out to Dionne's station. She would do the final count-down and tip out when the club closed at three.

I noticed her heading toward the door, carrying a box of decorations.

"You gonna be okay?" She asked.

I nodded. "Yeah, I'll be okay." I tapped the side of the box. "What's this?"

"Stephanie is throwing her aunt a birthday party, and I'm borrowing these decorations."

I laughed. "Borrowing? And y'all are speaking now."

"Of course. I knew she'd call eventually." She smiled. "Come on, I'll walk out with you."

We moved toward the front door, stopping in the entranceway. Linc was already outside on his phone. The door swung open and a few people blew in with the warm night breeze.

Dionne's freshly detailed black Chevy Camaro sparkled under the lights of the parking lot, the running lights from the marquee bounced off the rims, making the car glow. She hit the remote on her key chain and the car's lights flashed its hello.

She slid the box onto the backseat. "You don't have to go with him. You know that, right?"

"Oh, I'm not. I'm about to get into my car and go to my mother's."

I handed her the keys the office and club.

"Why don't you come back in and wait for me," she suggested. "You can keep me company at the bar."

I looked over at Linc and for a moment I thought about taking her up on her offer, but I really wanted to get back to my mom's. I had a lot to sort out, and I needed to do it without Lincoln hovering over me.

"No, I'll be okay. Once I get back to my mom's, I'll be able to sort out the best way to handle this."

"Handle what?" she asked.

"I'm leaving. I don't wanna do this anymore."

She studied me for a moment, waited to see if I was joking or not. "You're serious?"

I blew out some air. "Yes. I'm gonna talk to India tonight. See what I can come up with."

She smiled. "I'm so glad."

We walked over to my car and hugged good night. I saw her eyes go to movement behind me; it wasn't long before I felt Lincoln come up behind me.

"We need to go," he insisted, totally disregarding Dionne. "Now."

She sucked her teeth. "Call me as *soon* as you get home."

She turned and headed back inside the club, leaving me standing there with him.

I hit the button on the remote and unlocked my car doors. "Lincoln, I'm not leaving my car here. I'm going to get Cameron and I will see you at home."

I shoved my phone into my purse and tossed it onto the front seat, getting ready to climb in my car, hoping he'd take the hint.

Instead, he reached around me and slammed the door closed.

I spun around and looked at him. "What the hell is wrong with you?"

"You think I'm playin' with you?" His eyes were intense as he stood in front of me.

I could feel the anger radiating off his body like heat from a fire causing my heart rate to double.

"You know what, you're acting real crazy right now, and I ain't in the mood for it."

"Ain't in the mood for what?" he demanded through clenched teeth.

"I'm not doing this here." I tried to turn around to open my car door, but he held the door closed.

I stood there and shook my head in disbelief. "You know what. This is over, Linc. I'm *done*. I'm taking Cameron and I'm moving in with my mother."

I tried to push past him to head back in the club, but he grabbed my arm spinning me around and causing me to drop my keys.

"Let me go!"

He lifted up his shirt, showing me the butt of his Glock tucked in his waistband. "Get in the fuckin' truck, Idalis."

I kept my eyes on the glass doors that led inside 404 hoping that Dionne would come back out, but she never did.

Linc stayed behind me, waiting as I climbed up in his truck then slammed the door closed. Before I had a chance to clear my clouded vision he was merging his truck onto 285 speeding north.

"Slow down!" I screamed, as the outer perimeter flew by the tinted windows. My plea was met with a backhand that caused my head to slam against the window.

His dash glowed along with the phone in his armrest. He snatched his phone up. "What!"

I watched intently trying to get some sort of feel for what the hell was going on, but he wasn't saying anything and *unkown* flashed across the dashboard screen.

"So can you do it or not?" he snapped at whoever was on the other end.

He got quiet as he listened intently to whoever was on the other end.

My blood was coursing through my veins so fast I could hear it pounding in my ears. My head was pounding from hitting the window, I reached up and touched the spot to see if it was bleeding. It wasn't but I could feel the warmth of my blood trickling down the side of my face. I reached up and dabbed at it with the back of my hand.

A scowl spread across his face. "I'll do it myself then. You just let me know when he leaves."

He tossed his phone back in the armrest.

"Do what Linc?"

"Take care of Supercop once and for all."

Chapter Twenty-seven

Trip

The text I got telling me to come to the hospital had me on edge.

My mind was racing faster than my truck could slice through the soggy city streets. A wave of showers came through leaving behind humid air quicker than a rapper could wife a stripper.

I caught a glimpse of myself in the rearview mirror. I was doing exactly what I wasn't supposed to be doing, getting caught up with Idalis. She definitely wasn't the same person I'd grown up with, and she definitely didn't trust me the way she used to. There was a time when she would tell me things that India didn't even know. I knew that her relationship with Lincoln wasn't the picture-perfect story that everyone thought it was, long before the first bruise showed up on her brown skin.

But there was nothing I could do, if she didn't want my help.

I didn't know what to expect when I got to Phil's room, but I knew I needed to brace myself for anything. No matter how healthy he was a gunshot wound is still a gunshot wound.

When I bent the corner to the hall leading to Phil's room, I was met by Lenny and a crowd of agents and I immediately thought the worst.

Lenny read the expression on my face and calmed my nerves. "Phil's okay, but we got a bigger problem."

He turned and started walking toward Phil's room. Instinctively, the other agents and I followed. We all filed into the room. Commander Harris was talking to Phil, who was propped up, and two APD officers, who were standing next to the bed. Their conversation looked serious.

The intense look on everyone's face put me on edge. There were no smiles, nothing jovial about the fact that my partner up and talking after all this time.

I didn't like that.

I directed my attention toward Phil. "About time your lazy ass woke up," I joked, trying to lighten the atmosphere.

Phil turned, looked at me, and smiled. "About time you got here."

"What's up, partner? How you feeling?"

"Like I been hit by a truck."

Lenny spoke up. "Doctor says he's gonna be fine. Should be outta here soon."

I laughed. "Oh, is that right?"

"Damn right," Phil answered. "Did you really think I was gonna let you corrupt a new partner?"

Everyone in the room chuckled.

"Look, man, I'm really sorry about not being there for you," I started to say.

"Partner, I need you to table that shit for right now. I can kick your ass about that later," Phil retorted with a somber tone.

Lenny's facial expression suddenly changed too. It went from humorous to serious in the blink of an eye. "Spencer, we got a hit on the sketch and some evidence pulled from the last scene."

I looked at him, waiting for him to fill me in.

Commander Harris spoke up this time. "One of the men found dead at the scene was an APD officer, Nathan Daniels."

"Undercover?" I asked.

He shook his head. "No. His girlfriend worked at headquarters," he said.

I dropped my head and let out a sigh. "Let me guess, in the clerk's office."

"She was found dead this morning along with two others, we believe to be connected with the breach," the commander said.

"All signs point to it being a hit," Lenny continued explaining.

I scanned the room. There were too many eyes on me. My body was hot.

Still too much tension for what was supposed to be good news.

There was something they weren't saying.

I felt the muscles in my arms tighten.

"What aren't y'all telling me?"

Lenny took a deep breath. "Briscoe."

"What about him?" I asked, fire slowly rising up and lapping around my ears.

"He's been flipping the coke from the Four Horseman bust," Phil said.

I stood there for a second. I felt like I'd missed something. "What did you just say?"

He proceeded to go into the details of what went down at the bust. The more he talked, the angrier I got. I paced the floor as I tried to digest what he was saying, but it wasn't sitting right. I stopped at the window and stared out into the traffic going up and down the street.

I turned around and faced him. "Man, are you sure?"

"Hell *yeah,* I'm sure. His punk ass shot me."

"You mean to tell me all this fucking time—" I couldn't even finish my sentence.

Commander Harris cut me off. "We already got officers out looking for him to pick him up."

"Trip you should've told me what was going on with you and Briscoe," Lenny scolded.

I looked at Lenny. "Would you have taken me off the case if I had?"

Lenny nodded slowly. "Probably."

"Then there's your answer."

Lenny spoke; his tone was sympathetic. "I just sent a team to your friend Idalis's house."

I made a break for the door.

"They better find him before I do."

Chapter Twenty-eight

Idalis

"Lincoln, would please put the gun down."

I sat on the edge of the couch and watched him pace the living room floor. I kept eyeing the hall that led to the front door, trying to psyche myself up to make a run for it, but fear had me bolted to the couch. Every time I thought about how I had taken my phone out of my pocket and put it in my purse, I wanted to shoot myself.

"You know, Idalis, this shit didn't have to go down like this."

"I never said—"

"Let's keep it real shawty, you don't have to say shit," he shot back. "Your actions are enough."

His voice boomed, making me jump.

The sudden movement caused the cut on the side of my face to hurt. I reached up and touched the bruise I'd received in the truck, on the way over here. It had stopped bleeding, but it hurt like hell.

"Why are you doing this?"

He stopped his pacing and stared at me like I'd just insulted him. "You already know the answer to that, stop playin' stupid, it's startin' to get under my fuckin' skin for real."

Anger mixed with adrenaline took over and I jumped to my feet.

"You're the one who has been acting possessed! Since we putting it out there, let's keep it real. I've been walking around on fucking eggshells ever since Trip got back in town. It's like you don't even like me and I don't even know what I did! But you want me to believe you love me? Fuck you, Linc!"

This time it was his fist that caught my jaw, sending me to the floor. I pulled myself up on the couch just in time for him to reach down and pull my hair, yanking my head backward.

I swallowed the scream in my throat.

He bent down and got in my face. "You know what? You right. I don't like you, 'cause I don't fuckin' *trust* you! You been layin' up under me, fuckin' me, plannin' this bogus-ass weddin', and you don't want this shit."

"I just wanted us to push the date back until things settled down that's all, Linc. I never said I didn't want to marry you," I cried.

He tossed me back onto the couch and stood there, glaring at me. Just when I thought he was gonna hit me again, his phone rang. I froze as he put it to his ear, never taking his eyes off me.

"Yeah."

I watched as he listened to the person on the other end. He was emotionless. Nothing gave me an indication of what the conversation consisted of, one way or the other.

"He just left?" He looked at his watch. "I'll call you back." He slid his phone back into the holster.

"Showtime."

My eyes darted to the hallway, then back to him. He stepped into my line of sight, but I looked down at the floor, refusing to look at him.

So he stooped down. Got eye to eye with me.

"What? You gon' try to run?" He looked over his shoulder to the hallway then back to me. "Go 'head and see how far you get."

That's when I did look up at him. He looked like the same person, but his eyes were emotionless, like someone had flipped a switch and turned him off. Yeah, he'd always been hard and at times unemotional, but I figured that just came with the job, but now . . . Now it was like he was a shell. Like he was being manipulated by remote control. His anger was replaced with malice, and he was completely out of control.

The house phone rang and both of us looked in its direction. He stood up and holstered his gun. "Let it ring."

"I . . . It's probably India. I was supposed to pick up Cameron."

"I don't give a damn! I said, let it ring."

He walked to the front door, then made his way back into the living room. Before he could get back down the hall good, the phone started ringing again.

"Lincoln, please. If I don't call her, she's gonna start to worry."

"You know, Idalis, I like how you do a playa dirty, then wanna cry like you didn't bring this shit on yourself."

"Lincoln, we been together since college. How can you say that?"

He sat on the arm of the chair. "Man, get the fuck outta here with that. You pissed that history away a long time ago."

"So if you've felt like this, why didn't you just leave? Why stay and make both of us miserable?"

"Because it only seemed fair."

"Fair? What do you mean *fair?*" I stood on wobbly legs as he made his way back toward me. He got in my face; he was so close that I could see the flare of his nostrils. I could feel his breath on my face.

"Did you really think I was gonna walk away so you could run yo' ass to Trip?"

I took a step back and let that bounce around in my head for a moment.

"Why would you think I would run to Trip? Lincoln, we were getting married. We have a son together."

He cocked his head to the side. "You sure 'bout that?"

My mouth went dry and I felt light-headed. I stood with my eyes fixed on him. I wasn't sure what direction to go with this conversation. I just knew whatever direction we went in, it wasn't going to be good.

He raised his eyebrows, leaned in a little closer. "What's wrong, Idalis? Cat got your tongue?"

I sank down on the couch. "I don't know what you're talking about."

He pulled his gun from its holster and walked over to me. My heart raced as I prepared for another blow. Instead, he crouched down in front of me and tapped me on my knee with the barrel. "Speak up. I can't hear you."

Tears rolled down my face. I could barely find my voice. "I don't know what you're talking about, Linc."

"So you tryin' to tell me, you don't remember fuckin' Trip the night of his pop's funeral? You really want me to believe you don't remember how you didn't know who got you pregnant, so you decided to lie all these years?"

We locked eyes.

Suddenly I couldn't breathe.

Chapter Twenty-nine

Trip

With sirens blaring, I weaved in and out of traffic, making my way downtown, almost running down some club goers who were trying to cross in the middle of Peachtree. I pulled out my phone and dialed Idalis, but I didn't get an answer.

Just as I was about to toss my phone onto the passenger seat, it vibrated against my hand. Without looking at the display, I answered.

"Spencer."

"Trip, it's Dionne."

She was sobbing into the phone. "What's wrong Dionne?"

"Idalis is missing."

"What do you mean?"

Her voice faded into the background as she yelled out to someone in the club telling them that she was on the phone with me, before she came back to the conversation. "Earlier tonight

Linc came by here and was acting really strange."
Her voice still shaking. "I told her not to leave. I
told her to wait for me."

"Dionne, calm down and tell me what happened?"

She took a deep breath. "He was acting strange
and he wanted her to leave. She promised she
wouldn't go with him. She said she was going to
break up with him and go to her mom's.

"But when I came outside"—she started crying
harder—"her car was outside, and she wasn't.
Her keys were on the ground next to the car, and
she was . . . She was gone."

Her sobs made anything else that she was
trying to say to me incomprehensible.

"Dionne," I said, trying to get her to focus on
my voice. "Dionne, did she say anything else
when she was there?"

"Um, no. She just kept going on and on about
too much time having passed, and not being able
to fix things with you."

"Fix things with me," I mumbled to myself.
"Okay, have you tried calling her?"

"Her phone was in her purse in the car. Trip,
I'm scared. Please find her."

"Have you talked to her mom?"

"No you're the first person I called."

I didn't want her mother having to deal with this right now, not after just burying their grandmother.

"A'ight, don't call her yet. Her mom don't need this right now. I'll call you back when I find out something."

I disconnected the call and cut across International Boulevard. Merging onto I-75/85 south, I sped toward a house, over in Cascade.

A house that was full of secrets.

Secrets that not even I couldn't imagine.

I jumped off I-285 and headed down Cascade. My phone lit up on the seat next to me and I snatched it up.

"Spencer."

"What's up, Supercop?"

My jaw clenched and my blood ran hot. "This shit ends now, Briscoe."

"This shit ends, when I say it ends, pot'na."

"Where's Idalis?"

"That bitch right here. I guess you on your way to save the day, huh?" He let out a sarcastic laugh. "I should've put a bullet in your pot'na's head when I had the chance. Then I should've put one in yours in that conference room."

"We was coming for you eventually, you was already fuckin' up."

"That's what you think."

"Let me talk to Idalis."

"She's busy." I heard some rustling on the other end before what sounded like glass breaking and her screams.

My heart ached with every slap I heard come across the line. I hit the gas and sped across Fairburn Road, passing Cascade Crossing. A moment later he was back on the line.

"You still wanna talk to her?"

"You better hope they get to you before I do—"

"Oh, you think just because you fucked her, you got claim to her?"

My grip tightened on the steering wheel as I bent the corner onto New Hope on two wheels. I had tunnel vision as I blew threw a light at the Camp Creek intersection. "Come on, man. Damn! Don't make me do this."

"Do what you gotta do, Supercop."

"Is that what this is about? Huh? You jealous of a fuckin' badge?"

"I ain't jealous of nothin'. You ain't got *shit!* As far as this bitch, Idalis, you want her? Come get her!"

"You have until I get there, to turn yourself in."

"And if I don't?" he taunted.

I responded through clenched teeth, "I'm gonna arrest you *myself.*"

He disconnected the call.

I hit speed dial and called Lenny. He answered on the first ring.

"Spencer, where are you?"

"Lenny he has Idalis."

He barked some instructions to someone there with him before coming back to me. "I know, we already got units setting up outside the house."

"I'm two minutes away."

"Spencer, you need to let us handle this one."

The house and the units came into sight when I bent corner. The flashing lights pierced the darkness of the otherwise quiet street; but my mind was on Idalis.

"Lenny, he made this personal, not me."

He let out a sigh. "I know, but we can't have you flying off on this one. It has to be by the book, or he walks. You know that."

"He shot my fucking partner, Lenny!"

Before he had a chance to try to continue trying to reason with me, and piss me off any further, I hung up.

My truck screeched to a halt next to the SWAT team's truck in front of the house on Fitzgerald Place. I threw it in park and jumped out and started for the house. I pushed by all the wide-eyed agents and officers, who were huddled around, undoubtedly trying to figure out the best way to handle this. Tension always ran high in these types of situations. When it involved a fellow officer, however, that definitely changed the rules. In all of my years in law enforcement, I'd dealt with more situations involving officers who had snapped than I liked to admit.

"Trip, don't," Lenny called out.

I stopped in my tracks and turned around. Lenny and another agent were rushing toward me.

"You can't go in there. We don't know what we're dealing with."

"Oh, I know *exactly* what we dealing with."

I stared at the front of the house, looking for any type of movement coming from behind the windows. Anything to let me know that Idalis was okay.

I listened as Lenny gave me a rundown. "We have a perimeter set up. We're trying to establish some sort of communication. He's not going anywhere, Trip."

My cynical brain was in overdrive.

I scanned the cars and the people who had started to gather on what otherwise would've been a quiet, suburban street in southwest Atlanta. Obviously, whatever had set Lincoln off ran much deeper than the regular "cop gone bad" scenario.

He'd made this personal for a reason, and I had to figure out what it was before something happened to Idalis.

Lieutenant Jackson, with SWAT, walked over and extended his hand. I shook it and waited to hear what he had to say.

"We're trying to get a line in there. He won't answer his cell phone or the house phone. We have Georgia Power on the way out here to cut power and hopefully flush him out."

"Flush him out, or piss him off." I shook my head.

"We're doing everything we can to defuse this as peacefully as we can," he continued.

"Well, cutting off the power and trying to have a heart-to-heart with him ain't the answer," I snapped.

A look of agitation spread across his face. "So you think kicking in the front door is, Agent Spencer?"

His authoritative attitude was annoying the hell out of me. "No, I think APD keeping a shorter leash on their fucking officers and clerks from the beginning is really the best answer, Lieutenant Jackson."

"So tell me, Agent Spencer, how would you handle it, then?"

"I would've never let the shit get this far, in the first place."

Lenny stepped in between us. "Trip, that's enough!"

An APD officer came running up, getting directly in the middle of our heated discussion. "We got him on the phone. He's asking for Agent Spencer."

We all stood there for a second. I watched as Lenny dropped his head and let out a sigh heavy with disapproval.

"Trip . . ."

Before he could say anything else, I was at my truck, securing my vest. Lenny was on my heels trying to talk me out of it, and Lieutenant Jackson was helping to secure me into the only thing that would stand between me and whatever bullet Lincoln had etched my name on. I tucked a smaller compact Glock 19 in the waistband at my back and shoved my 9 mm in my holster.

"Trip, this isn't a good idea. Let another agent handle this."

"I'm just trying to get you back to New Orleans, Lenny," I assured.

"This isn't a game—"

My eyes met Lenny's. "Let me do what I do."

I knew he was worried, but I didn't give a damn at this point. My only concern was Idalis; and right now, I needed to get her out of that house. My cell phone vibrated against my hip.

I snatched it off and answered. "Spencer."

"If anyone walks through that door but you, a bullet is goin' in her head. You feel me?"

"If you want me, then put Idalis on the fucking phone."

I heard a soft scream before her trembling voice came across the line. "T-Trip."

My body tensed with the sound of her voice. I closed my eyes and took a deep breath. I could feel everyone's eyes on me; it was starting to fuck with me.

"Baby girl, are you okay?"

She sniffed and cleared her throat a little. "Yes. I'm worried about my sister. I was supposed to go get Cameron—"

Before she could finish, he took the phone from her.

"That's enough. You got what you wanted, now give me what I want."

The line went dead.

Chapter Thirty

Idalis

Lincoln paced the living room floor, stopping every once in a while to look toward the door. His phone was beeping and vibrating on his hip, but he moved like a man who was focused on nothing other than what was going on right now.

"What happened to you?" I asked.

He stopped in his tracks. "You happened to me."

A flash of tension shot up my neck and into my head. I reached up and rubbed my temple. "I'm sorry, Lincoln. I never meant for any of this to happen."

"So let me get this straight. Are you sayin' you didn't mean to fuck Trip and lie to me about it? Or are you sayin', you didn't mean to lay up with me the last few years, like shit was all good, when you knew *damn* well shit wasn't right!"

"Okay. Yes, I slept with Trip! But that is *not* a reason for you to do the shit you're doing!"

He glared at me, his body projecting anger and disgust. In a flash he picked up a picture off the mantel and pitched it at me. I managed to roll out of the way, just in time for it to hit the wall behind me, raining down glass all over my head and shoulders.

I heard his gun cock.

"Do you honestly think I won't kill you just because you fucked Trip into a hero complex and he's outside trying to rescue you?"

I sat there and stared at the man whom I had agreed to marry, and had promised my happily-ever-after to. I listened as he painted a picture of a woman full of deceit and lacking a heart. A woman who had realized a moment in time had swollen into something much more, but she had done absolutely nothing to address it.

A small bubble of compassion rose in my chest as I looked up at him.

He was a man at the end of an emotional ledge—one that I had obviously pushed him out onto. And now Trip was outside, ready to risk life and limb to ride in here on a white horse and save me. And for what? Hell, I didn't even know at this point. I'd gotten pretty good at barricading myself in my nice, cushy fantasy world. And now that world had turned on me in the worst way.

"Lincoln, please. Just let me explain."

Suddenly there were three sharp hits on the door and his head whipped in that direction. "Hold that thought." He looked back to me. "We got company."

My pulse raced, causing blood to pound against the confines of my veins. I half expected to blow a vessel in my brain at any moment. And honestly, I would've welcomed a stroke at that point.

Lincoln moved to the entranceway to the hallway and pointed his gun at the door. My mouth went dry and my hands began to shake uncontrollably.

This can't be happening, I thought. *This is* not *happening.*

My heart skipped a beat when I heard the chime of my alarm system signaling the door had been opened, and Trip had stepped into this nightmare.

The sound of his footsteps coming down the marble hall echoed through the house. I ran my tongue across the cut on my bottom lip. The bleeding had stopped, and now it was throbbing, and my lip was starting to swell.

Trip's broad frame came into my line of sight.

He wore the anger on his face like a Halloween mask.

He and Lincoln stood there for a second staring each other down. Lincoln was an inch or two shorter, but both of them were full of rage. The fire coming from them threatening to send this house and everything around it up in flames.

"Go 'head and toss me that gun Supercop," Linc instructed.

Never taking his eyes off Linc, Trip pulled his gun out of his holster and popped the clip out. He cocked it, causing the lone bullet in the chamber to fly out. It hit the carpet with a thud before he dropped the gun next to it.

Linc walked over and bent down like he was going to pick up Trip's gun but instead he stood back up, hauled off and punched Trip in jaw causing Trip to stumble into the wall.

My hand covered my mouth stifling the scream that tried to escape.

"I owed your punk ass that one."

Trip straightened up, touched his lip and looked down at his hand for any evidence of blood.

"Did that make your bitch-ass feel better?" he asked.

The house phone rang out, catching all our attention. I swallowed a mouthful of nothing and attempted to speak.

"That's India. I know it. Would you please let me answer it?" I begged.

Trip kept his eyes on Lincoln during my plea. The way his jaw was flexing, I knew he wanted to pounce on him.

Lincoln's eyes met mine and he kept them there, waiting for the phone to stop ringing. I fought my tears, which were trying to force their way out. I didn't want my sister here; I knew that she wasn't going to allow too many more phone calls to go unanswered.

He walked over and sat down on the arm of our oversized chair. With his gun still in his hand, he crossed his arms against his chest. "So, Trip, how does it feel knowing you fucked another man's woman right out from under him?"

He clenched his fists. "Lincoln, I'm not about to have a showdown with you like two kids in a fucking cafeteria. You trying to tell me you shot my partner over some bullshit?"

My hand shot up, covering my mouth and silencing the scream lodged in my throat. My body shook as waves of sobs fought to get out.

"W—what is he talking about, Lincoln? Y—you shot Phil?"

Trip took a step closer to both of us causing Linc to stand to his feet. I took solace in the fact that he was tucked safely into his Kevlar vest.

Suddenly I wished I had one.

"Lincoln, this is between us. Let Idalis go. You got what you wanted. Leave her out of this."

"Can't do that. 'Cause without her this little reunion wouldn't be possible." He positioned himself in the middle of the living room, blocking my line of sight to the hallway, standing between Trip and me.

"Look, you and I both know that it's not gonna be long before they kick that door in and put a bullet in your head. Is that what you want? You want your son to know his father went out like a punk," Trip asked.

Lincoln started laughing. "You worried about what *my* son thinks?"

He aimed his Glock at Trip.

I jumped to my feet. "No, Linc, don't!" I had screamed.

The phone rang again.

Its intermittent ringing was starting to mimic the ticking of a time bomb—a constant reminder of how out of control this situation was about to become.

"What, Idalis? Huh? You don't want Trip to know that you ain't what you claim to be?"

Trip looked at me. "What is he talking about, Idalis? What the fuck is going on?"

I opened my mouth, but nothing came out. I stood there for a second. Jaw gaping. Eyes fixed on Trip. I closed my mouth and looked down to the floor.

"Somebody better answer me," Trip demanded.

Again . . . the phone rang.

I looked up just in time to see Lincoln pull an envelope out of his back pocket. Trip never took his eyes off me. I looked at the folded wad of paper. My mind raced at what my heart already knew was inside.

In one swift motion Lincoln pitched the paper in my direction, never taking his eyes off Trip. I felt sweat bead up and run down the center of my back.

"Read it!" Lincoln yelled out. His voice echoed through the living room, making me jump.

Trip's eyes bounced back and forth between the two of us.

Confusion was etched all over his face.

My hands fumbled with the envelope and its contents.

Again.

The phone rang.

Chapter Thirty-one

Trip

Idalis looked at me, a look of regret and despair washed over her face as she started to read:

"The alleged father, Lincoln N. Briscoe, is excluded as being the father of the child, Cameron Allen Briscoe. For eight different genetic systems analyzed with the polymerase chain reaction, the alleged father, Lincoln N. Briscoe, failed to match the obligate paternal allele present in the child, Cameron A. Briscoe."

I listened as she read the words, but I didn't hear them. They rolled around in my head until they hit on something and finally registered. Bells and whistles started going off like I'd just gotten the high score in a pinball game. But I knew immediately from the tear-filled expression on Idalis's face, this wasn't a game.

Rage rode my body like a freight train and I felt myself losing control.

"Still think she's perfect?" Linc asked.

His attitude was more than I wanted to deal with. I swear I wanted to shoot him, just to shut him up. I broke the stare I was holding with Idalis and looked at him.

"How long have you known this?"

"Known what? That you fucked my girl the weekend of your father's funeral? Or that she had been trying to pass your seed off as mine?"

"That's not true!" Idalis screamed out.

He turned to her. "Oh, it's not? Then explain what you're holding in your hand.

As he fussed with Idalis, I took a slight step to my right, watched as she fidgeted where she was standing.

I forced myself to see past her swollen lip and red, tear-filled eyes.

I fought the urge to run to her and wrap my arms around her.

Instead, I tried to give her an out.

"Baby girl, look at me."

She looked up and our eyes met as tears streamed down her face.

"Tell me *something*. 'Cause right there's a lot of fucking talking going on but I'm not hearing shit."

"I had an idea," she said, barely above a whisper.

"An idea? Why didn't you say something?" I asked.

She averted her eyes. "I didn't know how."

That answer pissed me the fuck off. I wanted to walk out of that house and leave her there with his crazy ass and never look back.

I wanted to forget that I ever knew her.

But I couldn't. Our fate was sealed almost four years ago.

For the first time in our lives we'd allowed our friendship to turn into something more the night of my father's funeral when Idalis came to sit with me at the hotel. She knew I refused to go to the funeral and shed tears for a man who'd gotten enough from me already and she stayed with me and never denied me anything, even, a night of lovemaking we neither regretted but agreed never to mention again.

The next morning, I cleared out of my room and was back in New Orleans before my father's body was cold in the ground and she went home to Linc. That was almost four years ago.

Cameron was just over three.

I turned my attention back to Lincoln. "So you been holding on to this all this time? What the fuck is wrong with you?"

"You're what's wrong with me."

"Don't blame your shit on me!" I growled through clenched teeth. "This ain't a fucking game, Briscoe! You fucking with people's lives."

He smirked. "Fuck outta here with that shit man, you don't give a damn about her! If you did you wouldn't have fucked her and rolled up outta here like you did.

"You would've manned the fuck up and stayed and fought for her ass, but instead you *got* the ass you been wanting since grade school and left."

"When did you get this test done?" I asked.

"About a month after he was born." He smirked at Idalis. "One of those afternoons when I told Idalis she could have some "mommy" time. Me and little man took a trip downtown to visit my friend in the forensic lab."

Idalis was sobbing so hard she could barely speak, "W—Why didn't you just s-say something?"

Linc rushed toward her and pulled her up by her neck. I fought the urge to pounce on him, at least not yet; not while he had that gun on her.

"That was all you needed to go runnin' off to be with his ass." He tossed her back on the couch. "You think I don't know how you feel about him? I've known that shit since college."

I dropped my head. Emotions rushed at me so fast. . . . I didn't know which one to address first.

A son.

I had a son.

The house phone rang. A few moments later the phone on my hip vibrated. I'd been dealing with that dance since I'd been in the house. I figured it was either Idalis's sister or Lenny.

This shit needed to end, now.

I gave Lincoln a quick once-over. Just like me, his Kevlar was secured around his chest. Other than the Glock, he kept intermittently pointing at me; I spied another gun tucked in the waistband behind his back. When he wasn't paying attention, I'd already moved to my right, getting out of his direct line of fire and clearing the entryway to the hall.

Fire rose in my chest.

I taunted him, made him focus his anger on me instead of her. "So because I laid pipe to your girl you decide to start shaking down dealers and knocking off people to make yourself feel like a man?"

He looked up and gave me a sly grin. "Hey, I ain't kill nobody pot'na. That dude Geech was outta control and all you got on me is a bunch of hearsay from some shady pushers lookin' to catch a deal."

"What's your defense for shooting my partner, other than stupidity?"

"Aye man, I was just a cop trying to maintain his position in a bust gone wrong."

He cracked a smile.

That was too much for me at that point.

The phone rang again and Idalis looked toward the kitchen.

Wide-eyed and frantic she looked up at me.

In that moment we were two scared kids.

And it was time for me to sneak her out of the house safely.

I took a breath.

And gave her a wink.

She made a break for the door, catching Lincoln off guard. When he spun around to reach for her, I snatched the gun from behind my back and popped a bullet in his leg, causing both of them to tumble to the carpet, and making him drop his gun.

I kicked the gun out of the way as Idalis scrambled to her feet and headed toward the front door. I saw him about to go for the gun behind his back and pointed my Glock at his head.

"*Please* give me a reason!"

The gunfire caused the house to flood with agents and officers. All of them with guns drawn.

"Spencer!" Lenny called out.

"In here!"

Lincoln lay there for a moment, glaring at me, before he slowly pulled his hand from behind his back and tossed the gun in my direction. It landed on the carpet, near one of the agents, with a soft thud, setting off something inside me. I tucked my gun behind my back and hit his jaw so hard—I'm surprised my hand didn't break.

I got in two more blows before being pulled off him for the second time in as many weeks.

Lenny pushed me toward the front door. "That's enough, Spencer!"

They pounced on him and started cuffing him. I heard his rights being read just as I approached the front door.

"This shit ain't over, Supercop! You'll see me again! Believe that!" he called out to me.

Without looking back I answered, "Looking forward to it, Lieutenant Briscoe."

I stepped out into the moist night air and took a deep breath. It was that time of night when yesterday passes off the baton to tomorrow. Usually, we're all asleep when the hand-off happens, and are lucky enough to wake to a new day of sun and possibilities.

Not this night.

The lights from the ambulance lit up the night sky.

Neighbors were gathering outside; some snapping pictures on cell phones while others positioned themselves trying to get a glimpse of what had disturbed their peace. News vans were coming from all directions trying to be the first to break the story. My phone vibrated and I pulled it out.

It was Trinity.

"Trip, what is going on?" She was frantic. "Dionne has been calling me and India texted me twice and I've been blowing up your phone. Are you okay?"

"I'm good. Where's Mama?"

"Asleep."

"Good."

"What's going on Trip? Is Idalis okay?"

At that moment I looked up and saw Idalis sitting on the back of the ambulance. An EMT was tending to her, and Dionne was huddled next to her. I moved toward them, keeping my eyes on Idalis. She looked up when she saw me coming.

"She's fine. Trin, I'll be by there in the morning, a'ight?"

"Okay. Love you."

"Love you too."

Just as I stepped onto the street, India pulled up. I stopped dead in my tracks as she hustled to get out of the car. I watched her open the back door and unbuckle Cameron from his car seat.

She pulled his tiny, sleeping body out and headed toward her sister, causing me to change direction and head back to my truck. This was too much for me to deal with right now. It was something that didn't need to be done in front of Cameron.

I opened the door to the truck and glanced at Idalis. The EMT was securing a bandage to her head, but her eyes were still on me, pleading for understanding and sympathy.

Two things that I couldn't summon for her right now.

As bad as I wanted to go to her, I couldn't.

Instead, I jumped in my truck and sped off into the night.

Chapter Thirty-two

Idalis

"India, just let it go."

I tried my best to get comfortable on the couch in my mother's living room. Cameron was laying on my chest sleep and his body was generating heat and making me uncomfortable. There were boxes of things stacked in the hall and in the corners of the small room. My life had been reduced to what was in those boxes, or rather, what the Feds let me take out of the house.

The investigation into Lincoln prompted them to seize a lot of things, including our home and my club. Luckily, my car was in my name and I had proof that I was making payments out of my own account, or they would've taken that too. Thanks to a good attorney and a word from Trip, I wasn't held accountable for anything that he'd done. But that didn't help the fact that I was now one of the many homeless people in Atlanta.

"Look, I know he's still here."

I rolled my eyes and looked up at her. "You know this how?"

"Dionne told me. She saw him at the J.R. Crickets, the one off Camp Creek. Phil got out of the hospital last week."

"And what does that mean? He's here and hasn't called me, so why should I call him?"

She put her hands on her hips. "You can't be serious. After what you did? After what Lincoln's crazy ass did? Hell, I can almost see why he is staying away from you."

After getting his gunshot wound treated, Lincoln was discharged into police custody almost three weeks ago. He'd been calling asking me to come by the hospital and see him, but I just couldn't bring myself to do it. Plus Dionne and India had threatened my life if I went anywhere near him. Once he got booked into the jail someone slipped him a cell phone, which was making it easy for him to aggravate the hell out of me. While he waited for trial, the threatening calls started coming and I knew that until he was tried, he was gonna make my life miserable. And the fact that he was in isolation gave him plenty of time to make all the calls he wanted. I threatened to report that he had a phone, but he just laughed and told me that he'd fuck another female CO and have another cell phone before the charge hit his file.

"Look, I understand where you're coming from. Just give me some time."

"Time for what? You've had long enough. And now that what you've been unsure about all these years is confirmed you just wanna sit on your ass and do nothing."

"Just because he knows doesn't change anything. I'm sure all he cares about is going back to New Orleans and putting this behind him."

"How do you know that, if you haven't talked to him? And what about Cameron? You're being selfish, Idalis."

"Whatever, India."

"Did you see him when you went to take the paternity test?"

I shook my head.

"No. He had already done his part and left before Cameron and I got there."

Trip wasted no time pulling strings and dumping court papers into my lap requesting his own set of paternity tests be done. I guess he needed to see it in black and white on his own terms. So I took my baby downtown and let them swab his cheek and mine. I told him that the test was so Santa could make sure he was the real Cameron. He just giggled and went along with the test without a problem.

She sucked her teeth. "So what now? Y'all just gonna avoid each other altogether? That's real smart."

I rolled my eyes. "What are you gonna do? Tell on me?" I shifted on the couch, trying not to wake Cameron. "Take Cam upstairs for me and go away, India."

I didn't need to look at her face to know she was pissed. She scooped my baby up off my chest and the next sound I heard was the front door opening as I rolled over and started flipping channels.

A few minutes later I heard the door open and close again and India appeared in the doorway to the living room.

"India, I'm not in the mood to argue with you. Would you please . . ."

I looked up and the expression she had on her face was disturbing. She stood there, holding a certified letter in her hand. "Idalis, the mailman just came. This is for you."

I sat up and stared at the certified letter she was holding.

She asked, "Do you want me to open it?"

I nodded absentmindedly, then watched as she ripped into the paper and pulled out the wad of thick documents.

I couldn't even bring myself to look at them, so I stood up and walked to the entertainment center. I focused on a picture of Cameron, willed that envelope and its contents spontaneously combust in her hands. I turned around and watched as my sister's eyes scanned the document.

"Just spit it out."

She took a deep breath and spoke. "There's a court date set for two weeks from today. He's asking for joint custody."

I let out a sigh.

The acknowledgment of paternity was just to put it on paper, make it legal in the eyes of everyone involved; custody was a sucker punch to me. I wanted to call and cuss him out, but I couldn't, because he was right, and I was wrong.

India flipped through a few more pages. "It says here that he is willing to come to an agreement out of court with a mediator. But if you aren't willing to sit down with him and talk, he is going to go forward with the suit."

"He's just doing this because he's mad."

She tossed the papers onto the couch. "Don't even get me started on that."

"You made it perfectly clear that you are on his side."

"It's not about sides but"—she motioned toward the papers—"this is not going to go away."

"Obviously."

I sank down on the couch and closed my eyes. I had played the scenario, over and over again, in my head; only in my version it involved him being loving and understanding.

Guess he didn't get his copy of the script.

I let out a low groan and made a wish, just in case there was a fairy godmother, whom I couldn't see, lurking around.

India asked, "What?"

I stood up. "Nothing."

My sister hugged me and promised that she would be there for me, no matter what. But that didn't make me feel better.

"Are you going to be okay?" she asked.

"Yeah. I need to go check on Cameron."

"I'll go. I'm going upstairs, anyway, to check on Mama. She told me to put him in bed with her."

I managed a weak smile. "Thank you."

After she left, I sat there and tried to rationalize what he'd done. The fact that he hadn't called was overshadowing a lot of things for me right now. I knew he had a right to Cameron; I had psyched myself out all of these years and just couldn't seem to see that as a reality.

I picked up the small stack of papers. My eyes scanned the court document, but I didn't read it.

I couldn't.

I wanted the words to evaporate like they had been written with disappearing ink. I knew Trip well enough to know that this wasn't him being vindictive.

This was Trip trying to get my attention.

Two weeks later, India and I sat on one of the wooden benches that lined the wall of the long hall of the Charles L. Carnes Justice Center. Trip had pulled some favors and had gotten the court date pushed through. The way I figured: the sooner we addressed it, the sooner we could both move on with our lives. India insisted on coming with me, and I told her the only way she could was if she promised not to make a scene.

The air was buzzing with people coming and going—some with lawyers, quite a few without. Our mediator had already come out and acknowledged we were there. There was still no sign of Trip, though.

I checked my watch.

It was nine forty-five.

"There he is," India said, nudging me with her elbow.

I looked up and saw him walking toward us.

His locs were neatly pulled back and he wasn't in his usual black DEA tee and jeans. He was in a black Hugo Boss suit that looked like it was cut just for him and the smell of his Burberry cologne swirled around making my head spin.

My heart began beating in my chest, and my palms got sweaty. I slid my hand out of India's and stood up.

"Hey."

"Hey," I responded.

"Look, this doesn't have to be a tense situation," Trip said. "I think we've had enough of them."

"I agree."

I glanced up the hall and saw the mediator heading toward us.

"Here she comes," I said.

During the mediation India remained quiet, which I appreciated. I didn't want to piss off Trip any more than he already was. The results of the paternity test were read again, more for the sake of the court records than anything: 99.9 percent conclusive.

Hearing it read by the mediator didn't lessen the impact of what I had done. I watched Trip's body tense and then relax as the words floated around the room then settled into everyone's world for good. As if he was no longer fighting against it.

Over the next two hours, we hammered out an agreement of one weekend a month in which Trip agreed to travel to Atlanta, and one week in the summer whereby I would travel to Louisiana. India damn near choked on her gum when that one was brought up. The court reporter actually had to get her some water.

When it came time to talk about child support, Trip was very generous.

"Whatever she needs," he said, looking at me. For some reason there was sadness in his eyes, like something inside of him had died.

"The fifteen hundred a month we agreed to is more than enough," I said.

The mediator looked at me. "Are you petitioning for back support?"

"No."

Trip said, "I have no problem providing it."

"That's okay. I'm fine," I said.

The mediator spoke again. "What about insurance? Who will carry that?"

We both answered at the same time, "I will."

"No," Trip responded. "He's my son. He goes on my insurance."

After going through another half hour of legal mumbo jumbo, we finally signed our preliminary agreement. The mediator hastily collected our paperwork before informing us that nothing would be final until the judge reviewed it and signed off on it.

"If he has any questions or problems, don't be surprised if you are called into court," she said matter-of-factly.

After dropping that little piece of information, the tall, thin white woman disappeared into the hall. She was probably off to referee another battle of the sexes.

Once back in the hallway, we all stood around and waited to see who would speak first.

Trip locked eyes with me.

India's cell rang, getting our attention.

I turned for a brief moment and watched as she fumbled trying to get her phone out of her purse.

When I looked back . . .

Trip was gone.

Chapter Thirty-three

Trip

"You got everything?"

I scanned the hotel room where my partner had been recovering ever since he'd been released from the hospital. Other than the flowers and the get-well wishes that were left lining the walls, it looked like he was about as ready to go as I was.

"Yeah. I can't wait to sleep in my own bed."

I threw his laptop bag over my shoulder. "Yeah, but you gotta admit, it was nice staying here on the department's dime."

He smiled. "You damn right. Wait until they see that room service bill."

I laughed as he pulled a Snickers outta nowhere and took a bite. "I see some things never change."

"You know me."

We headed out and down the hall toward the elevator. I could tell by the way he was acting that he wanted to say something, but he probably didn't want to piss me off.

"What?" I questioned.

He looked at me like he didn't know what I was talking about.

"Just spit it out, Phil."

He opened the door to the truck and climbed in. "Okay, but you're not gonna like what I have to say."

I hopped in and closed my door. "When have I ever liked what you had to say?"

"True."

I watched for a second as he got situated in the truck. I could tell from his guarded movements that he was still in some pain. I waited until he seemed comfortable before I cranked up the truck and pulled out of the circular drive of the hotel.

"I'm listening," I prodded.

"I just think that you're going about this all wrong. You think dragging her into court like that yesterday was the right thing to do?"

"What? You don't?"

"I just think maybe she's been through a lot and could use some understanding and support, especially now. I mean her grandmother dies,

Linc nuts the fuck up on her all around the same
time. That's a lot."

I looked over at him, wanted to be mad at
his reasoning, but couldn't. I made sure that
she wasn't implicated in anything that Lincoln
had been involved in. During his arraignment
he didn't have a regretful bone in his body.
The whole time I wanted to smack the smirk
off his face every time I thought about how he
destroyed her world.

"You're probably right. I acted on impulse. I
probably should've talked to her first," I agreed.

He continued recounting his observations.
"Look, I'm not condoning what she did, but put
yourself in her shoes. Look at what the fuck she
was dealing with. She was scared and probably
in denial."

"Yeah."

"And I'ma be honest—you and your fucked up
attitude probably didn't help."

"What?" I frowned at him. "My fucked up
attitude?"

"Hell yeah. You ain't give that girl much of
an alternative." Phil shook his head. "And now
you just blew her spot up and are about to leave
her to pick up the pieces. Just like that punk-ass
Lincoln did."

I turned my attention out the window for a second. I merged onto I-20 and sped toward my mother's house. Phil and I were going to sleep there tonight and then I was going to take him to the airport in the morning. "I don't know what I'm gonna do to be honest with you," I finally said.

"Look, you know you my boy," he said, "but . . . it's time for you to knock that chip off your shoulder."

"I don't have a chip on my shoulder," I countered.

"Yes you do, man. When you came to the NOLA division fresh off some emotional shit, I told Lenny you were gonna be a problem. But you got good instincts and you made it work.

"But take a look at all the bodies you been leaving in your wake. You can't just leave her like this, man. You walked away from Camille after that miscarriage like it didn't bother you at all, when I know it did. It's time to stop running, man.

"And if you don't do it for yourself, or your mom, do it for your son. He didn't ask for any of this. You about to let the ghost of your dead father keep you from actually having a normal life. That's crazy."

I looked over at him and shook my head, laughing. "Damn. Getting shot made you deep."

He laughed. "Nah, getting shot made me realize that life is short. And opening my eyes and seeing Lenny standing over me fucked up my head." His large frame shook with laughter. "I would've much rather had a woman, preferably my wife, holding my hand. Not his grumpy ass."

I couldn't help but laugh at that. "Yeah, that's enough to snap any playa outta some shit."

He rubbed his goatee. "Matter of fact, is your sister single?"

"Fuck you, Phil."

He laughed. "I'm just fucking with you. But you know with Atlanta's police force in shambles, they gon' need some Supercops like us to put it back together."

I smiled and looked over at my partner. "You lovin' Atlanta, huh?"

"Atlanta's lovin' me," he said, smiling back.

I nodded. "That's what's up."

Once we got to my mother's house, I got Phil situated in my old room, away from my sister, before I headed in the living room and took a seat across from my sister on the loveseat.

"Trip you can't do her like this," she said, staring at me with a pitiful look on her face.

I took a drink from the bottle of water I had in my hand. "I'm not doing anything to her. This is a lot to try to deal with."

"And you think being in New Orleans is gonna make it any easier to deal with? Trip that's your *son*. My nephew. And don't even get me started on Mama. She is fit to be tied, she can't wait to get her hands on that baby," she guilted.

"Come on Trin—"

She stood up and started pacing the living room floor.

"No Trip! First of all, I'm still pissed at you for sleeping with her and not telling me. Second of all, *I told* you that you should've never left after daddy's funeral!"

I sat there stunned, with my mouth hanging open. "So this is . . . my fault?"

"You damn right!" She plopped back down on the sofa. "If you would've just stayed none of this would've happened. I know Idalis, when she found out she was pregnant she would've came to you Trip and you *know* it."

I let out a hard sigh. "I know. So now what?"

"You need to talk to her. No lawyers, mediators. Just you and her. As scary as it may be for you right now, you have to talk to her." She smiled. "And if you don't I'm telling Mommy on you."

I couldn't help but laugh a little. "I never thought I'd be getting advice from you."

"I knew it wouldn't be long before you realized how brilliant I really am."

I stood up and headed in the kitchen. "I wouldn't say all that."

"So tell me something," she said.

I tossed my empty water bottle into the trash. "What's up?"

"Does Phil have a girlfriend?"

I checked my watch and headed toward the front door. "Bye, Trin. I'll be back."

"I mean, I'm just askin'. Are you listening to me? Where are you going?"

"I have something I need to take care of. And yes"—I winked at her—"I always listen to you. Tell Mama I'll be back in a few, and see if Phil needs anything, other than a girlfriend."

"Trip!" she called to my back.

"I'll be back."

Chapter Thirty-four

Idalis

Sitting outside and watching cars make their way up and down my mother's street; I fought hard the urge to scoop up my son and flee to some tiny country situated in some dark corner of the world. The sun was retreating to the west, leaving behind a cool breeze and darkening sky to keep me company. I fixed my eyes on the intermittent headlights as they poked holes in the darkness as they made their way up the narrow street. Sometimes I stared at a set so long letting my vision get so blurry in hopes that when my sight cleared up, all would be right with the world.

I supposed this was what they meant when they said Karma was a bitch, because that bitch certainly had me in her crosshairs.

India came out onto the porch and sat on the stoop next to me. We sat there for a moment, not saying anything. A Volkswagen shot by and she tapped me lightly on my shoulder with her fist.

"Punch buggy white."

My heart warmed and a smile spread across my face as I gave her a tap in return.

"What are you doing?" she asked.

I winked. "You didn't say: no punch backs."

She let out a laugh. "You always did cheat."

"What's Cameron doing?"

"He's upstairs, just put him down."

We both kept staring straight ahead.

"Idalis."

"Yeah."

"Are you scared about testifying against Lincoln?" She asked.

"A little. But his phone calls have fallen off a little since he's been booked in and is segregated from general population."

"Good."

I looked down at my watch, then back out into the street. I wasn't late for anything or expecting anyone, but I was anxious.

"Have you heard from the job in California?" I asked, rubbing my hands together.

"Yeah, I told them I couldn't take it," she said, staring straight ahead.

I looked at her. "Why?"

"If you're getting in all this trouble while I'm here, I can only imagine the mess you'd end up in if I was across the country."

"I'm sorry."

She looked at me. "About what?"

"I didn't want you to go, and it was for selfish reasons. Trip had already left and I didn't want to lose you too."

"I know," she said, leaning back on her hands. "I just wanted to hear you admit it."

I smiled. "I guess I really messed up, huh?"

"Yeah, you did." She reached over and took my hand in hers. "But we'll get through it."

"I really thought I was doing what was best."

She squeezed my hand. "I know you did. And I let you down. When you told me you found out you were pregnant and weren't sure, I should've said something then."

"Unfortunately, Twin, this is the one thing we can't share blame in."

She laughed. "Can you tell that to Mama?"

I looked at her. "I figured she wasn't too happy with me that's why I been staying out of her way."

She looked out to the street. "Yeah and she's blaming me." She let out a short laugh.

"Of course, she is."

"But you did get bonus points for your little hostage situation. So you should be good for a minute."

I shook my head. "Well, at least it can't get any worse."

"Yeah, I think it can."

I tapped her leg. "Twin, don't say that."

She nodded toward the street and stood up. "No, seriously, it can."

I looked up just as Trip's truck came to a stop in front of my mother's house. I stood up and wiped my hands on the front of my jeans. My heart was pounding in my ears. I tucked my hair behind my ears and took a deep breath. I watched as Trip emerged from behind the tinted windows and closed the door. His stride appeared heavy and unsure. My mind was working overtime. I mentally ran through so many different scenarios, conversations. I tried to prepare myself for whatever he had to say to me.

He kept his eyes on me as he walked toward us. His eyes never left mine as he spoke to my twin.

"Hey, India. How are you?"

They hugged. "I'm good. How are you?"

He nodded. "I'm good. Taking Phil to the airport in the morning."

She looked at him, then to me, and back again. "I . . . I'm going to go find something to do."

We made eye contact and she gave me a word-less bit of encouragement before she turned and disappeared inside. With the closing of the screen door, we were left alone.

"Idalis?" His tone was questioning, almost accusatory. The sound of his voice was heavy with every question mark that I'm sure he'd dug up over the past few weeks. His throwing court papers and seeking paternity results were his ineffective ways of communicating.

He was here because he had run out of things to throw.

"Trip . . ."

His eyes narrowed. "What?"

"Can I—"

He took a step toward me. "Can you what? *Explain?*" he asked. "Oh, now you wanna talk? Where was all this conversation back then?"

I looked back toward the house, then back to him. "I don't wanna argue."

"Why didn't you . . ." He tried to search for the same words that had eluded me all these years. It was just as hard for him to say as it was for me to admit. He turned like he was going to walk back to his truck; then he stopped on a dime and came back to me. He walked up and got in my face. I flinched, wanting to turn and run, but my legs felt like they were full of lead.

I said, "I wanted to tell you."

"Tell me *what*, Idalis?" Anger flashed in his eyes.

I swallowed hard. He wanted to hear me say it, but I couldn't. I fought against tears—and they were stronger than I was—as they rolled down my face.

"Say it, Idalis," he instigated. "Tell me how you didn't trust me enough to tell me the truth."

"Don't do that. There was more to it than just coming clean, and you know it. There was so much going on that night, we got caught up and—"

"What happened that night was more than two people getting caught up Idalis and you know it," he said, cutting me off.

His eyes scanned the front of the house. He studied it for a moment, like he was seeing it for the first time. He turned back to me.

"Do you want to come in and get something to drink?" I asked.

The question fell out because I didn't know what else to say, and I figured hydrating him was my best option at this point.

He looked at me for a few uncomfortable seconds before he slowly nodded.

Once inside, I got him a bottle of water out of the fridge and we made our way into the living room. I watched as he scanned the stacks of boxes that lined the hallway and the corners of the living room. He popped the top off the bottle and walked to my mother's entertainment center.

His eyes scanned the pictures of Cameron. I watched his facial expression soften when his eyes locked on one of Cameron's baby pictures. It was that scraggly picture that they take of the newborns in the nursery. My tiny boy looked like a drowned rat, all pink, with his jet-black hair plastered to his head, but I loved it and had it blown up to fit in a frame.

"Can I see him?" he asked, keeping his back to me.

I stood up and headed toward the steps. I felt him behind me, following me as we made our way up the steps and down the hall. We stopped at Cameron's door and I placed my hand on the knob. I looked at Trip. I knew he was angry, but I didn't want him disturbing Cameron's sleep.

"He's asleep. Please let him sleep."

He nodded in agreement as I pushed back the door.

The hall light fell across Cameron's angelic little face.

My baby was lying on his back, knocked out. Trip walked into the room and knelt down next to the bed. I watched from the door as he reached out and gently touched Cameron's little hand. He stared at him for what seemed like an eternity before looking at me. Guilt washed over me as I watched him try to cram so many missed years into this one moment. After a few more moments, he stood up and adjusted the covers over Cameron's little body.

He walked past me without saying a word and made his way downstairs. I followed in silence, not sure what to say or how to say whatever it was I was supposed to say. And for some reason right now "I'm sorry" didn't seem like enough. At this point, I didn't think anything I could say would ever be enough.

We stood in the middle of the living room, not saying anything. The sun had officially made its trip to the other side of the world and it was dark outside.

"So Phil's leaving tomorrow?"

He didn't respond. He just stood there staring at me.

I tried again. "I never got a chance to thank you for doing what you did."

He continued standing there, eyes burning a hole through me.

I ran my fingers through my hair and tried to steady my voice. "Trip, would you please say something to me."

"I can't do this."

He turned and headed for the front door.

"So you're just gonna stay true to form and leave?" I called to his back.

He stopped dead in his tracks.

When he turned around, I could see the resentment in his eyes. "Are you fucking serious?" he shot back, angrily.

"Yes, I am."

"Idalis, I didn't ask for this. What do you expect me to do? What you did was fucked up."

"I know! But I'm trying to make it right. All you kept saying is how much you hate Atlanta. How much you don't want to have kids. And the next thing I know, I'm pregnant. And Lincoln wasn't the best, but he was there, ready to give me what I needed and wanted."

"And?"

"And I felt I was doing what was best for everyone. In spite of all the shit I had to put up with, I thought I was doing the right thing. Making everybody happy."

"So what am I supposed to do, Idalis? How the hell am I supposed to step in and make up for all these missed years? How am I suddenly supposed to be somebody's *father* when I don't even know what the fuck that means?" he argued.

I dropped my head and rubbed the back of my neck. "I don't know."

He stepped a little closer. "What did you say? Speak up, I didn't hear you?" he taunted.

"I said I don't know," I snapped.

"That's what the fuck I thought you said." He turned and headed for the door. "I'm gone."

This time I didn't stop him.

I sank down on the couch and buried my face in my hands.

I didn't even hear India come in the room.

"What in the world is going on, why is he leaving?"

I looked up at her. "Nothing. Just let him go."

"Nothing?" She stepped in front of me. "What do you mean *nothing?* That didn't sound like nothing, Twin."

"Leave it alone, India. It's over."

She let out a loud sigh. "So that's it?"

I shrugged my heavy shoulders. "I guess so."

Her voice was shaky. "But what about Cam? What about you? He can't just leave."

The fact that she was about to cry made me feel even worse and forced my own tears up and out. "India, I can't make him stay. I can't make him do anything he doesn't want to do. I have to focus on me and my son now."

She sat down and put her arms around me and squeezed. "I'm sorry. I'm sorry. It's gonna be okay."

"I don't know if I'll ever be okay again."

She smoothed back my hair. "Why don't you get some sleep, Idalis."

"Sleep? You really think I can sleep? I have nowhere to live, they seized my club, froze most of my assets and I just let my son's father walk out of our life. And now he'll never know that I've loved him since I was ten. Not that it matters, though, because I'm pretty sure he hates me."

My cry turned into a soul-wrenching sob as my sister held me. I wanted to be strong, accept the choices I'd made and the consequences that came along with them but I had no idea how heavy they were. I was exhausted, both mentally and emotionally, and no amount of sleep was going to make what I'd done right.

"I could never hate you, baby girl."

India and I broke our hug, looked up and saw Trip standing in the hallway. Neither one of us heard him come back into the house.

He walked over and pulled me up off the couch. "Idalis, you are the first thing I think about when I wake up, and the last thing I think about before I go to sleep at night. I have loved you ever since the first time I laid eyes on you."

"I'm so sorry," I whispered. "I didn't mean for any of this to happen."

He reached up and wiped the tears from my cheeks. "We can't change the past; all we can do is move forward. It's not about us; it's about that little boy upstairs."

"So now what?" I asked.

"You do something you haven't done in a long time."

"What's that?"

"You can try trusting me again."

He wrapped his arms around me; and for the first time in as long as I could remember, I actually felt safe.

For the first time in a long time, everything felt right.

He chuckled. "Oh, and we gotta explain to my mother that I knocked you up."

We both laughed a little harder as I buried myself deeper inside his embrace.